"I've neve[r] husbands [a]nd other Mr a[nd Mrs,] Sam said.

"Especially in the bedroom."

Nikki stiffened as if someone had just shoved a pole down the back of her tailored jacket. "That hardly matters in our case."

If her eyes got any colder, he was likely to have icicles hanging off his chin, Sam thought. "No family?" he asked, ignoring her comment. "I'd think you'd want them here to witness the happy event."

"I don't see *your* family in attendance, either. I guess you don't want them to know you're marrying for money?"

"No. But you already knew that."

Tit for tat. A great way to start a marriage, Nikki thought, even one that wasn't really a marriage.

How was she going to survive an entire year married to this man?

Dear Reader:

We at Silhouette® are very excited to bring you this reading **Sensation**™. *Look out for the four books which appear in our Silhouette* **Sensation** *series every month. These stories will have the high quality you have come to expect from Silhouette, and their varied and provocative plots will encourage you to explore the wonder of falling in love— again and again!*

Emotions run high in these drama-filled novels. Greater sensual detail and an extra edge of realism intensify the hero and heroine's relationship so that you cannot help but be caught up in their every change of mood.

We hope you enjoy this **Sensation**—*and will go on to enjoy many more.*

We would love to hear your comments and encourage you to write to us:

Jane Nicholls
Silhouette Books
PO Box 236
Thornton Road
Croydon
Surrey
CR9 3RU

A Very Convenient Marriage

DALLAS SCHULZE

Silhouette, Silhouette Sensation and Colophon are
registered trademarks of Harlequin Books S.A., used under licence.

First published in Great Britain 1996
Silhouette Books, Eton House, 18-24 Paradise Road,
Richmond, Surrey TW9 1SR

© Dallas Schulze 1994

ISBN 0 373 07608 8

18-9612

Printed and bound in Great Britain
by Mackays of Chatham PLC, Chatham

Chapter 1

"Let me get this straight. You're suggesting that it's a good idea for me to marry a woman I've never laid eyes on?" Sam Walker leaned back in the big leather chair and gave the man sitting behind the desk a look that questioned his sanity. "You're kidding, right?"

"Do I look like I'm kidding?" Max Devlin braced his elbows on his desk and leaned forward, his dark eyes intent. "This is the perfect solution to both problems."

"Perfect solution?" Sam raised one eyebrow. "Marrying a woman I've never met? I think you've been spending too many hours reading legal briefs and not enough time in the real world. In the real world, people do not marry people they don't know."

"You might be surprised. When they get divorced, it turns out that they didn't really know each other as well as they thought."

"Don't get philosophical on me. You know what I mean. I've never even *seen* this woman."

"What difference does that make?" Max asked impatiently. "I'm suggesting you marry her, not put her in your will."

"There speaks the lawyer." Sam's grin revealed deep dimples that creased both cheeks. "It's okay to marry her as long as I don't leave her my estate." The grin faded abruptly. "If I had anything worth leaving to anyone, I'd sell it. And then I wouldn't be sitting here listening to this crazy suggestion of yours."

"Wouldn't do you any good to sell anything, anyway. Cole wouldn't take the money, and you and I both know it." Max spoke with the confidence of someone who'd known Sam since third grade when they'd bloodied each other's noses and then become the best of friends.

"He'd take it." Sam's tone held grim promise.

"No, he wouldn't. He's as stubborn as the rest of you."

"He'd take it because it's for Mary. He'd do damn near anything to see her well. We all would." Sam's face softened at the thought of his niece.

"I know."

Max was more than a little fond of five-year-old Mary Walker himself, which was one of the reasons he'd come up with this scheme. It would solve problems for two people who were more friends than clients. If he could just persuade the two of them to do what was good for them. He picked up a slim black-and-gold fountain pen and twisted it between his fingers, deciding on a small shift in tactics.

"I know Keefe has put his ranch on the market, but real estate is in pretty bad shape in Southern California right now. It could take him months to sell it, and Cole is going to hate taking the money even if Keefe can sell." He made his voice thoughtful and carefully free of any hint of pressure.

Sam winced. When Max got that reasonable tone, he knew he was in trouble. It meant Max was convinced that whatever he had in mind was best for whoever he was talking to. And once that happened, it was damned near impossible to get him to turn the idea loose.

"Tell me this brilliant plan again." Sam stood up and walked across the room to the coffeepot that sat on one end of the elegant wet bar. He topped off his cup and then turned to look at his friend. "Tell me in short, simple sentences. I was on stakeout all night, and about the only thing keeping me upright at the moment is caffeine."

"Where was this stakeout? The bottom of a sewer?" Max eyed Sam's scruffy clothing with exaggerated distaste.

"Too real world for you, Counselor?" Sam grinned.

"Let me put it this way—it's a good thing it's so early in the morning. Having someone who looks like you in my office is probably a violation of my lease."

"I could have a word with the landlord, show him my badge."

"He'd probably think you stole it." Since Max *was* the landlord, the conversation was nonsensical. It was simply a continuation of an ongoing joke between the two of them, contrasting Sam's working-class background with the world of wealth and privilege into which Max had been born.

Sam carried his coffee back across the room and sank down into the comfortable leather chair. It took a conscious effort to resist the urge to lay his head back and doze off. After spending most of the night sitting on a pile of garbage in an alley, he was more than ready for sleep—caffeine or no caffeine. But if Max had a way for him to get the money for his niece's surgery, no matter how crazy it was, he'd listen.

"Okay," Sam repeated, "tell me again about this brilliant plan."

"It's simple." Max dropped the pen and leaned forward, fixing Sam with the same intent look he used to sway judges to his point of view. "You need money for Mary's surgery. A lot of money. Nikki has a lot of money but she needs a husband to collect it. The two of you get married. Nikki gets her inheritance. You get the money for Mary's surgery. Everyone lives happily ever after."

"Yeah, right. And the moon really is made of green cheese." Sam shook his head. "All these years and I never knew there was any insanity in your family."

"What's wrong with the plan?" Max refused to let himself be drawn into an exchange of insults.

"What's *not* wrong with it?" Sam leaned forward and set his cup on the desk. "It sounds like something out of a movie or a book, Max. We're talking marriage here."

"We're talking about a perfectly reasonable business arrangement between two consenting adults," Max corrected. "Just because a marriage certificate is part of the bargain is no reason to turn it down."

"There's the lawyer again." Sam rubbed one hand over his face, wishing he'd had a chance to get some sleep. He was sure there were any number of logical objections to this crazy idea—he was just too damned tired to think of them. "I don't want to get married again."

Sam's wife, Sara, had died almost five years before. He'd never imagined himself marrying again. Certainly not under these circumstances.

"This wouldn't be a real marriage." Sensing victory, Max leaned forward. "You and Nikki would have to share a house for a year but that's all."

"That's *all?* You're suggesting I move in with some strange woman for a year and you say *that's all?*" Sam glared at him through eyes red-rimmed from lack of sleep. "What about her? Doesn't she have any problem with this?"

"She wants her inheritance, and the way her grandfather's will leaves things, she has to be married before her twenty-seventh birthday and stay married for a full year in order to get it."

"So she wouldn't have any money for a year," Sam said, pouncing on the obvious weak spot. "Which means Mary would have to wait a year for her surgery."

"Nikki can give you the money up front." Max's smile was smug as he eliminated that objection. "She has money of her own. Besides, it's my understanding that the doctors don't have any plans to do surgery in the next year. Possibly not in the year after that. So, even if you had to wait until the end of the year for the money, it wouldn't really make any difference, would it?"

Max was right but Sam didn't plan to admit as much, at least not out loud.

"If she's already got money to burn, then why does she care about the money from her grandfather? Or does she just figure that you can't ever have too much?"

"Nikki has her reasons for giving in to her grandfather's request."

"What reasons?"

"If she wants you to know, she'll tell you," Max said, suddenly very much the lawyer.

Sam gave him a sour look. "Is this part of some lawyer code? It's okay to marry your clients off but not to talk about their money?"

"Something like that. Look, just meet her. Talk to her. Then make up your mind."

Sam was silent for a moment and then shrugged and reached for his coffee cup. "What the hell, I can always say no. Set up a meeting."

Max cleared his throat. "Actually, I already have. She should be here any minute."

Sam choked on a mouthful of coffee. Once he'd stopped coughing, he glared at his friend. "Confident, aren't you?"

"I knew you'd see reason," Max said imperturbably. "Since timing is somewhat critical for both of you, I didn't see any reason to waste time."

Or to give either of them a chance to change their minds. But Max didn't say that out loud. It would have been easier to persuade Saddam Hussein to have tea with Mother Teresa than it had been to convince Sam and Nikki to consider his plan for solving both of their problems. Now all he had to do was hope that they didn't hate each other on sight.

It was a vain hope.

Five minutes later, Nicole Beauvisage walked into the office, smelling of Chanel and luxury. Sam's blue eyes swept over her, from the smooth twist of her pale gold hair, across the elegant perfection of her peach silk suit, to the Italian leather of the matching pumps with their three-inch heels. His gaze rose, lingering on a pair of legs good enough to cause accidents, taking in the trim lines of her figure, before settling on the perfect oval of her face.

For her part, Nikki paused just inside the door, her gaze widening a little as she looked at the man Max had suggested she marry.

"I've known Sam Walker since we were kids," Max had said. *"He's a great guy. You'll like him and you'll like his family. The Walkers are a close-knit bunch, a Norman Rockwell kind of family. Besides, he's a cop. How can you go wrong?"*

Nikki considered the answer to that question as she looked at Sam Walker, great guy, police officer and member of a Norman Rockwell kind of family. Funny, she didn't recall ever seeing a Rockwell painting with anyone who looked like him in it.

Shaggy dark blond hair, worn too long for her taste, a square-jawed face that couldn't quite be called handsome but she had to admit was arresting. There was a cleft in the middle of his chin that she refused to find attractive.

His shoulders were broad, and she guessed they were solid muscle, but it was difficult to tell beneath the layers of ragged coat, filthy sweater and torn shirt. The jeans he wore looked as if they hadn't seen a washer in at least a year of steady wear. He wore heavy boots that laced up the front, but the sole of one flapped loose, revealing a sock of indeterminate color.

Her green eyes widened in shock before meeting the cool blue of Sam's and reading his assessment of her.

Rich ice princess, his look said.

Filthy pig, hers responded.

It was instant antipathy.

Max nearly groaned aloud with frustration.

"Nikki. Come on in." He came around the desk to take her arm, ignoring her slight resistance as he led her toward Sam. "This is Sam Walker. Sam, this is Nikki Beauvisage."

"Mr. Walker." Her voice had the cool sound of ice tinkling in a glass. There was an almost imperceptible pause before she extended her hand.

"Nikki." Sam grasped her hand firmly, taking pleasure in her faint shudder as he leaned toward her. He knew exactly how bad he looked, not to mention smelled. It had taken considerable effort to achieve just the right look, and he wanted to be sure Ms. Nicole Beauvisage got the full effect.

"Max has told me so much about you," he said, giving her hand a hearty shake.

"I don't think he told me nearly enough about you." The look Nikki cast at Max held more than a trace of annoyance. She pulled her hand free and Sam noticed that while her manners were too good to allow her to look and see if any of his dirt had migrated to her, she was careful to hold her hand away from the pastel elegance of her suit. "I thought you said Mr. Walker was a police officer, Maxwell."

Max winced, recognizing the anger behind that coolly polite inquiry. He shot Sam a warning look with little hope that it would be heeded. Damn the pair of them, anyway.

"Sam was on a stakeout all night, Nikki."

"If I'd known I was going to be meeting you, I'd have swung by my apartment and changed into my best Armani suit."

"Not on my account, I hope. If it would make you more comfortable, I could ask Max for a few pieces of rotten fruit to put in my pockets," she offered sweetly. "Or possibly a bottle of cheap wine would be more appropriate." Her nose wrinkled subtly at the smell of stale wine wafting from his clothes.

"Sorry. I was out of Dom Pérignon." Sam's smile held an edge sharp enough to cut.

"Stop it, you two." Max stepped between them, physically as well as verbally. "Sit down, both of you. The cleaning service charges extra for getting blood out of the carpet."

He saw Nikki seated before turning to look at Sam. Sam hesitated a moment before sitting back down. Only when the combatants had retreated to their respective corners did Max step out from between them.

Nikki crossed one leg over the other and fixed her gaze on the tip of her pump.

Sam studied the grain of the wood on the desk, pretending not to notice the truly riveting length of leg she displayed.

Max looked at the pair of them and wondered if maybe Sam hadn't been right about the insanity in his family.

"So, I know the two of you must have questions to ask each other."

They both looked at him.

Nikki raised one shoulder in a delicate half shrug.

Sam rolled his eyes.

Max reached for a package of antacids. "We could start out slow. How about the weather? The weather report said it might rain."

"It's that time of year," Sam said.

"Actually, it's rather early for rain," Nikki corrected.

They both fell silent.

Max popped an antacid and chewed furiously. "Okay, we'll skip the small talk. What do you think of my idea?"

"It's nuts."

"It's insane."

The responses came one on top of the other.

Max smiled. "Well, at least you agree on something." His smile faded and he fixed them both with his best stern, lawyerly look. "Look, this meeting is for your benefit, not mine. You've both got problems. I came up with a solution. If you don't want to take it, it's not my problem. I've got better things to do with my time than play referee for the two of you. Are you going to get married or not?"

Sam looked at Nikki.

Nikki glanced out the corner of her eye at Sam.

He frowned.

She shrugged.

And Max wondered how many years he'd get for killing two clients.

"The idea is nuts," Sam said finally.

"Completely crazy," Nikki agreed firmly.

"Do either of you have a better solution?"

"No."

"Not at the moment."

"The moment is all you've got," Max pointed out. "You're both in somewhat time-critical situations."

Sam shifted uneasily beneath his look, thinking of his niece's surgery, of his family's worry.

Nikki frowned, reminded that she was running out of time to comply with the terms of her grandfather's will.

"It might work," Sam offered grudgingly.

"Of course it will work." Max's smile reflected his relief at having gotten a marginally positive response. "What's not to work? You just have to get married, live together for a year, and then you part company with no hard feelings."

"It's the living together that disturbs me," Nikki said, casting Sam's large frame an uneasy look.

"I can't say I'm all that crazy about it either," he threw back.

"Living together is one of the terms of the will," Max reminded them. "Nikki's house is big enough that you won't even have to see each other. It shouldn't be a problem."

Sam's mouth tightened at the reminder of her wealth. "Maybe I'd prefer that we live in my apartment."

Since he lived in a studio apartment in a rough area of Hollywood, it was a ridiculous suggestion. Max, who knew where he lived, gave him a disbelieving look. Nikki, who didn't, looked at him coolly.

"I have no intention of moving out of my home, Mr. Walker."

"Maybe I don't want to move out of mine, *Ms.* Beauvisage." He ignored Max's astonished look. "Not everyone wants to live in a mansion in Beverly Hills."

"Pasadena. It's a mansion in Pasadena," she corrected sweetly. "And unless you have room for a housekeeper and a maid in your apartment, it seems more logical that you should move into my home, rather than the other way around."

Housekeeper? Maid? Sam choked on the image of himself living in a house with servants. "I suppose you've got half a dozen gardeners and a chauffeur, too."

"One gardener and some part-time help. I drive my own car."

"Should I be impressed?"

"I really don't care one way or another. As long as it's understood that *if* we were to get married, we'd be living in *my* house."

Their gazes clashed, and it occurred to Sam that he'd never seen eyes of such a clear, deep green. It also occurred to him that he was making a production out of nothing. He really didn't give a damn where they lived.

"I guess I could sublet my apartment," he conceded grudgingly. He ignored Max's snort of laughter at the idea of subletting the scruffy one-room studio.

"So you'll live at Nikki's house," Max said cheerfully.

"There is one thing I want to make perfectly clear," Nikki said. A hint of color tinted her pale skin, but her eyes were steady on Sam. "You do understand, Mr. Walker, that this is to be strictly a marriage in name only. I don't want any question about that."

Sam's eyes chilled to an icy blue. He let his glance go over her, from head to toe and then back again to meet her look.

"You don't have to worry, Ms. Beauvisage. I don't think I'll have any trouble controlling my animal lust around you."

His tone made it clear that he didn't find her in the least attractive. Nikki's flush deepened, but she nodded as if satisfied with his response. "Good."

Sam returned his attention to the desk.

Nikki studied the tip of her shoe some more.

Max resisted the urge to tear his hair out.

"So, is it settled? Are you going to get married?"

"I want the money up front," Sam said abruptly.

"You'll get it. *I'll* have to insist on a prenuptial agreement."

"If you don't, I will," he snapped. His pride was already stung by the necessity of taking any money from her. "Other than the money agreed on, you don't have *anything* I want."

"Other than your name on a marriage license, you don't have anything *I* want, either. Isn't it nice that we can agree on something?" she purred.

Max chewed another antacid and considered another line of work. Something with less stress. Air-traffic controller at LAX, maybe.

"A prenup is a given," he told them. "To protect both of you. I can have one drawn up by tomorrow afternoon. It should be pretty straightforward. I'll specify that, aside from the agreed-upon sum of money, you both give up all claims to each other's property."

"Fine with me," Sam said, wondering what the odds were that Ms. Nicole Beauvisage would try to lay claim to his five-year-old Bronco or his collection of baseball cards, the only items of any particular value he owned. Somehow, he doubted either one would hold much appeal.

"There is one other thing that concerns me," Nikki said slowly.

"I promise not to play basketball in the ballroom or leave my dirty socks lying on the Louis XV," Sam offered facetiously.

"That's quite a relief." Her smile was as icy as her eyes. "But my concern is more basic, Mr. Walker. Once you have your money, what guarantee do I have that you'll stick around for a year?"

"You have my word."

"I don't know you, Mr. Walker. I hope you'll understand my hesitation at staking my financial future on your word."

He did understand. And if it had been anyone else, he wouldn't have been offended. But there was something about this woman that got under his skin and made him react in ways he wouldn't have normally.

"Sam's word is good," Max said hastily, reading the anger in his friend's face.

"Draw up a contract," Sam snapped without looking away from Nikki. "She's paying me in advance for a year of my time. Make sure it's nice and legal and binding. You can do that, can't you, Max?"

"Sure. But it's really not—"

"I wouldn't want Ms. Beauvisage to have any doubts about getting her money's worth." Sam's voice was smooth as silk and sharp enough to draw blood.

"Thank you," Nikki said calmly.

"You're welcome."

The deadly politeness had Max reaching for another antacid. Maybe he should buy stock in the company, he thought, studying the wrapper. The silence stretched.

Nikki waited for Sam to speak.

Sam waited for Nikki to break the silence.

Max waited for the antacids to settle his stomach.

None of them knew how much time passed before the sound of Max's secretary settling in at her desk in the outer office finally broke the stillness.

"Well, are you going to do it or aren't you?" Max demanded, no longer trying to hide his exasperation.

There was a brief silence.

Sam spoke first. "I want it understood that no one is to know this isn't a real marriage."

If he actually went through with this insane idea, he didn't want Cole to know what he'd done. It would be hard enough to get his younger brother to take the check without him knowing the full circumstances of how Sam had acquired the money.

"As I'm sure Max told you, one of the provisions of the will is that this should be a genuine marriage." Since Nikki was very carefully not looking at Sam, she missed the sharp look he shot in Max's direction, a look that made it clear that he had not been informed of this particular fact. "Of course, in our case, it would only have the *appearance* of being genuine," she continued, "even if the will didn't require it, I'm not particularly eager for the world to know I had to get married in order to receive my inheritance."

"That includes my family," Sam said. "As far as they are concerned, we'd have to appear to be a normal couple."

A Norman Rockwell kind of family. Nikki remembered Max's description and wondered if it was possible that the hostile, scruffy, irritating man in front of her really came from that kind of family.

"I think I could manage that," she said. "If you can manage to convince my friends and family that you married me for something other than my money."

The reminder stung, making Sam's response sharper than it should have been. "I think my acting ability will stretch that far," he said smoothly.

The color that tinted her cheeks made him regret the words. He *was* marrying her for her money, dammit. It shouldn't be so aggravating to be reminded of that fact.

"I hope so" was all she said.

"So you're agreed that the marriage is to appear real," Max said.

"I haven't agreed to a marriage," Nikki pointed out sharply.

"Neither have I."

Max reached for another antacid and chewed furiously. "Look, I'm not a white slaver. I'm not going to force you two to get married. But as your attorney, I'm going to point out that this is the perfect solution to both sets of problems and that I think you're a pair of fools if you walk away from this opportunity. And as your friend, I'm going to tell you that you're acting like a couple of idiots. Now, are you going to get married or aren't you?"

There was a long silence.

"I don't like him," Nikki said without looking at Sam.

"I'm not wild about you either, honey."

Max threw up his hands. "You don't have to like each other. You just have to get married! Are you going to or not?"

There was another pause.

Sam shrugged. "I'm game if she is."

Nikki nodded slowly. "I can't believe I'm saying this but, all right, I'll marry him."

"Don't act like you're doing me a favor, honey," Sam snapped.

"I *am* doing you a favor. And don't call me 'honey.'"

"You're doing each other favors," Max said, verbally stepping between them again. "You need each other, and for the next year, you're going to be living together. You might as well get used to the idea."

Sam glared at Nikki, thinking he'd never met a woman he disliked more. Or one with better legs.

Nikki glared at Sam, thinking it was a shame Max couldn't have found her someone a little less overwhelmingly male. And wasn't it a good thing she didn't find him in the least bit attractive?

Max looked at the pair of them and wondered if his own sanity would survive the next year.

Chapter 2

Once an agreement, however grudging, was reached, it didn't take long to work out the details of the arrangement. Aside from the fact that the bride and groom detested each other, the only possible barrier to the upcoming nuptials was the necessity of convincing Nikki's grandfather's attorney that they were getting married for the usual reasons.

Lymon Beauvisage had foreseen the possibility that his granddaughter might make a marriage of convenience in order to get her inheritance and had done his best to circumvent the possibility. As the final proviso in an already complicated bequest, he'd left his friend and lawyer, Jason Drummond, the final say in whether or not Nikki received her inheritance. If he believed the marriage was real, he'd release the money at the end of the year. If he didn't, the money went to Nikki's older brother, Alan, who'd already received—and squandered—his half of their grandfather's estate.

"You just have to convince Jason Drummond that you're in love with each other," Max said.

"Unless he's deaf, dumb and blind, that may not be so easy," Sam said, looking as if he were starting to reconsider the whole idea.

"All it takes is a little acting," Max coaxed.

"There's a limit to my acting ability," Sam muttered. Out the corner of his eye, he saw Nikki stiffen and realized that his comment could be taken as a slap in her direction, which wasn't what he'd intended.

"I'm surprised, Mr. Walker." Her voice was sweet enough to send chills down his spine. "You're so convincing as a rude, filthy wino." She paused and her delicate brows drew together in a small frown. When she continued, her tone was one of concern. "Perhaps that isn't as much of a stretch as convincing Uncle Jason that I might actually want to marry you."

Sam winced in acknowledgment of the hit, but restrained the urge to respond in kind. The last thing he wanted was to prolong this meeting, not even for the pleasure of continuing the verbal warfare with the woman he'd just agreed to marry. He wanted to go home, wash off the smell of that alley and get some sleep. Maybe when he woke up, this idea would seem as logical as Max claimed it was and not the insanity it looked to be at the moment.

"Uncle Jason?" he questioned.

"My grandfather's attorney is also a family friend."

"That should make him fairly willing to be convinced," Max put in optimistically.

"Less strain on your acting ability, Mr. Walker," Nikki pointed out with a saccharine smile.

"Thanks."

It was agreed that Nikki would contact Jason Drummond and arrange for him to meet Sam as soon as possible.

"The sooner you get his approval, the sooner you can get married," Max said.

"A thrilling thought," Nikki said as she rose, preparatory to leaving.

Sam, who'd been about to gather his energy to rise, a courtesy his mother had drummed into him, relaxed back into his chair. He was damned if he was going to waste his time on polite forms with this stuck-up little ice princess.

"I'll let Max know when I've arranged a meeting with Uncle Jason."

"You do that."

Max started to suggest that it would be easier if she contacted Sam directly, but immediately thought better of it. The way things stood right now, it was probably safer if the bride and groom had as little contact with each other as possible before the wedding.

"I'll be in touch," she said to Max. She glanced at Sam and gave him a cool little nod. "Mr. Walker."

"Ms. Beauvisage." He returned the nod, his tone mocking her formality.

Nikki's mouth tightened, and he saw fire flare in her green eyes. He waited for the explosion, but it didn't come. She turned and walked out of the office without another word. Sam watched her leave, surprised to realize that he actually felt a twinge of regret at her restraint.

He let his eyes drift down her narrow back to her legs. She had the disposition of a pit viper. It was too bad she also had legs like an angel. It didn't take much imagination on his part to picture those legs sliding into the expensive car she undoubtedly drove.

Or between a set of black silk sheets.

* * *

Nikki heard the rapid tap of her heels against the tile entryway of the office building and realized she was almost running. She forced herself to slow down as she exited the building and stepped out into the bright sunshine.

She *wasn't* running, she told herself as she pulled open her car door and slid onto the genuine imitation sheepskin-covered seat. Sam Walker might be a bit larger than life, and some women—susceptible women—might even find him wildly attractive, but she herself hardly noticed such things, and they certainly wouldn't send her fleeing from her lawyer's office.

She had an appointment with her mother, that was all. The fact that she wasn't meeting Marilee for three hours and that Marilee would probably not arrive for another forty-five minutes after that was irrelevant. She'd concluded her business here and she was leaving. Nothing odd about that.

Nikki's hands weren't quite steady as she put the car into gear and pulled away from the curb. She'd done it. She'd actually agreed to marry a man she'd just met. A man she didn't know and wouldn't like if she did. Her mind reeled at the thought.

When Max had suggested the idea as a way to get her inheritance, he'd made it sound so simple, so businesslike that she'd had no hesitation in agreeing to meet with his friend. But she hadn't been expecting Sam Walker and she hadn't been prepared for the jolt of awareness she'd felt when they shook hands. What had sounded like a simple business arrangement suddenly seemed much more complex.

Nikki turned the car onto the Glendale Freeway and headed north. She'd planned to do some shopping before meeting her mother for lunch, but that was before she'd met Sam Walker, before she'd agreed to marry him. Right now, she needed to talk to someone she could trust, someone who had no ax to grind.

Twenty minutes later, she parked the scruffy ten-year-old Chevy in front of a neat little house on a street lined with other neat little houses. The front door opened as she walked up the driveway and a short, thin man of about thirty came out. Bill Davis had married Nikki's best friend four years ago, right after Liz graduated from UC Santa Barbara. They had little money, a house made chaotic by a toddler and all the attendant problems of raising a family, but they loved each other deeply. Nikki was unabashedly envious of their happiness.

"Hello, Bill."

"Nikki." His plain face creased in a smile when he saw her. "Isn't it a little early for the idle rich to be out slumming?" he asked as he hugged her.

"I like to get started early. Slumming, properly done, takes more time than most people realize. Is Liz around?"

"In the kitchen, feeding the holy terror."

"Don't call my godchild a terror. He's adorable."

"You don't have to live with him," he said darkly. "When I left, Michael had just tried to put the goldfish in his oatmeal and Liz was trying to convince him that Oscar didn't need a hot breakfast."

"And you fled in the midst of that?"

"Like a coward," he admitted cheerfully. "I've got cars stacked up like cordwood, waiting for work."

"Nice to be busy." Bill was manager and chief mechanic at an auto repair shop in Montrose. He and Liz were saving money in hopes of buying the business when the current owner retired in a couple of years.

"Bring that junk heap by and I'll take a look at it," he said, nodding toward her car. "I still think you ought to sell it for scrap and buy a real car."

"Barney *is* a real car," she protested. "It had been Bill's four-year-old son who'd named Nikki's car, thinking the faded purple paint job was reminiscent of the dinosaur he watched every day on television.

They spoke a moment longer before Bill left for work. Nikki let herself in the house with the familiarity of an old friend. She called out Liz's name and received a frazzled-sounding response from the kitchen. Picking her way across the mine field of toys strewn across the living room floor, she could hear Liz telling Michael firmly that Oscar did not want his fishbowl filled with milk, any more than he wanted to swim in Michael's oatmeal.

"Aunt Nikki!" Michael's greeting was enthusiastic as only a four-year-old's could be. He scrambled off his chair and hurled himself at her, oblivious to his mother's command not to touch anything until his face and hands were washed. An instant later, Nikki had an armful of four-year-old boy and smudges of oatmeal and jelly on her silk suit.

"You have to learn to dodge," Liz said as Nikki stood.

"I don't want to dodge. The suit will clean." Nikki grinned down at the little boy, who was rifling through her cavernous purse, looking for the small treat she never failed to bring him. Today it was a palm-size dump truck, and Michael immediately began scooting it across the kitchen floor, making engine noises.

"You spoil him."

"He's too sweet natured to be really spoiled," Nikki said.

"Sweet natured?" Liz repeated disbelievingly. "Ask Oscar how sweet natured he is."

Nikki followed her gesture to the goldfish bowl perched on top of the refrigerator beyond the reach of four-year-old fingers. Oscar swam lazily around his small home, undisturbed by his close encounter with Michael's breakfast.

"Oscar looks none the worse for wear. I can't say the same about you, though." She gave her friend a critical look as Liz collapsed into a chair. Liz's hair stood out from her head in springy carrot-red curls and her hazel eyes held the dazed look of a disaster survivor.

"Michael woke us up at four-thirty. Then the toilet stopped up. Bill spent half an hour working on it and finally pulled out one of Michael's action figures. Apparently Michael wanted to send him on a diving mission. The remains were so mangled, there wasn't even enough left for a decent burial. I didn't get to the laundry yesterday, so the only clean underwear Bill could find is a pair of tiger-striped bikinis I bought him as a joke. He's convinced he'll be in some kind of accident and be rushed to the emergency room where the doctors will find him wearing kinky shorts. The bread was moldy, there was only one egg, which I cooked for Bill, and Michael has spent the morning trying to introduce Oscar to the joys of breakfast."

Nikki let a few moments go by at the end of Liz's recital of the morning's disasters and then lifted her brows in surprise. "Is that all?"

"Get out." Liz threw a paper napkin in her direction, watching as it drifted into Michael's half-eaten bowl of oatmeal. "If I had the energy, I'd throw something more lethal. Worse, I'd send the holy terror home with you."

Grinning, Nikki lifted the kettle off the stove and carried it to the sink. "A cup of tea will restore your energy. And anytime you want a couple of days off, you know I'd love to have Michael." She set the kettle on the stove.

"Friendship only goes so far," Liz said broodingly as she watched her son crawling across the floor with his new truck. "I may hit you up for enough money to run away from home instead."

"Yeah, right." Nikki found the tea bags and two cups. "You wouldn't give up your life for anything, and you and I both know it."

"This morning I'd sell it for a wooden nickel and consider myself lucky."

"Liar." Nikki poured the water over the tea bags before carrying the cups to the table. She sat down across from Liz. "You adore Bill and Michael."

"Maybe." Cradling her hands around the mug of tea, Liz looked as if she might be getting her second wind after her hectic morning. "Enough about my miserable existence. What's up with you?"

Nikki took a sip of tea and considered possible responses to that question. In the end, she chose the simplest and most direct. "I'm getting married."

The stark announcement brought Liz's head up so fast Nikki had visions of whiplash. "You're what?"

"I said I'm getting married." Repeating the words didn't make them sound any more real. "In a few days," she added, feeling a flutter of panic at the thought.

"Who?" Liz looked bewildered. "I didn't know you were even dating anyone."

"I'm not."

"But you're getting married?"

"Yes."

Liz stared at her, and then her eyes widened in understanding. "Your grandfather's will? You're getting married because of that?"

Nikki nodded. "Max set it up. It's a friend of his. A police officer."

"Have you met the guy?" Liz's tea was forgotten as she leaned forward, her eyes bright with interest.

"This morning." Nikki shifted uncomfortably, remembering that meeting. "In Max's office."

"What's he like?"

What was he like? Sam Walker's image sprang into Nikki's mind, far more vivid than she would have liked. Why couldn't Max have found her the kind of guy you forgot as soon as they were out of sight?

"He's tall," she said slowly.

"How tall?"

"I don't know. Six-one, six-two. I didn't have a tape measure with me."

"Skinny, fat, somewhere in between?" Liz asked briskly.

"Somewhere in between." The lackluster description hardly did justice to Sam Walker's broad shoulders and narrow hips, but it was close enough.

"Is he handsome?"

"No. Yes. Sort of." Nikki flushed as her friend's eyebrows rose.

"Nice to hear you sounding so decisive," she commented.

"If I'd known you were going to be so interested, I'd have taken a snapshot." Nikki winced at the defensive sound of her own voice. She had to get a grip. "He has...dents in his face."

Liz choked on a mouthful of tea, coughed briefly and then stared at her friend. "Dents? You mean a birth defect or scars of some kind?"

"No." Nikki waved one hand to dismiss that idea. As far as she could see, Sam Walker was as close to perfect as it was possible for a man to be. If you liked that type, anyway. She'd never really seen the appeal of shaggy dark blond hair, blue eyes, a smile to die for and muscles like a Greek god. No appeal at all. "He's got a cleft chin and creases when he smiles,'' she said, aware that Liz was still waiting for her to explain what she'd meant by dents.

"Creases?" Liz frowned. "Dimples? You mean the guy has dimples?"

"Yes." She didn't want to think of them that way. Dimples sounded...attractive, and she didn't want to find anything about Sam Walker attractive. Not his dimples, not anything.

"So, is he good-looking or not?" Liz asked, her frustration clear in her voice.

"What difference does it make? I don't care if he looks the way Danny DeVito did in *Batman Returns*. All I need is a husband for the next year so I can get my hands on my money."

"That's true. Still, if you have to spend a year married to some guy, it wouldn't hurt if he was attractive and pleasant to be around. Is he nice?"

"Nice? I guess." *Nice* wasn't the word she would have used, but she supposed he hadn't exactly been un-nice. Or, at least, no more un-nice than she herself had been.

"And the two of you hit it off?" Liz pursued anxiously.

"Well enough," Nikki temporized. There was no reason to mention that they'd hit it off about as well as oil and water. "Since this is just a business arrangement, we don't have to be bosom pals."

"True." Liz took a sip of her tea, her expression thoughtful. Michael was scooting his new toy up and down the wall, making engine noises more suited to a 747 than a three-inch-long dump truck. "It's ridiculous that you should have to go to these lengths to get your inheritance. Your grandfather didn't make your brother get married before he got his money."

"Grandfather didn't think much of women and their ability to manage money." Nikki got up and refilled the teakettle, more for something to do than out of a desire for more tea. "I gather Grandmother had feathers for brains, and I can't say Mother is much better."

"There's nothing wrong with your mother's ability to manage money. Every time she starts running out, she marries someone rich. Efficiency itself."

Nikki snorted with laughter at this blunt summation of her mother's money management techniques. They'd known each other long enough and well enough for Liz to speak her mind without fear of offending.

"I don't think Grandfather had your appreciation for Marilee's methods." Nikki glanced at her watch. "I'm supposed to be having lunch with her today. She's on her way to Europe tomorrow to look for husband number five. Or is it six? If I'm lucky, she'll marry another count or earl or something and stay in Europe for the next year. If I'm really lucky, I can be divorced before she even knows I'm married. Let's face it, my mother is a ditz, my grandmother was a ditz. Ergo, according to my grandfather, *I* must be a ditz. He figured he was protecting me by forcing me to get married because everyone knows men are better at managing money." There was more resignation than anger in her voice.

"Yeah, right. Bill couldn't balance a checkbook if his life depended on it. And look at your brother. He ran through the money your grandfather left him in a couple of years. Why didn't Alan have to get married to inherit his half of the money? I know, I know." Liz waved one hand, forestalling Nikki's response. "We've had this discussion before. Alan's a man and the last of the Beauvisage name. Therefore, he gets his inheritance up front instead of being forced into marrying some total stranger."

"I don't *have* to get married," Nikki said as she poured fresh hot water into both of their cups. "I could just let the money go to Alan, which it will do if I'm not married by the time I'm twenty-seven. I do have a trust fund that's mine whether I marry or not. It's not like I'll starve without it.''

''No, but you couldn't afford to keep your house.''

''It's too big for one person anyway.'' Nikki tried to sound as if the thought of losing the house she'd grown up in didn't bother her. But in reality she loved the big old house and hated the thought of letting it go.

''And you couldn't afford to keep the Rainbow Place going,'' Liz finished, playing the trump card.

Nikki was silent for a moment, thinking about the day-care center she funded in a low-income area. She'd started it four years ago when she'd graduated from college and realized that a degree in American history didn't do much to prepare her for a job in the real world. Not that she'd needed a job, but she had needed something to occupy her time, something to make her feel as if she were making some contribution to the world.

She not only provided the operating capital, she also worked there three days a week. It had become a vital part of her life and it would leave a real hole if she had to give it up. But far more important was the impact it would have on the mothers and children who'd come to depend on Rainbow Place. Without safe day care available, many of the women would have to quit their jobs to stay home with their children. Many of them would end up on welfare.

No, she couldn't let the center close. With the money she'd inherit when she got married, she could afford to keep it open. Without that money, the center's future was in serious jeopardy. She sighed.

''How'd you like to come to a wedding?''

''You and the guy with the dents in his face?'' Liz's hazel eyes sparkled with laughter.

"Me and Sam Walker," Nikki confirmed. She picked up her cup and cradled it between her hands, staring down into the amber-colored tea. "Of course, we still have to get Uncle Jason's approval," she added, not sure whether she hoped to get it or prayed that they didn't.

Chapter 3

Nikki adjusted the cuff of her kelly-green suit jacket, using the motion as a cover for a discreet glance at her watch. It was almost one-thirty and the message she'd given Max had been for Sam Walker to be here at one o'clock.

He was late and she was going to kill him with her bare hands.

He knew how important this meeting was, knew they had to have her uncle's approval in order for her to get her inheritance. But he couldn't even bother to show up on time. This was probably some macho attempt to show her that he didn't have to take orders from her. Not that she'd given him any orders. She'd simply left a message with Max stating the time and place of the meeting she'd arranged.

Perhaps she had been a bit peremptory, but Max would have softened that when he passed the message on to Sam. Which meant that there was no excuse for him being late at all. Except to annoy her, and he was certainly succeeding in that. She became aware that Jason was speaking and forced her attention away from plans for Sam Walker's demise.

"...so I drew out my sword and ran him through, which was an unconventional way to win a trial but effective nonetheless."

"What?" She stared at Jason in bewilderment, wondering just what it was she'd missed. "What are you talking about? Who did you run through?"

"The opposing attorney, of course." He seemed surprised that she had to ask. "A very annoying man with an irritating habit of rubbing his hands together like Uriah Heep gloating over his coins. I never could stand him, and neither could anyone else, which is probably why the judge cited me for contempt of court rather than murder."

His blue eyes, only slightly faded by his sixty-five years of living, twinkled at her through the lenses of his neat horn-rimmed glasses. "You missed all the best parts, Nicole. It was a very good extemporaneous effort on my part, if I do say so myself."

"I'm sorry, Uncle Jason." Nikki's smile was both regretful and affectionate. "I guess I faded out on you."

"That's quite all right, my dear. Worried about your young man, are you?"

"Just a little." She nearly choked on hearing Sam referred to as *her* young man. "It's not like him to be late." She didn't have any idea whether it was like him or not. For all she knew, Sam Walker was always late for incredibly important appointments.

"Would you like to call and find out what's delaying him?"

"No, that's all right. I'm sure he'll be here any minute." She could hardly admit that she didn't know where to call. All she knew was that Sam was a cop; she didn't have the slightest idea what city he worked for.

Luckily, before her nerves were completely shot, Jason's secretary ushered Sam into the office.

"Mr. Walker." Jason rose and went to greet him, which was just as well because Nikki was momentarily paralyzed by her first sight of her husband-to-be.

She'd wondered what he'd look like cleaned up and wearing decent clothes. Even covered with several layers of dirt and rags, he'd had a definite impact on her senses, but that was nothing compared to what she felt now.

Not that he looked all that different, it was just that he looked...different. Taller, even broader through the shoulders, lean hipped and with a long, rangy walk that bespoke confidence and maybe just a touch of arrogance. His dark blond hair was neatly combed and considerably cleaner than it had been the first time they met, but there was still something a little untamed about the way it curled against the back of his collar.

He wore a well-tailored gray suit and a white shirt. Paired with this conservative attire was a fuchsia-and-black tie, patterned with indescribable swirls and dots. Just looking at it made her dizzy.

Or was it looking at Sam Walker that made her light-headed?

"Mr. Drummond. I'm sorry I'm late. I had to testify at a hearing this morning and the proceedings were delayed."

"I understand. The legal system is many things, but timely it's not."

The two men shook hands. "I think Nicole was beginning to get a little worried, though," Jason continued, turning toward her with a fond smile. "I thought she was going to wear out her watch, she looked at it so many times."

"I'm sorry you were worried, darling. I should have thought to call from the courthouse." Sam's smile was a masterpiece of concerned affection.

"Darling" stared at him, barely managing to keep her mouth from gaping. *This* was the unwashed, unkempt, uncivil man she'd met less than a week ago? This attractive, well-dressed man looking at her as if he adored her?

She realized that Jason was watching them, waiting for her response, and she managed to force a smile that she hoped looked more natural than it felt. "That's all right. I knew it had to be something important that kept you." She stood up so that she wouldn't feel at quite such a disadvantage.

"Next time, I'll be sure to call and let you know I'm running late."

He crossed the room to where she stood and reached toward her. Momentarily confused, Nikki half extended her hand, thinking he meant to shake it. But that wasn't what he had in mind. He did take her hand, but only to use it to draw her toward him.

The wicked glint in his eyes dispelled the illusion of loving affection and gave Nikki warning of his intention. She turned her head slightly and the kiss aimed at her mouth landed on her cheek instead. Even that small contact had more impact than she liked. He was too close, too large and too male. She could smell the subtle, woodsy scent of his cologne, feel the faint, masculine roughness of his chin. She didn't like him being so close, forcing her to be so aware of him.

Sam lifted his head and looked down at her with every appearance of adoration. "I'm sorry I worried you, sweetheart, but I'm glad you care enough to worry."

Nikki guessed there were women who would have been charmed by his boyishly wicked smile. Foolish women who might actually enjoy this little game he was playing. If they'd been alone, she would have shoved him away and probably planted her fist in his face. But with Jason looking on, she couldn't do either. A quick glance told her that the other man was standing behind his desk, watching them with an indulgent expression.

"That's all right, darling."

Her smile was enough to chill Sam's blood but there was no time to avoid the spike heel that was planted squarely on the toe of his soft leather dress shoe and then slowly ground down. Pain sliced across the top of his foot.

If they'd been alone, he wouldn't have bet money on his ability to resist the urge to shake her until her perfect white teeth rattled. Probably caps, he thought uncharitably. His hands tightened on her shoulders and their eyes did battle.

She was a spoiled, rich little brat and the next year stretched ahead of him like an eternity.

He was an overbearing, obnoxious, mercenary male and the next year was going to be absolute hell.

"You two will have time for that later," Jason said, smiling at the pair of them. "Why don't you have a seat, Sam. I hope you don't mind if I call you Sam. I don't see any need for formality, do you?"

"Not at all." Sam released Nikki's shoulders and swallowed a sigh of relief as she removed her heel from his foot. He resisted the urge to check for blood. From the feel of his foot, she must have sharpened the heel of the damned shoe into a stiletto.

He sat down in the chair beside Nikki's and tried not to notice the subtle floral scent of her perfume, which was like a summer breeze wafting across a bed of roses. An ounce of the stuff probably cost as much as he made in a week, he reminded himself.

"Nikki told me that she'd explained the situation with her grandfather's will to you and the necessity for this interview," Jason said. "She tells me that you'd just as soon walk away from this inheritance rather than rush her into marriage."

The look Sam shot Nikki held grudging approval. He'd wondered how he was supposed to convince her grandfather's attorney that he wasn't marrying Nikki for her money. She'd done a perfect job of smoothing the path.

"I don't want her to feel as if she has to make any decisions in a hurry. It's not like I'm marrying her for the money," he added, with a smile. Which was more or less true, since *his* money, the money for Mary's surgery, was coming out of what she already had. One thing he'd learned from doing undercover work was that it was always best to stick as close to the truth as possible.

"I'm glad to hear it." Behind the smile in Jason's eyes was a shrewdness that warned Sam that it would be foolish to underestimate him. He steepled his hands together on the desk. "Nikki hasn't really told me much about the two of you. Where did you meet?"

"Meet?" Sam looked at Nikki. He cocked one eyebrow, as if to suggest that she should answer the question. She swallowed and searched her suddenly blank mind for a reasonable response. God, why hadn't they worked out these kind of details ahead of time?

When the panic in her eyes made it clear that she didn't have a clever response handy, Sam answered Jason's question himself. "We were intoduced by a mutual friend, actually. After everything Max told me, I knew even before I met her that Nikki was the perfect woman for me."

Nikki was torn between gratitude and anger. There was nothing in what he'd said that could arouse Jason's suspicions but she was not blind to the double meaning behind his words. "After everything Max told him," indeed. All Max had had to say was that she was rich.

"Max?" Jason asked. "Didn't I meet him at your house, Nicole?"

"Yes. We've been friends for years."

"A lawyer, isn't he?"

Nikki swallowed. He couldn't possibly suspect the truth just because Max was a lawyer, could he? "Yes, he is."

"Seems like there are a lot of us around," Jason said casually. He leaned back in his desk chair and studied the two of them for a moment. "Nikki tells me that the two of you haven't known each other long."

"Not long," Sam admitted. "But I knew exactly how I felt about Nikki from the first moment I saw her." He threw a loving glance at Nikki, who fumed under the laughter in his eyes.

"Love at first sight, hmm?" Jason's smile was indulgent.

"Something like that."

Nikki would have given a great deal to have planted her fist smack dab in the middle of Sam's smiling mouth. She could only hope that Jason would take her blush for one of modesty rather than rage.

"I didn't approve of the way Lyman drew up his will and I made no secret of that. But he was a stubborn man." He peered at Sam from under bushy gray eyebrows. "You might be warned that stubbornness is a family trait," he added, smiling.

"I'll keep that in mind." Sam glanced at Nikki, hoping he looked fond rather than irritated.

"I couldn't persuade him to change his mind, so I drew up the will as he'd requested and agreed to be executor. And neither my disapproval of the provisions of the will nor my fondness for Nicole can be allowed to color my judg-

ment,'' Jason said firmly. "Lyman may have been stubborn and, I think, misguided in this, but he did love Nicole
and he honestly felt he was doing what was best for her. As
his friend, as well as his attorney, I must do my best to carry
out his wishes.''

There was a moment of silence while the potential bride
and groom considered the import of his words. Obviously,
Jason was not averse to approving their marriage, as long
as he was convinced that they were getting married for the
right reasons.

An image of Mary's small face flashed through Sam's
mind and his jaw tightened. He'd walk through fire to get
her the help she needed. But, while walking through fire
might be easier than spending the next year with Nikki
Beauvisage, it wouldn't do Mary any good.

Without taking his eyes from Jason Drummond, he
reached for Nikki's hand, which lay on the arm of her
chair. She jumped in surprise and automatically tried to
pull away, but he tightened his hold ruthlessly.

"I understand your concern," he said to Jason. "And I
appreciate it. Nikki is a very...special woman. She certainly deserves the very best." His shrug was self-
deprecating. "I don't know if I'm that, but I can tell you
that marrying Nikki means more to me than anything else
in the world.''

He threw Nikki a look that held both warning and command. The next few minutes were critical. A five-year-old's
health hung on whether or not Jason believed they were in
love.

Jason nodded as he leaned back in his chair. He let his
eyes drift from the couple in front of him, focusing instead on the swath of smoggy sky visible out the window.
Sam and Nikki waited, unaware that they were still hold-

ing hands, unconsciously drawing support from the contact.

The silence seemed to stretch forever, but in actuality, it couldn't have been more than a few minutes before it was broken. Jason slowly looked away from the window, his faded blue eyes drifting from Nikki's face to Sam's before settling on their linked hands.

"The two of you are very sure this is what you want? That you really *want* to marry each other?"

"More than anything, Uncle Jason." There was so much sincerity in her voice that Nikki almost believed herself.

"Absolutely, sir." Sam was startled by the fervor of his own response. But he *did* want to marry her, just not for the reasons Jason Drummond thought he did.

Jason pinched his lower lip between thumb and forefinger, looking at the pair of them with eyes that seemed able to penetrate the suddenly flimsy-seeming fabric of their charade. They waited, hands clasped, neither of them breathing. Once again, Jason's gaze dropped to those linked fingers and his expression took on a pensive air.

After a moment that seemed an hour long, he nodded slowly. "All right. You have my blessing."

His acceptance, when it came, was so simple that it took a moment for it to register. When it did, Sam's hand tightened over Nikki's fingers until she squeaked a protest. With a quick apology, he released her.

He had it. The money for Mary's surgery was all but in his hands. So what if he had to spend the next year living with the ice princess. It was worth it.

Nikki flexed her fingers absently after Sam released them. It was done. She'd be able to keep the Rainbow Place open without spending her time begging money from other sources. The price was steep: twelve months of sharing her house with a man she couldn't stand. But she could survive that.

She glanced at Sam. At least, she was fairly sure she could.

Chapter 4

With only a little effort, the bride and groom were able to avoid seeing each other again before the wedding. The few communications necessary were filtered through Max, who also made the wedding arrangements.

It was Sam's suggestion that they simply go to Las Vegas and, as he put it, get it over with. Nikki's response to this, via Max, was that no one who knew her would ever believe that she'd get married in such a tacky place.

Sam, taking this, quite rightly, as a comment on his good taste or lack thereof, responded that she could do whatever she wanted as long as she didn't expect him to dress up in a powder-blue tuxedo and ruffled shirt. Or at least that was the portion of his message Max chose to pass on, deeming it unnecessary to get too literal. His suggestion that he make the arrangements was gratefully accepted by the engaged couple.

He found a small chapel in Burbank for the ceremony, traditional enough to allay any suspicions anyone might have about the authenticity of the marriage, but simple enough to satisfy the bride and groom.

Liz and Bill brought Nikki, and the four of them—Michael included—arrived a few minutes early and waited outside for Sam and Max to arrive. They could have waited inside, but the woman who was to marry them had shown a definite tendency to wax sentimental and Nikki wasn't in the mood for hearing homilies about the joys of wedded bliss.

Aside from Max and the Davises, the only other guest was to be Jason Drummond. When she'd refused Sam's suggestion of a Vegas wedding, Nikki hadn't stopped to consider that Jason might not have come to an out-of-town wedding. As it was, having him in attendance meant that they'd have to keep up the facade of being a happy couple, which wasn't easy when she'd rather have had a root canal without anesthetic than marry Sam Walker.

"He's late." Bill glanced at his watch and then scowled at the quiet street. He'd made no secret of his dislike of the whole idea. When he'd heard of Nikki's plan, he'd said bluntly that it was crazy. He'd agreed to attend the wedding, but Nikki knew it was as much to vet Sam as it was to offer her support.

"Less than five minutes." Liz gave her husband an exasperated look. It wasn't often that he put on his protective male attitude, but when he did, he did a thorough job of it.

"If the guy is so anxious to get married, you'd think he'd show up on time."

"You were thirty minutes late for our wedding." Liz reached out to grab Michael's hand, pulling him away from the brick planter he'd begun to dig in.

"I got caught in traffic," Bill said defensively. "That was different."

"My mother didn't think it was different. She spent the entire half hour telling me that if you loved me, you'd have left plenty of time to get to the church."

"Only your mother could translate being late into not loving you," he groused, but he shut up about the groom not having arrived.

Nikki barely heard the exchange. She was too busy trying to convince herself that this was a good idea, that she shouldn't turn and run as far and as fast as she could. A week ago, it had seemed like her only choice. Now, standing outside the plain stucco facade of the chapel, waiting for her groom to arrive, the idea of marrying a man she'd only met twice seemed absolutely insane.

There had to be another way. She could sell the house and use that money to keep the Rainbow Place open for a while. And she could do fund-raising once that money ran out. Other people managed to keep worthwhile projects going without marrying complete strangers. Why couldn't she do the same?

"There's Max." Liz's announcement brought Nikki's head up. She stared at the approaching men, feeling like a doe watching the approach of a hunter.

"*That's* Sam Walker?" Liz's incredulous question broke Nikki's paralysis.

"Yes." The single word was all she could get past the sudden lump of panic that clogged her throat.

"Dents?" Liz hissed in her ear. "Dents? You're marrying a guy who looks like this and all you can tell your best friend is that he has dents in his face? He's gorgeous!"

Max and Sam reached them just then, saving Nikki the necessity of finding a reply. She really didn't need Liz to point out Sam's attractiveness. It was bad enough that she was marrying him; it was an added source of irritation to be forced to admit that the man was a bona fide hunk. He was wearing the same gray suit he'd worn to the meeting with Jason, paired with a plain white shirt. She'd thought the crazy tie he'd worn then might have been a quirk, but the one he had on today was an indescribable concoction of turquoise and hot pink on a dark gray background.

She let Max make the introductions, grateful for the small delay before she had to speak to Sam. But she still wasn't ready when he turned those deep blue eyes in her direction. She lifted her chin and met his look, hoping she looked as cool and unemotional as he did.

Sam had spent a week telling himself that Nikki Beauvisage couldn't be half as beautiful as he remembered. But seeing her, he knew he'd been lying to himself. Bathed in the ruthless glare of the afternoon sun, she was every bit as beautiful as she had been in kinder indoor light.

Her pale gold hair was pulled back from her face and twisted in some kind of knot at the back of her head. It was the kind of style that made a man's fingers itch to pull out the pins that held it. Her eyes were an even more vivid green than he'd remembered, contrasting with the milky paleness of her skin. If it hadn't been for the lush fullness of her lower lip, she could have been a painting of an angel. But he didn't think angels had mouths that made men think of smooth sheets and smoother skin.

Not to mention a body that curved in all the right places. Those curves were nicely displayed in an ivory-colored suit, worn with a green shell that echoed the color of her eyes. Sam didn't need to look at the labels to know that both items were pure silk. He was vaguely aware that the others had moved away a little, giving him and his soon-to-be bride at least the illusion of privacy.

"Mr. Walker." Nikki's greeting was as cool as her image. If it hadn't been for the slightly panicked look he'd seen in her eyes as he and Max approached, and the nervous tightness of her fingers on the tiny leather purse she carried, Sam might have believed that she was completely unmoved by what they were about to do.

"Call me Sam. I've never been crazy about husbands and wives calling each other Mr. and Mrs. It's cumbersome." He could have stopped there. He *should* have stopped there but some demon made him add: "Especially in the bedroom."

Nikki stiffened as if someone had just shoved a pole down the back of her tailored jacket. "That hardly matters in our case."

If her eyes got any colder, he was likely to have icicles hanging off his chin, Sam thought. "No family?" he asked, ignoring her comment. "I'd think you'd want them here to witness the happy event."

"My mother and my brother are both in Europe." Not that it was any of his business, Nikki thought, immediately sorry that she'd given him an answer. "I don't see your family in attendance. I guess you don't want them to know you're marrying for money?" She was unreasonably pleased when the sweetly asked question made Sam's mouth tighten.

"No. But you already knew that."

Tit for tat. A great way to start a marriage, Nikki thought, even one that wasn't really a marriage. Less than five minutes and already he'd managed to get under her skin in a way she couldn't remember anyone else ever having done. How was she going to survive an entire year married to this man?

"Drummond is here." Max stepped forward, his words both warning and announcement.

Sam slid his hand through Nikki's arm, his tight-lipped expression relaxing into a fond smile. Only Nikki was close enough to see that the smile stopped short of his eyes. "Smile, darling. It's show time."

Nikki tensed as Max's look swung from Sam to her, his expression questioning. "Ready?"

This was her last chance to back out of this whole crazy arrangement. She could walk away right now, kiss her inheritance goodbye and never have to see Sam Walker again. But she'd also be saying goodbye to the needs of a lot of people who depended on her, not to mention her own hopes and dreams for expanding the center, maybe even opening another one.

Over Max's shoulder she could see Jason approaching and she knew that the final moment of decision had arrived. She could say she'd changed her mind and never have to see Sam Walker again. Or she could marry him and start counting down the next three hundred and sixty-five days to freedom.

Her hand tightened unconsciously on Sam's arm, feeling the hard strength of muscle under the fabric of his sleeve. For one crazy moment, she had the urge to bury her face in his shoulder and hide from the world. The idea was so ridiculous that her shoulders stiffened and she took a quick step away from him. She'd been standing on her own two feet for a long time. And if the time ever came that she needed someone to lean on, it certainly wouldn't be Sam Walker.

"I'm ready," she said, aware that she'd never felt less ready for anything in her life.

Afterward, Nikki remembered her wedding in bits and pieces, like images caught in a photographer's flash.

Sam being introduced to Michael, shaking his hand with a grave courtesy that made the four-year-old's eyes widen in wonder.

Then the chapel itself, with the sun slanting through the lattice-and-ivy roof, casting dappled shadows across the stone floor.

Jason's loving smile as he watched the two of them in front of the altar.

The sound of a soft female voice reading the marriage vows, which Nikki couldn't hear through the humming in her ears.

And Sam Walker.

His image was the clearest of all. His big frame standing so close to hers, his face expressionless as he listened to the words meant to link two people who loved each other, meant to create ties that would last a lifetime.

Nikki jumped when he reached out and took her hand in his. Her eyes locked on his face. As if in a dream, she heard him repeating his vows, promising to love, honor and cherish her. Till death do us part. *Or until she inherits her money,* she thought, suppressing a wild urge to giggle hysterically.

And then she felt the cool weight of a ring slide onto her finger. She looked down at the circle of plain gold that sat so snugly at the base of her third finger. A wedding ring. She hadn't even thought about a wedding ring. But Sam had thought of it. And not just for her. Nikki stared blankly at the much larger gold band he pressed into her palm. She could barely hear her own voice as she repeated her vows, making promises she had no intention of keeping, vows she planned to break. Her hands were shaking so badly that she had a difficult time sliding the ring on Sam's finger.

He closed his fingers around hers, holding her hand in a sure, steady grip. Nikki lifted her face to his and he felt something twist in his chest at the look in her eyes. She looked young and vulnerable and just a little frightened.

His hand tightened over hers, offering a silent reassurance he wasn't sure was justified. What they were doing was crazy—a devil's bargain made in a house of God.

"You may kiss the bride." The minister's words sounded unnaturally loud.

Liz and Bill looked at the couple standing before the simple altar and wondered if Nikki knew what she'd just done.

Max looked at his clients and friends and wondered if putting them together had been a stroke of genius or an act of madness.

Jason Drummond looked at them and hoped he'd done the right thing when he gave his approval to their marriage.

Sam looked at Nikki and realized that he'd been wondering what her mouth would taste like since the first moment they'd met.

Nikki looked at Sam, feeling a flutter of panic uncurl in her chest, a feeling that, once he kissed her, some indefinable line would have been crossed and there'd be no going back.

Later, she told herself that she might have pulled back at that moment if it hadn't been for the fact that Sam was still holding her hand. But if she were completely honest, with herself if with no one else, it wasn't his grip on her hand that held her in place. It was a deep, feminine curiosity, a need to feel his mouth on hers, to know his taste and touch.

It was a plain, unadorned kiss, a simple pressing of his lips to hers, certainly nothing to justify the sudden quivery feeling of her knees—that had to be nerves. Nor was there anything in his kiss to explain the urge she had to curl her fingers around the edges of his jacket and cling, to burrow against him as if he could shield her from the rest of the world.

Sam lifted his head slowly. There was a dazed look in Nikki's eyes that he could relate to. He felt a little dazed himself. He'd certainly shared more passionate kisses in his time, but he couldn't remember the last time he'd had the urge to gather a woman close and hold her, to protect her from harm. Or maybe he could remember. He'd had a similar feeling when he held Sara.

The thought of his first wife made him drop Nikki's hand and step back. He'd loved Sara. That was why they'd married. His marriage to Nikki was an entirely different story, purely a business proposition. He had no intention of forgetting that.

Nikki saw the barriers come up in Sam's eyes as he released her hand and moved away. Her spine stiffened. If he hadn't stepped back, she would have.

It had only been a kiss, she reminded herself. It was a momentary delusion that made it seem as if she could feel it all the way to her toes. She was tired and stressed. That's what was causing this slightly weak feeling in the knees. It certainly wasn't caused by a simple kiss from a man she didn't even like.

This was a business arrangement. That was probably the only kiss they'd ever share.

And she refused to admit to even a twinge of regret at that thought.

The bride and groom left the chapel in separate cars. The only unfortunate thing about the arrangement, as far as they were concerned, was that their destinations weren't also separate. From their terse farewells, it was clear that, given a choice, they'd have parted company at the chapel and never seen each other again. But even if the terms of the will hadn't made that impossible, Jason had been kind enough to make arrangements for the small wedding party to go out to dinner after the ceremony.

"I couldn't let you get married without having a celebration, Nicole," he'd said with an affectionate smile.

The last thing Nikki wanted to do was celebrate her marriage, which already felt like a prison sentence, but she forced what she hoped was a pleased smile and gave the older man a warm thank-you.

Jason was the first to leave the chapel. Nikki had been standing next to Sam, his hand resting on the small of her back, presenting the picture of connubial bliss. The door shut behind Jason, and Sam dropped his hand as if he'd been touching a hot coal. At the same moment, Nikki stepped away, putting distance between them.

"If I'd known he was going to do this, I would have found a way to prevent it," Nikki said, directing her words to no one in particular.

"Things might have been simpler if we'd gone to Vegas." Sam's comment was aimed directly at his bride.

"Some people might think it's perfectly normal to be married by an Elvis impersonator standing under a flashing neon heart, but no one who knows me would ever believe *I'd* get married that way."

"Since there's no one here but us chickens, I don't see what difference it makes where the damned ceremony is performed. We could have gotten married on top of a flagpole and no one would ever know."

"It's a moot point now," Max said before Nikki could snap out a response. "You're married and Jason has arranged a reception and you're just going to have to make the best of it."

There was a moment's silence while the combatants digested the simple truth of his words. Nikki was the first to speak.

"You're right, Max." She gave him a gracious smile. "We'll just have to make the best of it. Why don't I go with Liz and Bill and show them the way to the restaurant? Perhaps you can do the same for him?"

She nodded her head in the direction of "him" without taking her eyes from Max. In some indefinable way, she managed to imply that Sam would probably need considerable guidance in order to find the restaurant.

Sam ground his teeth together but refrained from comment. He might as well start practicing restraint now. Over the course of the next year, he had the feeling he was going to need a great deal of it.

"If I don't throttle her by the end of the first month, it will be a miracle," Sam said without taking his eyes off the road.

"After tonight, you'll probably barely see each other," Max said soothingly. "Besides, she isn't that bad."

Sam gave him a sour look. "Not if you like a woman with a tongue like a pit viper and a temper like a rabid wolverine."

"You haven't exactly been a picture of sweetness and light," Max pointed out. "I think the two of you are about even at this point." Sam's silence was as good as an admission of guilt. "All you have to do is look happy for a couple more hours and then you two can pretty much go your separate ways for the next year." He gave Sam a sideways glance, his bland look giving way to one of gentle malice. "Besides, a wedding deserves a celebration."

The look Sam shot him made it clear that he wasn't in the mood to appreciate the humor in that remark. "The only thing I'm looking forward to celebrating is my divorce a year from now. I do *not* see any reason to celebrate this farce of a marriage."

Seeing their exit coming up, he flipped on the turn signal, putting so much force into the simple gesture that Max wouldn't have been surprised to see the lever snap off in his hand. He hid a smile. It wasn't often that he saw Sam Walker with his feathers ruffled.

"Then look at it as a celebration of the fact that Mary will be able to have her surgery."

"Yeah." Sam rolled that thought around as he guided the Bronco off the freeway. Max was right. He should be thinking of his niece and his brother, of what this marriage would mean to both of them. The fact that he and his new wife got along about as well as the Gingham Dog and the Calico Cat faded into insignificance beside the thought of Mary being able to run and play like other five-year-olds.

"That's something worth celebrating," he conceded grudgingly. "But I still think the idea of all of us going out to dinner together is stupid."

"The two of you are going to be living together for the next year."

"Don't remind me."

"You're bound to share a few meals in that time. You might as well start now."

Sam turned into the parking garage near the restaurant. "I married her. That doesn't mean I have to eat with her."

"I can't imagine how I let Max talk me into this," Nikki said, speaking as much to herself as to Liz and Bill.

"I don't remember seeing any bruises from him twisting your arm," Liz pointed out. She was sitting in the back seat where she could keep an eye on her son. Since Michael was busy orchestrating a ferocious battle between two action figures, she was free to give her attention to her friend in the front seat. "You seemed to think marrying Sam was a good idea."

"I was wrong. It's a crazy idea."

"It's a done deal," Bill said. He glanced in the rearview mirror before changing lanes. "Besides, Sam seems like an okay kind of guy. I thought the whole idea was nuts, but I feel better about it after meeting Sam."

"Me, too," Liz agreed.

"I'm glad you both like him." Ridiculous as it was, Nikki felt a little betrayed by their ready acceptance of Sam. "How would you like to have him living with you for the next year?"

"It won't be so bad. In a house the size of yours, you'll barely know he's there. Besides, you're the one who married him, not me."

"Don't remind me." She was being unreasonable and she knew it. She couldn't blame Liz for not seeing past Sam's ruggedly handsome exterior and charming smile. Not that *she* thought it was charming. At least, not very. Grudgingly, Nikki admitted that he probably seemed like the embodiment of a woman's dreams—*some* women's dreams, anyway. Certainly not hers.

"I can't remember the last time Michael took to someone the way he took to Sam," Liz said, determined to point out Sam's attributes. "He really has a way with children."

"It seems that way." Nikki couldn't argue with her there. Sam had developed an immediate rapport with her small godson. Ordinarily, that would have gone a long way to softening her attitude toward the man she'd just married, but she wasn't interested in having her attitude softened. She'd just as soon keep up the mutual dislike they had going. It seemed safer.

"He seems very nice," Liz pointed out ruthlessly.

"Mmm." Nice wasn't exactly the word Nikki would have used. Pushy, annoying, overbearing, maybe. But not nice. She pretended a fascination with the traffic outside the window, hoping Liz would take the hint. She should have known better.

"You've got to admit he's very attractive."

She had no intention of admitting any such thing. "If you like that type, I suppose."

"You mean the tall, blond, blue-eyed, built-like-a-god type? It is a little passé, isn't it?"

"Should I be jealous?" Bill asked, frowning at his wife in the rearview mirror.

"Just because I happened to notice that Nikki's new husband is a hunk?"

Nikki only half heard the byplay going on between her friends. They'd just driven into the parking lot of the restaurant and she'd seen Sam and Max standing outside, waiting for them so that they all could enter the restaurant together and Jason wouldn't know the bride and groom had parted immediately after the ceremony. The fact that her heart was suddenly beating much too fast was caused by pure dislike. It had nothing to do with Sam Walker's broad shoulders or his craggy good looks. Liz might be impressed by those things, but *she* certainly wasn't. Not even a little bit.

Nikki was grateful for the dimness of the parking garage as Bill pulled the car into it. She didn't want Liz's sharp eyes to see the additional color in her cheeks and question the reason for it. Knowing Liz, she'd put some ridiculous interpretation on it and suggest something like Nikki being attracted to her new husband. Which was obviously absurd. Even if she did happen to notice that he was attractive, it was only on a purely intellectual level and certainly wasn't the cause of the sudden fluttery feeling in her stomach.

And no matter what Liz said, this was all Max's fault. It would be a miracle if she made it through the next couple of hours without wringing his neck. Of course, if she was going to commit murder, Sam Walker might be a better target. Then she wouldn't have to worry about how she was going to get through the next year with him as her husband.

Two hours later, Nikki was no longer worrying about the next twelve months. Her focus had narrowed to the next twelve hours.

Her wedding night.

Throughout dinner, all she'd been able to think about was how much she wished it were over. Sitting in the restaurant, playing at being a happy newlywed, had been sheer torture. She could hardly wait for the meal to be over with so she could go home. It was only when the meal finally ended and everyone was preparing to leave that it hit her that when she went home, she wouldn't be going alone. Liz and Bill had agreed to drive Max home, which meant she was going to be left alone with her new husband.

It had taken considerable effort to refrain from clinging to Liz and begging her friend not to leave her alone with Sam. In the ten minutes since Nikki and her husband had left the restaurant, the silence had reached an almost deafening level. Sam drove with the easy competence she'd expected. She might not like him, but he struck her as the kind of man who did most things well.

She twisted the wedding ring on her finger. The plain gold band felt as if it weighed ten pounds, dragging her hand down. Or was that her conscience feeling the weight of the lies she'd told? Her gaze was compulsively drawn to Sam's hands on the steering wheel of the truck. Light glinted off the wedding ring on his left hand.

"Is the ring too big?"

Nikki jumped. It had been so long since either of them had said anything that the sound of his voice was startling.

"The ring?"

"The one you've been fiddling with ever since we left the restaurant," he clarified.

"No. No, it's fine." She forced her hands to relax. "It just feels odd. I'd forgotten all about rings. I'm glad you thought of them. It would have looked odd if we hadn't had them."

"Very odd."

Well, that had been an almost pleasant exchange, she thought. A first for the two of them. It had been very thoughtful of him to provide the rings. She touched her ring and frowned. She didn't have the slightest idea how much a police officer was paid, but she seemed to recall hearing that it wasn't all that much. Could he afford these rings? She cleared her throat. "It's a nice ring."

"Glad you like it." He didn't take his eyes off the road.

"I think I should pay you for it."

There was a moment's silence before Sam spoke. "That's not necessary."

Something in his tone suggested that it might be wise to drop the subject, but she chose to ignore it. She didn't like the idea of him buying her a ring. It was too reminiscent of a real marriage. And this marriage wasn't real. Not in any way.

"No, really. If you want to pay for your own ring, that's one thing, but there's no reason for you to spend your own money on a wedding ring for me. If you'll tell me how much they were, then I'll pay half. It's only fair."

"It's not necessary," he said again.

"I insist." She wasn't sure why this had become so important, but it had. "There's no reason for you to buy me a ring."

"You can insist until you turn blue in the face." Sam's tone was soft as silk and sharp as a razor. "I don't want you to pay for the damned ring."

"But this is a business arrangement, and any expenses incurred should be shared."

Sam's hands tightened on the wheel as visions of murder and mayhem danced before his eyes. With an effort, he kept his voice level.

"I appreciate the offer, but—"

"Really, it's a simple matter of good business," Nikki interrupted. "I should have provided my own ring, but since I didn't think of it and you did, that doesn't mean I shouldn't pay my fair share."

"If you don't shut up about the damned ring, I'm going to pull off and dump you in the emergency lane and let you walk the rest of the way."

His tone was so calm that it took Nikki a moment to realize what he'd said. Shock was followed almost immediately by indignation and anger.

"That caveman attitude may impress some women, Mr. Walker, but I'm not accustomed to being spoken to like that."

"Too bad. It might have improved your disposition."

"There's nothing wrong with my disposition. You're the one with the personality traits of a—a Neanderthal. I can't believe I let Max convince me that this idea would work. I'd rather live on the street than spend the next year married to you."

"It's not my idea of a really fun time, either, honey."

"Don't call me honey."

"Would you prefer Mrs. Walker?"

"What I'd prefer is for you to take a long walk off a short pier," she snapped. She sat back in her seat and threw him a furious look. "And I will pay for the ring!"

Sam's only response was to glance in the rearview mirror as he flipped on the turn signal. Nikki sat in stunned silence as the truck coasted to a stop in the emergency lane.

"You can't stop here. This is for emergencies." It was a weak protest at best.

Sam unbuckled his seat belt and half turned in the seat so that he faced her. "Are you going to shut up about the ring?"

Wide-eyed, she stared at him, trying to read his expression in the dimly lit cab. She couldn't believe he was acting like this. Just because she wanted to pay for her own ring—a perfectly reasonable thing to do. "You wouldn't dare leave me here."

By way of an answer, he leaned toward her. Nikki gasped as she felt his arm brush against her. She pressed her spine so tight to the seat that she practically melted into the upholstery. But Sam simply grabbed hold of the latch and pushed open the door.

The freeway noise immediately rushed in on them, but Nikki was barely aware of it. Her eyes were locked with Sam's in silent battle. There was no softening in his expression. She looked away and unlatched her seat belt. Picking up her purse, she started to slide out of the truck, intending to call his bluff.

She paused. It was awfully dark out there. A tractor trailor roared by, and the truck rocked in its wake. She considered the three-inch heels on her pumps, not exactly the proper footwear for a stroll along the freeway. Of course, he wouldn't really let her walk.

Would he?

Sam waited, wondering what the hell he was going to do if she actually got out. Obviously, he couldn't let her walk to the nearest emergency phone. She wasn't exactly dressed for strolling along the freeway, and it would be just his luck some maniac would get hold of her and then he'd have her murder on his conscience. Besides, if anyone was going to have the pleasure of strangling her, it was going to be him.

He shouldn't have threatened to dump her on the freeway. And her offer to pay for the ring shouldn't have made him so angry. It wasn't even an unreasonable suggestion. It was just something about the way she'd said it, as if she thought he couldn't afford to buy a wedding ring. And the fact that it had taken damn near all of his savings to buy the rings didn't make him feel any more cordial toward her. There was just something about her that got under his skin and touched off his temper in a way he couldn't remember anyone else ever doing.

He waited to see what she was going to do.

Nikki waited for him to tell her he was just kidding. That he had no intention of making her walk. But he didn't say anything. She weighed her pride against her safety. It was a tough choice. Another truck roared by and she tried to imagine what it would be like to be standing beside the road when one of those metal behemoths rushed past.

Without a word, she pulled the door shut and faced forward in her seat. If she hadn't been so angry, she might have noticed Sam's almost silent sigh of relief.

They finished the drive to Nikki's house without another word being spoken between them.

Chapter 5

Sam pushed the restaurant door shut behind him, closing out the cool, damp air. Winter, or what passed for it in Southern California, had arrived abruptly the night before, blowing in with the first storm of the season and drenching the southern half of the state. The rain had tapered off to a miserable drizzle, just enough to make visibility poor and keep the roads slick. Sam spared a moment of gratitude that he wasn't with the highway patrol. Or driving a tow truck.

Brushing the rain from the shoulders of his denim jacket, he looked around. He'd never been in the Wagon Wheel Café but he'd been in places like it. The decor, if you could call it that, was strictly functional. A black-and-white-tile floor that showed signs of age, faded red vinyl booths and a few dusty plastic plants in pots scattered at random throughout the single room. He didn't have to look at a menu to know that the food would be plainly cooked, plentiful and reasonably priced.

"Find yourself a place and light, sugar. We don't stand on formality here." The woman who spoke was in her fifties. Her hair was a shade of red that owed nothing to nature, but her smile was genuine.

"I'm looking for someone."

"He's in the corner booth," she said immediately. "Said he was meeting his brother." She looked Sam up and down. "There any more like you at home? Maybe a few years older?"

"There's four of us, but I'm the oldest."

She sighed. "Ain't that always the way of it? Either too young or married or both."

Sam's smile lingered as he made his way between the rows of booths to the corner one. Keefe looked up as he stopped beside the table. He smiled, but Sam was shocked by the lines of exhaustion etched around his brother's eyes. Keefe was the younger, though by less than two years. At the moment, he looked ten years older.

"Sam." The single word served as a greeting.

"Keefe." Sam had barely slid into the booth when the red-haired waitress arrived. She set a thick white china mug in front of him and filled it with steaming coffee without asking.

"You two want to look at a menu, or should I tell you what's good?" She topped off Keefe's mug as she spoke.

Sam glanced at Keefe who shrugged indifferently. "What's good?" Sam asked.

"The steak and eggs is about the best thing on the menu, but don't ask for the eggs scrambled. Clive, he thinks a scrambled egg ain't done unless it crunches when you bite down."

"We'll take the steak and eggs," Sam told her after another glance at Keefe, who shrugged again. "Eggs over easy. Steaks rare."

"Comin' right up, sugar."

After she'd left, Sam looked at his brother. "You look like hell."

"Good to see you again, too." Keefe lifted his coffee cup and took a deep swallow. "I've been putting in a lot of hours."

"Including working all night? You look like you haven't slept in a week. I thought ranchers went to bed at sundown. Are you out branding cattle at midnight?"

"Don't pull the big-brother act on me." Keefe's smile was tight around the edges. "The only ranchers who go to bed with the sun are the ones who ranch for a hobby. I'm trying to make a living from the Flying Ace, remember?"

"I remember. How's it going?"

"I'm breaking even this year, which is about as much as I'd hoped. I wouldn't be doing that much if Jace Reno hadn't busted his butt for me this past year."

"He's a good friend."

"And a hell of a rancher. He should have a place of his own." Keefe swallowed the last of his coffee and set the cup on the edge of the table for the waitress to refill. "If I want a lecture on my life-style, I'll go see Mom."

"Sorry." Sam forced back the questions he wanted to ask. "Old habits are hard to break."

"Even bad ones." Keefe grinned and some of the tension seemed to leave his eyes. "You always did act like the nineteen months between us were nineteen years, especially after Dad died."

"I was the oldest. Someone had to keep the rest of you in line."

"You're lucky Gage and Cole and I didn't get together and beat some sense into you."

"I wasn't that bad," Sam protested.

"Worse." Keefe pulled a cigarette pack out of his pocket and tapped it until the end of one came loose. As he lit it, he caught Sam's frown and grinned tiredly. "Like I said, even bad habits are hard to break."

"I thought you quit when you and Dana got married."

The humor instantly disappeared from Keefe's eyes and the lines around his mouth deepened, making Sam regret mentioning Keefe's ex-wife. "Yeah. Well, you may recall that we haven't been married for a while now so if I want to rot my lungs, there's no one around to nag me. Unless I have breakfast with my big brother, of course."

"Sorry." Sam shook his head. "I didn't drive all the way up here to harass you."

"Could have fooled me." But there was no anger in Keefe's response. "Why did you ask me to meet you? Thanksgiving is only a couple of weeks away. I'd be seeing you then."

Sam shifted uncomfortably in the vinyl booth. He'd driven three hours from L.A., leaving before dawn. And Keefe had driven down from his ranch in the Sierra Nevadas. There was so much to say, but now that he was here, he didn't know where to start.

The waitress's arrival with their food gave Sam a moment more to think. When she was gone, he watched Keefe stub out his half-smoked cigarette.

"Have you talked to Mom?" Sam asked finally.

Keefe picked up his knife and fork before glancing across the table at his older brother, his dark eyes shrewd.

"I know you're married, if that's what you're pussy-footing around mentioning."

"A couple of weeks ago." Sam cut a piece off his steak and stared at it.

"Mom says nobody's met her." Keefe chewed and swallowed. "I don't think she was real thrilled about the way you did things—not having any of the family at the wedding and all."

"We were in a hurry," Sam muttered as he reached for his coffee cup.

"She pregnant?"

Sam choked on the coffee.

Keefe waited calmly until he'd stopped coughing. "Is that a yes or a no?"

"No!" Sam gasped the word out, reaching for a glass of water. "God, no."

Keefe's brows rose at Sam's adamant response. "That's the usual reason people get married in a hurry."

"Well, it wasn't our reason," Sam said shortly. He sliced another piece off his steak and chewed it without tasting.

"Okay." Keefe reached for his coffee. "You plan on telling me what the reason was?"

"How's Mary?"

Keefe looked surprised by the abrupt change of topic, but he went along with it.

"About the same, as far as I know. I haven't talked to Cole in a while, but I asked Mom and she said there was no change. She still needs surgery and Cole still doesn't have the money for it. I've got my place listed, but there aren't many people buying ranches these days." His expression was grim. "I guess it's a good thing they're not going to be doing the surgery right away. Gives us a little time to come up with the money."

"Take it off the market."

"I might as well, for all the good it's doing to have it listed."

"You don't need to sell it."

Sam gave up the pretense of eating and looked across the table at his brother. He'd made the long drive to see Keefe because he wanted to tell him the truth. He might be able to convince everyone else that his marriage to Nikki was a real one, but he knew Keefe would never believe it. Of his three brothers, he was closest to Keefe. They'd fought the most when they were young, but they'd still ended up friends.

"I don't have to sell the ranch?" Keefe said slowly. "If you're saying that, then it must mean you've found a way to come up with the money Cole needs." Sam could see the wheels turning in Keefe's head, adding things up and coming to the obvious conclusion. "Does this have something to do with you getting married in such a hurry?"

"It has everything to do with it." Sam's grin was crooked. "I have just made what is called a marriage of convenience, Keefe. And considering the circumstances, it's a *very* convenient marriage. I'll have the money for Mary's surgery by Thanksgiving."

There was a long moment of silence, and then Keefe pushed aside his half-eaten meal and gave all his attention to his brother. "You want to run that by me again?"

"You heard me the first time."

"I heard you, but I don't believe what I heard. You married some woman to get the money for the surgery?"

"That's right."

There was another long silence and then: "Are you nuts?"

"Just desperate. It was Max's idea."

"Max knows about this?" Keefe asked, surprised.

"He set it up. Nikki is a friend of his."

"Nikki? Is that your wife?"

"Yeah." Sam frowned over the description. The word *wife* didn't sound right. Sara was his wife, the only wife he'd had, the only one he'd wanted.

"Maybe you'd better explain this whole thing to me from the beginning," Keefe said. He reached for his cigarettes as if they were a lifeline.

Sam was surprised at how little time it took to tell the whole story. Keefe's cigarette was burned only halfway down when he finished talking. It seemed as if something that had such a cataclysmic effect on two lives should take more than a couple of minutes to describe.

"So she gets her inheritance and you get the money for Mary's surgery," Keefe summed up when Sam was done. "And all you've got to do is stay married for the next year."

"There's only eleven and a half months left now," Sam corrected him.

Keefe's brows rose and one corner of his mouth twisted in humor. "You sound like a prisoner marking off the days to parole on the cell wall."

"That's about how I feel."

"Is she that bad?"

Sam started to say yes but caught himself and shook his head instead. "It's not Nikki. We barely see each other. Which is just as well, because we get along about as well as oil and water."

"She hard to get along with?"

"Yes." Sam's mouth twisted in a self-deprecating smile and he shrugged. "But I probably haven't been much better. On the way home from the wedding, I threatened to dump her out on the freeway and make her walk the rest of the way. She damn near did it, too."

Keefe's eyes narrowed speculatively at the reluctant admiration in his brother's tone. He wondered if Sam was even aware of it.

"She's stubborn as hell," Sam was saying.

"And you're a picture of sweet reason." Keefe's tone was dry as dust.

"That's me." Sam grinned. "Not a stubborn bone in my body."

"Tell that to someone who didn't grow up with you." Keefe shook his head as he stubbed out his cigarette. "I can't believe you actually did this—got married like this, I mean."

"You'd have done the same thing."

"Probably." Keefe reached for his cigarettes, caught Sam's eye and dropped them back in his pocket without taking one. "You're as bad as Mom," he complained without heat. "What does this new wife of yours look like?"

There was that word again. *Wife.* It was technically correct but it made him uneasy to hear it said out loud. He shook off his uneasiness and considered the best way to answer Keefe's question. What did Nikki look like?

An image of her, more vivid than he would have liked, sprang to mind. She was exquisite, like a fine china figurine or a painting by one of the masters. She was golden hair and porcelain pale skin and eyes the color of jade. She made him think of cold winter nights and soft rugs in front of a fireplace. Or hot summer days and cool green grass and the feel of her skin beneath his hands.

"You *do* know what she looks like, don't you?" Keefe's quizzical question made Sam realize that he'd been staring into space as if struck dumb by the question about Nikki's looks.

"Of course I do." He lifted one shoulder in a half shrug and reached for his coffee. "She's about five feet four inches, weight maybe a hundred and twenty pounds. Blond hair, green eyes."

"You sound like you're giving a police report," Keefe said, disgusted by the lack of information. "That description fits just about anyone from Michelle Pfeiffer to Attila the Hun. Details, bro. Details."

"I think Michelle Pfeiffer is taller," Sam muttered.

"So are half the women in the country. What does Mickie look like?"

"Nikki. Her name is Nikki. And she's...attractive." The word hardly did her justice, but if he tried to describe her to Keefe, Keefe was going to end up with the idea that he was attracted to her, and he wasn't. At least, no more than any living, breathing male would be. It was impossible *not* to find her attractive.

"Attractive. That tells me a lot. It's a good thing you're a cop and not a writer. I can see your description of the characters now—the woman pointing the gun at Fosdick was...attractive."

"I never claimed to be Hemingway," Sam pointed out sourly.

"Good thing, too." Keefe lit another cigarette, ignoring Sam's pointed frown this time. "You going to tell the family the truth about this marriage?"

"No." Sam shook his head. "You're the only one I'm telling. It's going to be hard enough to get Cole to take the money without him knowing how I got hold of it. Gage spends most of his time out of the country. As long as he knows Mary's okay, he won't question the whys and wherefores. And I don't see any point in worrying Mom."

"You think you and this Nikki can pull off the happy couple act well enough to fool the family?"

"I hope so." Sam didn't need his brother's raised eyebrow to tell him that he didn't sound as positive as he might have liked. That was still a big question. Could he and Nikki maintain the facade of loving newlyweds when they could barely be in the same room without going for each other's throats?

* * *

Sam was no surer of the answer to that question a few
hours later, when he turned onto the narrow street that led
to Nikki's home—his home for the past two weeks. In those
two weeks, he and Nikki had done a fine job of avoiding
each other, which wasn't difficult in the large house. But he
didn't doubt that they could have managed to keep a certain distance, even if they'd been sharing a one-room studio apartment.

Luckily, his new residence was far from a studio apartment. The house was nestled in the hills that surrounded the
Rose Bowl. Even after having lived there for two weeks,
Sam still found himself surprised by it. He'd had a certain
image of the place before he married Nikki. He'd been
picturing pillars and a veranda, a sort of latter-day Tara. He
should have known better. Everything about Nikki Beauvisage—now Walker—spoke of money, but it wasn't flashy
money. It was quiet money, the kind that had been around
so long that it didn't need to be flashy.

And the house in front of him could be called many
things, but flashy wasn't among them. A sprawling, two-
story, Spanish style home with off-white stucco walls and
clay tile roof, it nestled gracefully into its setting. Three
ancient pepper trees, their delicate branches shifting in the
slightest breeze, stood near the house, contrasting with the
darker green of the oaks that created a ragged line along the
edges of the property. The landscaping was beautiful but
modest, giving the impression of nature gently curbed.

Sam parked in front of the house, at the end of the long
driveway. As soon as he cut off the engine, he was struck by
the quiet. Like a lot of other things about his new living
arrangements, he still wasn't used to the silence.

He'd grown up in a lower-middle-class neighborhood in
Glendale, a place with lots of families, lots of kids and

dogs, and not much silence. His own apartment was situated not far from Hollywood and Vine, a fabled corner that had little to recommend it these days, unless one liked taking a chance on getting mugged. The street noise was so prevalent that he'd long since stopped hearing it.

Here he listened to a silence broken only by the sound of a mockingbird working its way through the scales. In the distance, he could hear a subtle rushing noise that was the traffic on the Foothill Freeway, but the sound was far away and unobtrusive. The house was set so far back from the small winding road that he couldn't even hear a car go by.

For no particular reason, the quiet was suddenly irritating, and Sam took some pleasure in slamming the door of the Bronco when he got out. The mockingbird paused, as if shocked by the rude interruption, and then continued with his song, graciously ignoring the ill-mannered human in his territory. Sam glared in the bird's direction. Even the birds were high-class.

The complete irrationality of that thought brought him up short. He was losing it. The stress of this past month had finally gotten to him. He brought his hand up to run his fingers through his hair, but his eyes caught the glint of sunlight on the gold band nestled at the base of his finger and the movement was never finished.

It felt odd to be wearing a wedding ring again. He rubbed his thumb over the band, remembering. He'd worn a ring during his marriage to Sara. It had been buried with her, along with a good part of himself. When he'd bought Nikki's wedding band, he'd hesitated a moment over the matching band for himself, but he knew his family would expect it.

It had been tough enough to spring the news that he was married again, he didn't want to do anything that might make them question the reasons for that marriage. It was important that they all believe this was a real marriage, particularly Cole. His youngest brother had more than his fair share of pride, and knowing the reasons for Sam's marriage would grind that pride into the dust.

He'd have to stress to Nikki that his family was not to know the truth behind their marriage, any more than her family could.

Nikki. His wife.

Sam shook his head in disbelief as he started toward the house. He just couldn't quite connect the words *Nikki* and *wife*. Not his wife, anyway. Maybe by the time the year was up, he'd get used to the idea. He paused to consider that possibility and then shook his head. Nope, Nikki Beauvisage and Sam Walker just didn't go together. Not in a year, not in five years, not in a lifetime.

He glanced at the beat-up old Chevy parked directly in front of the house. It was painted an improbable shade of purple that made him shudder every time he saw it. He still couldn't believe the vehicle belonged to Nikki. It was a long way from the sleek luxury car he'd envisioned her driving. The first time he'd seen it, he'd assumed it was the housekeeper's and thought that if it was the best she could afford, maybe it was time to suggest a raise. But the housekeeper, Lena Sinclair, drove a respectable, late-model sedan and the purple bomb was Nikki's.

Sam shook his head as he passed it, wondering, as he did every time he saw it, why a woman who wore silk suits and Italian leather shoes drove a car that looked—and sounded—as if it were on its last legs.

He pushed open one of the heavy wooden doors and stepped inside. The entryway was all Spanish tile and white stucco. There was a fountain in one corner, and a profusion of potted tropical plants. The stained-glass skylight overhead provided enough light to keep the plants luxuriantly green. The exterior landscaping was the province of the gardener, an elderly Scotsman named McDougal, but the indoor plants were Lena Sinclair's pride and joy.

When Sam entered, she was nipping faded fronds from one of the several ferns that hung from wrought-iron hooks on the wall above the fountain. The thud of the door closing behind him made her turn. She dropped a faded leaf into the basket that hung over her arm as she came to greet him.

"How was your drive?"

"Long and wet," Sam said with a smile. Nikki's housekeeper had proven far more welcoming than Nikki had been, and Sam liked her.

Lena was one of those women who could have been any age from forty to sixty, though Sam thought she was closer to the latter than the former. He guessed that, in her youth, she'd been strikingly beautiful. In late middle age, she was still a handsome woman. She was tall, with a trim figure and a subtle elegance to her carriage that made him think of deposed queens rather than housekeepers.

"Supper's in an hour," she told him.

"Thanks, but I'll probably just get a sandwich later."

They had the same conversation or a variation of it nearly every evening. He wasn't comfortable with the idea of her cooking for him, but, even more than that, he had no desire to share a meal with Nikki. They'd managed to be civil for the past two weeks, a feat that could be attributed, in large part, to the fact that their paths rarely crossed. He didn't see any reason to tempt fate by having a meal with her.

"I've got my best baked chicken in the oven, fresh wholewheat rolls and an apple pie to die for," Lena coaxed.

Sam felt his stomach stir with interest. Aside from a couple of stale doughnuts in the early hours of the morning, the only thing he'd eaten all day was half of a steak-and-egg breakfast with Keefe. The meal Lena had just described sounded wonderful. On the other hand, the odds of him and Nikki making it through an entire meal without getting into an argument were slim to none.

"Is Nikki home tonight?"

Lena's patrician features tightened with annoyance. "I swear, the two of you are acting like a pair of children. Nikki going out to dinner and you eating sandwiches in the kitchen like a sneak thief just to avoid sitting down to dinner together."

"I don't think sneak thieves normally take time for a sandwich," Sam pointed out.

She ignored the facetious interruption and continued her scolding lecture. "The two of you agreed to live together for the next year. Do you plan on spending all that time avoiding each other?"

"It's worth a try."

"Well, it won't work. My nerves won't take it, even if yours will. Besides, the holidays are coming up." She waved her pruning shears for emphasis. "Seems to me it's going to look a little odd if you spend them apart."

"We'll work something out," Sam assured her, without the least idea of what that something might be.

"Not if you don't talk to each other."

"We'll talk. And I'll be ready for dinner in an hour. I wouldn't miss your baked chicken for the world." After all, from what she'd said, it sounded like Nikki wasn't home, so there was no sense in wasting a perfectly good chicken dinner.

Lena watched him disappear up the stairs and considered her conscience. She hadn't actually told him that Nikki was going to be out. She could hardly be blamed if he chose to infer that from what she'd said. Her conscience was in fine shape, she decided as she turned back to her plants.

Besides, she was tired of watching the pair of them walk around like a couple of unfriendly cats forced to share a barn. It was time and past that they sat down and actually talked to one another.

Nikki approached Sam's room with all the enthusiasm of a dental patient anticipating a root canal. At least a dentist gave you novocaine, she thought, stopping in front of his closed door. She could have used an anesthetic to still the butterflies in her stomach.

It was ridiculous to be so nervous at the thought of talking to him. In the two weeks since the wedding, they'd managed several perfectly civil exchanges. Of course, none of those had consisted of much more than hello and goodbye, but they *had* been civil, which was more than could be said about any of their exchanges prior to their marriage. Or after, for that matter. Her mouth tightened at the memory of Sam threatening to put her out on the freeway on their wedding night.

But she wasn't going to think about that now, she reminded herself firmly. She had business to discuss with him. It should only take a moment and, once it was done, he could continue avoiding her. For the moment, she chose to ignore the fact that she'd been doing a considerable amount of avoiding herself.

Nikki smoothed her palms down the sides of her pale grey wool trousers and then adjusted the collar of her jade green silk shirt. Fussing with her clothes was a delaying tactic and she knew it. The truth was, Sam Walker made her just a little nervous. He was large and he was ridiculously male. Worse, she was married to him. It wasn't as easy as she'd hoped to forget that.

She suddenly became aware of the picture she must make, hovering in the hall like a schoolgirl dreading a meeting with the principal. Her soft mouth tightened with irritation. This was *her* house and she wasn't going to stand here getting butterflies in her stomach at the thought of talking to the man she'd married.

Nikki lifted her hand and rapped briskly on the door. The response she received was muffled but she thought she heard the words *come in*. The sound of that deep voice renewed the tension in her stomach and her hand was not quite steady as she reached for the doorknob. The fact that they were married was irrelevant, she reminded herself. He was practically an employee, if she chose to look at it that way. Not that she could imagine ever hiring Sam Walker for anything. But, husband or employee, he was still just a man, no different from any other man.

On the other hand, maybe there were a few differences.

Nikki stood transfixed in the open doorway. Sam was across the room, his back to her, his attention on the open drawer in front of him.

And he wore not a stitch of clothing.

She forgot how to breathe as her stunned eyes skimmed the muscled width of his back to the tight globes of his buttocks and down the length of his legs.

There were, most definitely, differences between Sam Walker and other men. She'd seen a lot of men in bathing suits that covered little more than the bare necessities, but this was the first time she'd found it hard to breathe. As if compelled by some outside force, her eyes moved upward, tracing every corded muscle on the way.

There was a towel bunched casually in his left hand, held against his hip. From that and the dampness of his hair, she assumed he must have just taken a shower, which explained the fact that he was naked. But it didn't explain him telling her to come in.

She was angry, of course. Or she would be as soon as she caught her breath. How dare he expose himself to her like this, as if . . . as if they were really married!

There was a jagged white scar across one shoulder and she wondered how he'd gotten it. Would it feel rough in contrast to the smoothness of his skin? What would it feel like to put her hands against the hard muscles of his arms?

Not that she'd want to do that, of course. But the mental denial sounded a little weak. And there was a faint tingling feeling in her fingertips that hinted at a curiosity she had no business feeling.

It seemed as if she stood there forever, but in reality, it was probably less than a minute. Sam reached for something in the open drawer. The simple movement made the muscles ripple across his back and shoulders.

Nikki swallowed hard.

She didn't make a sound, but something must have alerted Sam to the fact that he was no longer alone. He turned suddenly, spinning around in a half crouch, his right hand going across his chest—reaching for a shoulder holster, she realized. Of course it wasn't there.

No shoulder holster. Nothing at all to cover the solid wall of muscle that was his chest. Nikki stared wide-eyed at the mat of dark gold hair that covered his chest, tapering downward across a tautly muscled stomach to—

"What the hell are you doing in here?" Sam's irate demand jerked her eyes upward, but not before she'd seen enough to make her mouth go dry.

"You said to come in," she stammered, thrown momentarily off balance by her own reaction to the generous display of male pulchritude before her.

"I said 'just a minute,'" he snapped. He jerked open the crumpled towel and wrapped it around his hips.

Nikki was surprised and dismayed by the twinge of regret she felt. What on earth was wrong with her? It wasn't as if she found the man attractive.

The thought was enough to stiffen her spine.

"I distinctly heard you say 'come in.'" She hadn't *distinctly* heard anything, but she certainly couldn't admit that now.

"Then you need your ears cleaned." Sam finished knotting the towel, his jerky movement revealing his irritation. "Why the hell would I say 'come in' when I'm standing here bare beam and buck naked?"

"I have no idea." Nikki had regained her poise, or at least a portion of it. "I thought perhaps you had exhibitionist leanings."

"And maybe the heart of a voyeur beats beneath that prim exterior. Maybe you're sorry I covered up?"

The fact that she *had* felt a twinge of regret added to the color in Nikki's cheeks. "Don't be ridiculous," she snapped.

"Shall I drop the towel?" he asked in a tone that made her want to smack him. "I certainly wouldn't want to spoil your fun."

Though her face felt as if it were on fire, Nikki managed to give him a look of cool indifference. "You don't have anything I haven't seen before." She paused, letting her eyes flick downward. "And in somewhat greater quantity."

Color tinted Sam's cheekbones, but the look in his eyes suggested it was caused more by anger than by any blow she might have dealt his male ego.

"Was there something you wanted? Or did you just barge in here to leer at me?"

"I was invited in," she said through clenched teeth.

"You stick to that story, if you like." He nodded agreeably, and Nikki's hands clenched against the urge to wipe the bland expression from his face.

"Max called. There are papers you need to sign. *That's* what I came to tell you."

"Thanks. I'll call him."

He didn't look in the least apologetic, damn him. "Next time, I'll slip a note under the door."

"You do that. Now, if you don't mind, I'd like to get dressed."

Nikki stood there for a moment, wishing desperately for a clever response, something that would make it clear just how much she disliked him, how little desire she had to ever speak to him again. And most of all, how little attraction he held for her. But she couldn't come up with the words to convey all those things. Worse, from the gleam in Sam's eyes, she suspected that he knew exactly what was going through her mind and was amused by her frustration.

The only option was to withdraw with as much dignity as possible. Which was what she did. She stepped back into the hall, pulling the door closed with a gentle click, not allowing him the satisfaction of seeing her slam it.

She stood in the hallway, feeling as if steam must be coming out her ears. She'd never in her life met anyone who made her want to commit violent acts. Never—until she'd met Sam Walker.

And she'd had to go and marry him.

She cast a last frustrated glance over her shoulder at the blank door, wishing desperately that she hadn't let Max convince her that this marriage was a good idea, that she'd married someone else, *anyone* else.

But she was stuck with Sam Walker, at least for the next eleven and a half months.

Nikki forced herself away from the door. He was an obnoxious jerk, but she probably wouldn't have to deal with him again for days. With luck, maybe she could stretch it to a week.

Chapter 6

Luck was not smiling in Nikki's direction.

Half an hour after her encounter with Sam, she left her room to go down for dinner. She'd been avoiding eating in the dining room for the last couple of weeks, not wanting to share a meal with Sam. But Lena had expressed considerable annoyance over Nikki's new habit of taking a tray up to her room, asking if she planned to eat her meals in her room for the next year. The idea didn't sound bad to Nikki, not if it meant less time spent in Sam Walker's company.

Lena must have read the answer in Nikki's eyes, because she'd clicked her tongue in exasperation and pointed out that Sam hadn't eaten a single meal in the dining room since he'd moved in. The two of them were acting like a pair of children. She would have continued, but Nikki lifted a hand in surrender and promised to come down to dinner. After all, what were the odds that Sam would choose tonight to eat in the dining room?

Apparently, they were much better than she'd hoped.

She saw him as soon as she entered the room. He was standing in front of the floor-to-ceiling window, looking out into the courtyard that was tucked into the corner of the L-shaped house. The rain was a glistening curtain sliding through the lights that illuminated the naturalistic waterfall and small pool that dominated the center of the courtyard.

It was a beautiful view, and one she'd often admired herself, but Nikki wasn't in the mood to appreciate it. Obviously, Sam had decided to come down to dinner tonight. Equally obvious was the need for an immediate change of plans on her part. The last thing she wanted to do was sit across a dinner table from Sam Walker. Talk about a prescription for indigestion.

She took a step backward, intending to slip out of the room before he saw her. Better to face Lena's wrath than to spend time with her reluctant husband.

But before Nikki could make her escape, Lena came through the door across the room. She was carrying two bowls from which steam was rising. Her dark eyes immediately spotted Nikki, who was poised for departure in the doorway.

"There you are, Nikki. Just in time."

At the sound of Lena's voice, Sam turned and saw Nikki. He was wearing a pair of softly faded jeans and a chambray shirt that echoed the blue of his eyes, but a sudden image of how he'd looked wearing only a towel—and not even that—flashed through Nikki's mind. She could only hope that the light was dim enough to conceal the color that came up in her cheeks.

From Sam's expression, it was clear that he was no more enthused about the idea of sharing a meal than she was. The knowledge carried a perverse sort of pleasure. At least she wasn't the only one who'd be miserable.

"The soup smells wonderful, Lena," she said as she strolled into the room, giving no hint that she'd rather have been walking into a lion's den.

"There's nothing like a good bowl of soup on a chilly night like this," Lena said as she set the bowls down.

Nikki was dismayed to see that she'd arranged the place settings together at one end of the long table, one on either side, so that she and Sam would be staring at each other across the width of polished mahogany.

"Lena said you were eating out tonight," Sam said, making little effort to conceal his displeasure at finding out otherwise.

"Actually, I just said she'd been eating out lately," Lena said serenely. She reached out to straighten a spoon, bringing it into perfect alignment with the fork beside it. "Why don't the two of you start on the soup. I'll bring in the rest of the meal."

There was a moment's silence after her departure. The hiss of the rain outside suddenly seemed very loud. Nikki stared at Sam's hand where it rested on the back of one of the chairs. His hands were large, long fingered and strong. She thought of the corded muscles in his thighs, of the way the muscles in his shoulders rippled beneath his skin.

"I think I'll see if there's anything I can do to help." She was halfway across the room before the sentence was complete. At the moment, she didn't care if he knew she was running. She just wanted to get out of the room before he noticed that she was blushing like a girl in the throes of her first crush.

Lena glanced up as she entered the kitchen. Her sharp gaze took in Nikki's flushed face and the panic in her eyes. Her smile was subtly smug as she returned her attention to the steamed vegetables she was transferring from pan to bowl.

"If you've come to offer help, I don't need any," she said.

"I've come to ask what you think you're doing." Nikki kept her voice low, not wanting Sam to hear her.

"I'm finishing up dinner." Lena raised her dark brows in surprise.

"You know what I mean. You told me he wouldn't be here tonight." Nikki took the pan Lena handed her and set it in the sink.

"I said he hadn't eaten in the dining room since he'd moved in." Lena shrugged her innocence. "How was I to know he'd choose tonight to do something different?"

"Because you told him *I* wouldn't be here."

"That's not what I said. I just said you hadn't—"

"I heard what you said. And I know perfectly well you were setting the two of us up. What I don't know is *why.*"

Lena finished garnishing the vegetables with parsley sprigs and slivers of red pepper before raising her head to meet Nikki's indignant look.

"I set you up," she admitted without the smallest show of guilt. "I told your Sam, and I'll tell you—it's more than past time the two of you sat down and talked."

"I don't want to talk to him. And he's not *my* Sam. He's not *my* anything."

"He's your husband."

"Only for the next year, and I don't know how I'm going to get through it."

"Well, you're not going to get through it by acting like a couple of children. Sneaking around the house to avoid each other. If I hadn't come in when I did, you would have gone back up to your room tonight, wouldn't you?"

"I don't want to eat with him." Nikki flushed at the childish sound of her protest, but it was nothing more than the truth.

"Do you plan on going the whole year without eating a meal together?" Lena demanded.

"If I can manage it, I'll go the whole year without setting eyes on him."

"Well, you can't manage it. You know it, I know it and he knows it. If the pair of you weren't too old for it, I'd smack your heads together to knock some sense into you."

Nikki's eyes shifted away from Lena's. She suddenly felt as if she were five years old again and had just been caught with her hand in the cookie jar. When she was a child, it had always been Lena who'd provided a sense of discipline and stability in her life.

Her father had been killed in a boating accident when she was a baby, and her grandfather had moved her and her mother and brother into his house, making no secret of the fact that he didn't trust Marilee to take care of his grandchildren. It had proved a wise move since Marilee had embarked on a series of affairs and marriages that had spanned the years since. During the marriages, she'd moved out of the big house, but, at her father-in-law's insistence, her children had stayed.

Marilee had flitted in and out of her life like a beautiful butterfly, never quite with them even when she was living in the same house. Nikki's brother, Alan, had been old enough to reject any attempt at filling the gap Marilee's periodic disappearances left in his life, but Nikki had desperately needed Lena's stable presence in hers. Lena was much more than a housekeeper to her, and her disapproval stung.

"I don't like him," Nikki muttered when the silence had gone on longer than was comfortable.

"You don't know him well enough not to like him. And if you didn't like him, you shouldn't have married him."

"Max didn't exactly provide me with a lot to choose from," Nikki pointed out.

"Well, there's not a thing wrong with the choice you made. And you might find that out if you'd take a minute to get to know him. I don't see what you're complaining about. He's well-spoken, a police officer, and he's a good-looking man. Not like some of the namby-pamby types you've dated these last few years."

Nikki stared at her, horrified. "You're not matchmaking, are you?"

"You're already married to him. Why would I matchmake?" Lena lifted the foil off the chicken and rice she'd just taken out of the oven and transferred the chicken to a platter.

"But it's not a real marriage," Nikki shouted in a whisper.

"You said the words. You signed the papers. And your Sam looks pretty solid to me. I'd say that makes it a real marriage."

"You know what I mean. And he's not *my* Sam."

"What I know is that it's time and past that you met a man who won't lay down and roll over for you or your money." Lena began transferring the rice to a bowl.

"He *married* me for my money," Nikki pointed out, surprised to realize that the thought stung.

"I'm sure he had his reasons," Lena said, undisturbed.

"Like greed," Nikki muttered.

"I don't think so. Your Sam doesn't strike me as a greedy man."

"He married a woman he didn't even know in return for a nice, fat check. Which he demanded up front, by the way. If that's not greed, I don't know what is. And he's *not* my Sam," she added without much hope of being listened to.

"I'd guess he had his reasons," Lena said comfortably. "Besides, you did the same thing—married him for money."

"But it's *my* money."

"No, it's not." Lena shot her a stern look. "It's your grandfather's money and you're cheating to get it."

The criticism stung all the more because Nikki had felt a few guilt pangs over the way she was circumventing her grandfather's intentions.

"Grandfather shouldn't have put such a ridiculous clause in his will," she muttered.

"No, he shouldn't have. And if he hadn't been such a blind, stubborn fool, he'd have realized that you'd do exactly what you have. Heaven knows, you're as stubborn as he was. I don't blame you for doing what you did, but now that you've made your bed, I think you should lie in it with a bit more grace. Both of you," she added, nodding toward the dining room to include Sam in her disapproval. "If you can't share a meal without arguing, then you're going to have a hard time getting through the next year, now aren't you?"

She didn't seem to expect a response, because she nodded to a cloth-covered basket.

"Bring the rolls with you when you come," she ordered as she picked up the platter of meat and vegetables.

Frustrated and confused, Nikki stared after her. Just what she needed—Lena lecturing her on Sam Walker's attributes. Not to mention the possibility that Lena had matchmaking in mind. It was going to be difficult enough to live with him for the next year, without adding Lena's interference to the picture.

But she was right about one thing—they certainly should be able to make it through a meal together without arguing. The question was whether or not they would.

* * *

The soft hiss of the rain in the courtyard seemed to thicken the silence inside, making it an almost tangible presence. Neither of the room's occupants had said a word since Lena's departure. The housekeeper had gone home as soon as the meal was served, leaving the newlyweds alone in the big house.

Sam ate with the methodical precision of an assembly-line worker building widgets. And with about as much pleasure.

Nikki picked at her meal, rearranging the food on her plate and forcing down an occasional bite. She was vividly aware of the man sitting across the table from her.

"I think we were set up."

Nikki jumped, startled. The silence between them had been so thick that it was a shock to have it broken. Her eyes jerked to his face.

"Set up?"

"For this meal. I think Lena set us up." There was a hint of rueful humor in his eyes, and Nikki felt the knot of tension in her stomach ease a little.

"I think so, too," she agreed.

"You'd think I'd recognize a sting when it's staring me in the face, but I fell for it like a rookie."

"I've known her long enough to be suspicious, but I didn't see it coming."

"She's very good. I mean, she didn't actually tell me you weren't eating in tonight. She just held out the bait and I jumped for it." There was real admiration in Sam's tone.

"She did the same thing with me. Said you hadn't been eating here at all."

"She said the same thing about you."

"I haven't been. Not since the . . . since we . . ."

"Got married?" Sam said the words she couldn't quite get out.

"Yes." Nikki gave up the pretense of interest in her food and pushed her plate aside. "It seems so incredible, I have a hard time saying it."

"I know what you mean."

Sam pushed his own plate aside and reached for the thermal coffeepot Lena had set on the end of the table. He held it up, lifting one brow questioningly. Nikki nodded and pushed her cup across the table. Sam filled both their cups, nudged the cream and sugar in her direction and then leaned back in his chair, cradling his coffee between his palms. The bone-china cup looked ridiculously small and fragile in his large hands.

Nikki added a spoonful of sugar and a healthy dollop of cream to her coffee. The only sound in the room was the soft rush of the rain outside and the musical chime of her spoon against the delicate porcelain of the cup as she stirred her coffee. But the tension that had characterized the silence only moments before was gone.

"I think this is some kind of record," Sam said.

"What is?"

"We've been together for—" he glanced at his watch "—almost twenty minutes without getting into an argument."

"We didn't speak for seventeen of those twenty minutes," she pointed out dryly.

"And that's another record. Three minutes' conversation without attempted murder on either side."

"Where's Ripley when you need him?"

There was a short, almost companionable silence. Nikki took a sip of coffee and shot a surreptitious look across the table at Sam, wondering if he was as surprised as she was that they were actually managing a civil exchange. From the look in his eyes when they met hers, he was.

"I was out of line this evening when you came to my room," he said. "I'm sorry."

The reminder of the scene—was it only an hour ago?—brought an extra tint of pink into Nikki's cheeks. She looked away from him, trying to banish the image of his nudity. "I really did think you'd said to come in," she said, hoping he wouldn't notice her blush.

"I guess your finishing-school ears just aren't accustomed to my middle-class accent."

Nikki's shoulders stiffened. So much for their brief cease-fire, she thought. He couldn't go more than a few minutes without making snide remarks about the differences in their backgrounds. She was surprised by the depth of her disappointment. The last few minutes had been so pleasant.

She lifted her head, a cutting response hovering on the tip of her tongue. And she saw the humor in Sam's blue eyes. There was nothing sarcastic or critical in his expression, and Nikki realized she'd misjudged him.

Maybe not for the first time?

It was a novel thought, the idea that she might have misjudged him. Not that she'd been completely wrong. Certainly she hadn't misjudged his determination to dump her on the Ventura Freeway in the middle of the night. But maybe he wasn't quite as hopeless as she'd thought.

"Next time, I'll ask you to repeat yourself," she said. And it was hard to say who was most surprised by the faintly teasing note in her response.

"Maybe I should ask you to repeat what you think you heard." Sam's half smile became a full-fledged grin, and Nikki's heart bumped ever so slightly. He really was a remarkably attractive man, if you liked the type. And wasn't it a very good thing that she didn't?

"Lena thinks we should try to get along," she said abruptly.

"So I gathered." Sam cradled the cup against his palm. "I assume that's why she set us up tonight."

"Yes."

"It would certainly make the next twelve months a little easier."

"True."

There was a brief silence while they both considered just how long a year could be.

"I guess I haven't been the easiest guy in the world to get along with," Sam said finally.

She could have commented that that was the understatement of the year, but she didn't. He'd offered an olive branch and the least she could do was respond in kind. "I haven't been an angel of sweetness and light."

"I'm the one who's been at fault in most of this."

Nikki shook her head. "I can't let you take all the blame. I know my temper's been short."

"I don't blame you. I've been a real s.o.b."

She felt a flash of irritation. Did he have to argue with everything she said? "Really, I'm just as much to blame as you are," she insisted in an aggressively reasonable tone.

Sam's smile tightened subtly and his eyes took on a faint chill. "I launched the hostilities in Max's office the day we met. You're not to blame for responding in kind."

Nikki fought to control her annoyance. Really, he was the most obnoxious man she'd ever met. And wasn't it typical of him to insist on having the final word and taking all the blame—

Suddenly it hit her that they were actually on the verge of quarreling over who was most to blame for their past quarrels. The absurdity of it brought her eyes to Sam's face. The same thought must have struck him, because his eyes reflected her own surprise and disbelief.

"This is ridiculous. I can't even believe we're arguing about this," he muttered.

Neither could Nikki. She wasn't normally an argumentative woman. What was it about the man she'd married that brought out this side of her? And how were they going to dig themselves out of this latest hole?

"You're right, it is ridiculous. If you want to take all the blame, I won't stop you." She nodded her head graciously.

"Gee, that's big of you," Sam said dryly. "Thanks. I think."

"You're welcome."

Nikki saw the laughter in Sam's eyes, and a soft giggle escaped her. Sam chuckled. The moment of shared laughter banished the last of the tension between them.

"Maybe we can blame everything on the situation," Sam suggested. He shook his head as he reached for the coffee pot. "I thought arrangements like this only existed in books and movies."

He raised the coffeepot and gave her a questioning look.

"No, thank you. One cup is my limit."

"You'd never make it as a cop." Sam twisted the lid back onto the thermal pot and picked up his cup.

"Do you have to drink a lot of coffee to be a cop?"

"At least a pot a day," he confirmed solemnly. "We've got to have something to go with all those doughnuts."

"I can imagine." Though from what she'd seen of him— which, come to think of it, was a considerable amount—she doubted that Sam spent much time eating doughnuts. A man didn't end up with all that lean muscle by spending his time at Winchell's.

"Do you think we could manage to maintain this level of civility for more than a few minutes?" he asked, his tone pitiable.

Nikki shot a quick glance across the table, taking in the humor in his eyes, the warmth of his smile and the tousled thickness of his dark blond hair. She was shocked to realize that she didn't think it would be difficult at all.

"Maybe if we worked on it," she conceded.

"I'm willing to try if you are. A year is a long time to be at odds with someone you're living with. We could try and think of each other as roommates. My brother Gage has a woman roommate, and they manage to rub along together fairly well."

"In a way, I guess that's what we are," Nikki said slowly.

"Truce?" He offered his hand across the table.

Nikki hesitated only a moment before accepting the gesture. She felt an immediate jolt of awareness, the same tingling feeling that she'd had the first time they shook hands in Max's office. She'd had it again, only much stronger, when he'd kissed her in the chapel.

His fingers seemed to swallow her hand, making her very aware of how much larger and stronger he was. The thought should have been frightening. They might share a marriage license, but he was still a stranger. It wasn't fear Nikki felt, though. It was a deep feminine awareness of the masculinity of the man across from her, of the differences between them.

"Truce." She heard the breathy tone of her response and hoped Sam would attribute it to the surprise of finding them in agreement. She pulled her hand free.

"Maybe we'll make it through this next year without killing each other after all," Sam said, giving her another of those grins that made her pulse jump.

"It just might be possible."

Somehow, twelve months didn't sound nearly as long as it had a few minutes ago.

"So, how's married life?" Liz's eyes were bright with curiosity. "I don't see any wounds, so I assume you and your new hubby haven't come to blows yet."

Once a month, she and Nikki got together to have lunch, go shopping or catch a movie together. Liz deposited Michael with a baby-sitter and, as she put it, escaped long enough to confirm that the real world still existed. Nikki thought that Liz's husband and son *were* the real world, but she enjoyed a chance to spend a few hours with her friend. This was the first time they'd seen each other since the wedding and Liz was bursting with a curiosity she didn't even try to hide.

"He's not my *hubby* and married life is just fine, especially since it's not really a marriage."

Liz clicked her tongue in disgust at this boring response. "Details. I want details."

"What kind of details are you hoping for?" Nikki asked. She gave her friend a stern look. "As if I didn't know. You're hoping for some lurid tale of passion."

"Lurid tales have gotten a bad rap in recent years. And what's wrong with passion?"

"Nothing. But that's not why I got married. For heaven's sake, Liz, I'm not going to jump into bed with a man I barely know just because we share a marriage license."

"You've thought about it, though, haven't you?" Liz asked wickedly. "I mean, there he is. And there you are. All alone together in that big house."

"I think you've been spending too much time watching soap operas. Things don't work the same way in real life as they do on TV. Maybe we should get together more often so I can give you a reality check," Nikki said, giving her a concerned look. "There's nothing going on between Sam and me."

"If I were living with a man as gorgeous as Sam Walker, I don't think I'd be boasting about the fact that nothing was going on."

The waiter's arrival with their meals gave Nikki a momentary respite, but she knew Liz too well to think the topic would be forgotten. She was right. The moment he was gone, Liz pinned Nikki to the booth with an intense look.

"And you can't tell me that you haven't given some thought to the possibilities inherent in this whole setup."

"I hardly even know he's in the house," Nikki said, lying through her teeth. She gave Liz a quelling look as she reached for the saltshaker. "This is strictly a business arrangement and that's all it's ever going to be. Enough said. Now, can we please change the subject? How is my adorable godchild?"

From Liz's expression, it was obvious that she didn't think there'd been nearly enough said, but she accepted the change of topic. And in a gesture of true friendship, she refrained from bringing up Sam's name for the rest of the afternoon.

Nikki appreciated her restraint. She only wished that he'd stay out of her thoughts as well as the conversation. And she wished she'd been telling the truth when she said that she hardly knew he was in the house. But if she'd told Liz the truth, she'd have had to admit to thinking about her new husband more than she liked.

It had been a week since they'd agreed to a cease-fire. As she'd crawled into bed that night, she'd wondered if it was possible that she and Sam could really get along. From the moment they'd met, they'd struck sparks off one another.

Now, driving home after her time with Liz, she found herself considering the possibility of a whole new kind of sparks between them. She dismissed the idea almost immediately. Even if she were to become attracted to Sam, and assuming the feeling was mutual, it wouldn't make any difference. This was still a business arrangement and, if there was one thing she'd learned from her grandfather, you did not mix your business and your private lives.

"And you forced me to break that rule, Grandfather, when you came up with that ridiculous clause to put in your will," she said out loud as she turned into her driveway. "Because you forced me to mix business with my private life in a major way."

Sam's truck was parked in front of the house. Nikki's heart jumped a little, but that was easily explained. She and Sam might have been getting along this past week, but she still wasn't accustomed to the idea that she no longer lived alone. And it wasn't as if she and Sam had become friends overnight. The overt hostility was gone, but they were still strangers. They'd hardly seen each other this past week, which could be why their truce had held, she thought as she pushed open the front door.

Sam was coming down the stairs as she entered the house, as if he'd been conjured by her thinking about him. He smiled when he saw her, and Nikki was struck by how much more pleasant it was to be on speaking terms. Prior to their truce last week, they'd probably have exchanged little more than a nod.

"Nikki, I'm glad I caught you," he said, taking the last two stairs in one stride.

He was wearing jeans, well-worn and faded, clinging to his long legs in a way that made her aware of the muscles beneath the snug denim, and the light from the chandelier picked out the gold in his dark blond hair. All in all, he looked altogether too attractive. It was too bad Max hadn't come up with a nice, mousy type for her to marry, someone with a plastic pocket protector and safety glasses that slid down his nose—someone who wouldn't have even the slightest effect on her pulse.

With an effort, she forced herself to concentrate on what Sam was saying.

"I was hoping I'd get a chance to talk to you before I left for work."

"I thought you worked today," she said. Walking to the narrow mahogany side table that sat along one side of the entryway, Nikki set her purse down and picked up the stack of mail there before turning back toward Sam. The little bit of extra distance made it easier to breathe.

"No rest for the wicked." His smile couldn't completely banish the tired lines beside his eyes. "Thanksgiving is next week." Sam was shrugging into his jacket as he spoke. "I never thought to ask if your family is coming back from Europe for the holidays."

"My family?"

The questioning tone of her voice made Sam's brows go up. "Your mother and your brother," he clarified. "Are they coming home for Thanksgiving or Christmas?"

"Not that I know of. I think Mother planned to spend the holidays in Monaco. I don't know what Alan will be doing." She shrugged. "We're not really very close." Which was a bit of an understatement, particularly when it came to her brother, whom she hadn't seen since their grandfather's funeral two years before.

"Then there's no conflict," he said with satisfaction.

"Conflict?"

"With your family and mine both expecting us to join them. We can go to Los Olivos." He pulled his keys out of his pocket, apparently satisfied that the decision had been made.

"I can't spend the holiday at your family's home," Nikki protested, horrified at the idea.

"Why not?"

"Because they think we're married."

"We *are* married."

"You know what I mean." Agitated, she set the mail back down and shoved her hands in the pockets of her slacks.

"You mean they're going to expect us to act like a couple." He took the lift of her shoulder as agreement and continued. "You didn't think we could make it a whole year without running into situations where we'd have to pretend we were really married, did you?"

"It's too soon. We could never carry it off. Besides, I was planning on spending the holidays with Jason. Otherwise, he'll be alone." She finished on a note of triumph, confident that she'd solved the question of the holidays.

"Isn't Jason going to think it a bit odd if we spend our first holiday together apart?" Sam's tone was dry. "We're supposed to be madly in love, remember?"

Nikki stared at him. She wanted more than anything to argue with him, but she couldn't. Jason would think it very odd if she spent Thanksgiving with him and left her new husband to go off and join his family.

"Why don't you see if Jason wants to join us?" Sam asked, accepting her tacit agreement that they'd be spending the holidays together. "Thanksgiving is pretty much of an open house and I know he'd be welcome."

"I'll ask," Nikki said, giving in to reality.

"Don't look so glum," Sam chided. "We haven't burned anyone at the stake in at least five or six years."

"That's reassuring."

He grinned at her gloomy tone, lifted his hand in farewell and disappeared out the door. Nikki stayed where she was, listening to the delicate sound of the fountain in the corner and trying to convince herself that this visit didn't have disaster written all over it.

Chapter 7

Thanksgiving dawned gray and cloudy, a perfect reflection of Nikki's expectations for the day. She'd had a full week to anticipate meeting Sam's family, a full week in which to consider all the things that could go wrong. The possibilities were awful enough to make her pray the clouds would open up and rain so hard that they'd have to give up the idea of driving north. Unfortunately, by midmorning, the sun was starting to nudge its way through and the radio was announcing that it was going to be a beautiful holiday.

Sam drove to Los Olivos. With a vague idea of having a quick getaway available, Nikki had suggested they take her car. But neither Sam nor Jason made any secret of their doubts about it being able to make the three-hour trip. Nikki's protests that Barney was a great deal more reliable than he looked were ignored. And since Barney's heating and air-conditioning system consisted of opening or closing windows, she didn't pursue the argument.

Besides, she didn't really want to drive. She was better off climbing into the back seat of the Bronco and leaving Sam to carry on the bulk of the conversation with Jason, giving her yet more time to brood about meeting his family.

It would have been difficult enough to meet them if she'd really been his wife, a genuine addition to the family. But the fact that the marriage was simply a business transaction made it even more nerve-racking.

If there was a good time to be introduced to Sam's family, it surely wasn't in the midst of a major holiday. Nikki stared out the window at the passing scenery and wished she'd insisted on meeting the rest of the Walker clan sooner. Never mind the fact that, until two weeks ago, she'd barely been able to exchange a civil word with Sam and that she'd probably rather have had her nose pierced than spend any time with him, let alone meet his family.

The fact was, if they were going to pull off this charade for the next year, she really should have met his family before this. What kind of a daughter-in-law didn't want to meet her in-laws? They'd probably already figured out that it was a sham. And if they hadn't, they undoubtedly soon would. It would have been nice to believe Sam's assurance that they wouldn't be looking for evidence that his marriage was anything less than what it seemed and would, therefore, take it at face value and accept her as his wife. But she couldn't shake the feeling of impending disaster.

They'd take one look at her and know she was a fake. Then they'd tell Jason, and she'd not only lose her inheritance, she'd probably go to jail for fraud of some kind. She'd lose her friends, her money, have to wear ugly clothes and probably spend the rest of her life as the girlfriend of some woman named Bubba.

It was, perhaps, fortunate that lack of sleep caught up with her before Nikki's imagination could paint even more lurid pictures of the disasters that lay ahead. She dozed off shortly after they left the outskirts of Los Angeles behind them, sleeping until Jason reached back to shake her awake minutes before they arrived at the Walker home.

"You should have had Jason wake me sooner," she said, keeping her voice low as Sam opened the back door. She was rummaging through her purse for her brush. "I look like a disaster survivor."

"You look fine."

"If you like the hair-on-end, ruined-makeup look," she snapped in a whisper. She was vividly aware of Jason standing on the other side of the car and of the need to present a happy-couple image to him.

Sam's smile tightened. "You're meeting my family, not filming a shampoo commercial."

"I wouldn't want to meet a dog collector looking like this." She jerked the brush through her hair, smoothing it into a thick gold fall around her shoulders.

"It's a good thing none of my family work for Animal Control, then, isn't it?"

"Problem?" Jason walked around the car, curious about the delay.

"Nikki's worried about how she looks," Sam said, sounding so like an indulgent husband that Nikki almost believed it herself. "I was just telling her she doesn't need to primp. She always looks beautiful."

"That's true," Jason agreed, and Nikki could only hope that the sun in his eyes prevented him from seeing the hostile look she shot her loving husband.

She slammed the brush back in her purse and jerked the zipper closed. The Walkers would just have to take her as she was, because she wasn't going to sit here, and put on lipstick after she'd just been accused of primping. She would have liked to ignore the hand Sam offered to help her out of the car, but Jason would surely notice. Besides, her left leg was asleep and she didn't want to risk falling face first onto the sidewalk.

"Don't look so nervous," Sam chided, taking her hand to steady her as she got out of the truck. "They're going to love you."

Nikki knew his assurance was given, at least in part, for Jason's benefit, in keeping with Sam's role of loving husband. But she wanted desperately to believe it. Not necessarily that they'd *love* her, but that they wouldn't take one look at her and know her for the phony she was.

She didn't think she could have been any more nervous if she really had been a new bride. Though she knew it was strictly for show and she was still annoyed with him, she found herself grateful for the strength of Sam's fingers around hers as they walked up the slightly erratic brick path.

The house was a simple, one-story stucco, painted white with deep blue trim. The yard was small and beautifully kept. There was a split-rail fence made of cedar that had weathered to a soft gray. Along the street, and set just inside the fence, were rose beds. Roses in every possible color dipped and swayed in the cool breeze. Pansies lined the walkway, their cheerful faces nodding a welcome.

It was a friendly picture, and Nikki found herself insensibly soothed by it. It didn't seem possible that anything bad could happen in a house with such a cheerful yard.

They'd just reached the foot of the steps when the door burst open and a tall, dark-haired man stepped out.

"I'm probably going to have to raid a turkey farm," he was saying over his shoulder. "Wouldn't it be easier just to roast the damned dog?"

It was apparently a rhetorical question, because he pulled the door closed, cutting off any possible reply. He turned, saw Sam, and a smile banished the somewhat intimidating frown on his face. "Sam!"

"Gage! I thought you were in the wilds of Borneo or Brazil." Sam released Nikki's hand and took a quick stride forward, meeting his brother as he stepped off the porch.

"It was Africa. And I was able to wangle six weeks' leave."

Nikki hung back, watching as they hugged, a little surprised by their obvious pleasure at seeing each other. She couldn't remember anyone in her family ever being quite so enthused about getting together. An air kiss next to her cheek was about the most she'd ever gotten from her mother, and her brother had never expressed anything stronger than indifference to her presence.

The family resemblance between the brothers was slight. Both men were tall and broad shouldered, but Gage Walker's hair was a brown so dark it hovered on the edge of black, his features more even than Sam's. But the clear blue of his eyes was familiar, as was the humor in them.

"I understand you've got big news," Gage said, looking past Sam with unconcealed interest. "I hope this isn't your wife. She's too pretty to waste herself on someone like you."

Nikki flushed at the compliment, but the butterflies in her stomach subsided a bit. At least one member of Sam's family seemed friendly.

"Nikki, this is my brother Gage." Sam turned and caught her hand, drawing her forward. "He spends most of his time in uncivilized parts of the world building bridges and dams and other things for which the natives have no use."

"He's just jealous because he spends all his time writing parking tickets." Gage's hand swallowed hers, and his smile held nothing but welcome.

Nikki dared to draw a shallow breath, listening with half an ear as Sam introduced Jason. One down and heaven knew how many to go.

"What were you saying about robbing a turkey farm?" Sam asked when the introductions were complete.

Gage's dark brows hooked together in a frown, though Nikki thought she saw laughter in his eyes. "You just missed all the uproar. Mom got the turkey out and set it on the counter to baste it. The phone rang, and while she was answering the phone, Hippo stole the turkey off the counter. Mom screamed bloody murder, which scared Hippo, and he took off through the living room, still carrying the turkey, Cole and Keefe and I in hot pursuit. We got the turkey back, but the uproar upset Mouse, and now there are feathers and half-cooked turkey all over the living room."

"You can grin if you want," he told Sam with mock indignation. "But you aren't the one being sent out to find another turkey, with instructions to find one even if I have to drive to L.A."

"Hippo?" Nikki questioned faintly. He didn't mean a *real* hippo. Did he?

"One of the mutts Mom collects," Gage explained. "She usually finds homes for them, but no one was willing to take on an animal the size of a small truck, so Hippo has become a fixture. Cole's little girl named him after she saw him yawn."

"And Mouse isn't a mouse?" *And why didn't Sam tell me he had a niece?*

"A cat," Gage explained, grinning. "She's timid. She was sleeping on an old pillow when Hippo and the turkey made their entrance into the living room. I think she tried to dig her way into the pillow to hide."

"Which explains the feathers," she said, relieved to have a reasonable explanation.

"Which explains the feathers," Gage agreed. "I've got to go see if I can find a turkey, or Mom will wring my neck. Good to meet you, Jason. Welcome to the family, Nikki."

"Thank you." Nikki turned to watch him stride down the walk and slide into the sleek black Corvette parked at the curb. She looked at Sam.

"Maybe we should give your mother time to get things straightened out. We could come back later."

"Don't be ridiculous. Mom won't mind."

Without giving her a chance to argue, he walked up the porch steps, pulling her with him. If Jason hadn't been with them, Nikki might have argued more vehemently. If she and Sam had really been married, she might have insisted that her first introduction to his mother not come in the midst of a domestic crisis. Caught between reality and facade, she said nothing.

The door opened into a small entryway, which opened directly into the living room. The room seemed full of people, but after a moment Nikki was able to sort it out into two men, a woman and a little girl. The woman was kneeling in the middle of the floor, rubbing a damp rag over a spot on the carpet. One of the men was standing in front of a window, trying to pry a large tiger-striped cat loose from the top of the curtain. The other man was scooping feathers off the sofa and dropping them in a brown paper grocery sack. The little girl was picking up an occasional feather, but the bulk of her attention was on the operation at the window.

"Be careful, Uncle Keefe," she instructed now. "Mouse had a bad scare."

"*Mouse* had a bad scare," Keefe muttered under his breath. "Don't forget she went over *me* to get to the top of the drapes. The damn thing has claws eight inches long."

"Don't curse in front of Mary," Rachel Walker ordered without glancing up from the spot she was scrubbing. "If the cat drew blood, I'll put some iodine on the scratches later. Right now, I want this place in some kind of order before Sam and his new wife get here."

"Trying to fool your new daughter-in-law into thinking the place isn't a loony bin, Mom?" Cole asked, dropping another feather in the sack. "It might be better if she knew the truth right off."

"Just pick up those feathers, Cole," Rachel ordered, shifting her attention to another spot.

"Wouldn't it be easier to vacuum them up?"

"Not until your brother gets Mouse off the curtains. She's afraid of the vacuum."

"She's afraid of her own shadow," Keefe muttered in disgust. "I've met rocks with more brains." But Nikki noticed that he was very gentle in prying the frightened animal loose from the curtain.

Sam opened his mouth to announce their arrival, but his niece had seen them and beat him to it. She darted toward them. "Uncle Sam!"

As she jumped to her feet, her arm hit the sack of feathers, which her father had set on the back of the sofa. Cole made a quick grab for it, but succeeded only in bumping it again. The sack tumbled off its perch, trailing feathers in its wake like big, fluffy snowflakes.

Startled by the little girl's shriek, Keefe tightened his hold on the cat he'd just succeeded in prying loose from the curtain. It was too much for Mouse's already traumatized nerves. With a yowl loud enough to wake the dead, she sank four sets of claws into her rescuer's arm. Keefe yelped and dropped her to the floor. She streaked across the carpet like a furry orange missile and disappeared toward the back of the house.

Rachel Walker's head jerked up. Still on her hands and knees, she stared at the new arrivals. Her horrified expression made Nikki's heart sink.

Sam caught his niece up in his arms, balancing her easily on his hip. His greeting broke the momentary stunned silence. "Hi, urchin."

"Oh, no." As first greetings from a new mother-in-law went, it could have been worse, Nikki decided. It could have been "Get out."

"Hi, Mom."

"Oh, Sam. How could you do this to me?" Rachel groaned as she stood up.

"*I* didn't steal the turkey," Sam protested with a grin.

"You were a wretched boy, and you've grown into a wretched man." She glanced down at the rag in her hand and then, with a sigh, let it drop. "Everything was going so well," she muttered, to no one in particular.

"Hippo stoled the turkey," his niece informed him. She leaned forward in his arms and fixed Nikki with big brown eyes. "I'm Mary. Are you my new aunt?"

"I . . . Yes, I guess I am." This was getting more complicated by the minute, Nikki thought. Now she was lying to small children. "I'm Nikki."

"I had everything organized," Rachel said. Her eyes drifted from the feathers dusted over the sofa to the spots on the rug to the doorway through which the cat had disappeared. "It was the phone," she announced, fixing Nikki with a sudden look. "Everything was going fine until the wretched phone rang."

"I'm sure it was," Nikki agreed hesitantly, wondering if Sam had forgotten to tell her that his mother's mind was starting to go.

"I've never liked phones." Rachel bent down and picked up the damp rag, looked at it a moment and then stuffed it in the pocket of the pink gingham apron she wore over a pair of lavender slacks and a white blouse. "They always ring at the most awkward moments, like when your hands are covered in mud."

"Or when you're basting a turkey," Cole added helpfully.

"I only turned my back for a moment."

"If you didn't insist on keeping that wolf in the house, you'd be able to leave a turkey sit on the counter without posting guard over it," Keefe said. He was dabbing droplets of blood off the series of scratches that decorated the back of his hand.

"It's not poor Hippo's fault." Rachel immediately leapt to the dog's defense. "How was he supposed to know the turkey wasn't for him?"

"Do you normally feed him half-roasted turkeys that happen to be sitting on the counter?" Keefe asked, not troubling to conceal his annoyance.

"Of course not. But I didn't explain that it *wasn't* for him, either."

"Most dogs understand that the counters are off-limits without needing to have each specific item of food pointed out to them."

"If you hadn't yelled at the poor thing, he wouldn't have run off with the bird. You scared him."

"Excuse me, but when I see a dog absconding with the Thanksgiving turkey, that seems reason enough to yell."

Nikki felt like a spectator at a tennis match as her eyes followed the conversation back and forth between mother and son. None of her worried imaginings had included a scene quite like this one.

"Welcome to the Walker family, Nikki." Sam's tone was dry and laced with amusement.

"Oh goodness!" Rachel turned a stricken gaze in their direction. "I didn't even say hello, did I?"

"Not exactly," Sam said.

"I'm so sorry, Nikki. You must think you've married into a family of savages." Rachel crossed the room to where they stood and reached out to take Nikki's hands. Her grip was firm and strong, surprisingly so for such a small woman. "I did so want everything to be nice when you arrived." She gestured to the chaos behind her. "This isn't the first impression I'd planned, but welcome to the family, my dear."

Nikki stepped awkwardly into the embrace Rachel offered, her thoughts spinning at the realization that *Rachel* had been nervous about meeting *her.*

"Thank you, Mrs. Walker." Up close, Nikki found it hard to believe that this woman could be the mother of four strapping sons. She didn't look old enough, for one thing. Her soft dark hair was cut stylishly short and framed a face of remarkable sweetness. Any impression Nikki might have had that Sam's mother was a few bricks short of a full load was dispelled by the quick intelligence in her dark eyes.

"Call me Rachel, please. 'Mrs. Walker' always makes me think of my mother-in-law, whom I never liked. And since the feeling was mutual, I don't consider that speaking ill of the dead. I swore I'd never be a mother-in-law of the sort she was, so you don't have to worry about me poking my nose in things that are none of my business."

As if on cue, Mary, who'd been watching and listening from her position in Sam's arms, piped up. "Are you going to have a baby?'' she asked, fixing Nikki with a bright, curious gaze.

Instant silence greeted her question. Nikki could feel her smile freezing solid. Her voice came out a little wheezy. "What?"

"Daddy told Uncle Gage that was prob'ly why you and Uncle Sam got married so quick," Mary explained. "'Cause you were going to have a baby."

"My brother, Ann Landers," Sam muttered, shooting Cole a fierce look. "No, Nikki is not going to have a baby."

"Talk about little pitchers," Cole said on a groan. He crossed the room to take his daughter from Sam. "Your ears are entirely too big, you little pest."

"If you don't want me to hear things, then you shouldn't talk so loud," she pointed out, with unarguable, five-year-old logic.

"When you're right, you're right," Sam said, giving his brother a pointed look, which Cole ignored. He smiled at Nikki.

"Hi, I'm Cole. The one with the overactive imagination. Welcome to the madhouse."

Nikki took the hand he offered. There was a rueful apology in his eyes. The resemblance between him and the little girl he held was marked. Both were fair haired with chocolate brown eyes. But Cole's smile was reminiscent of his brother's, tailor-made for breaking female hearts.

"The one nursing the scratched hand is Keefe," Sam said, completing the introductions as Keefe came to join them.

"I think I'll live," Keefe said dryly. "Glad to meet you, Nikki. It's not always this bad."

"Sometimes it's worse," Cole offered.

"Ignore him," Keefe suggested as he shook her hand. "Aside from a few neurotic pets, we're a fairly normal bunch."

Nikki wondered if it was her imagination that put something watchful in the look he gave her, something more than curiosity. As if he knew something the rest of his family didn't.

Before she could follow that line of thinking any farther, she suddenly remembered Jason, who'd been standing quietly behind her. She turned immediately, slipping her hand under his elbow and drawing him forward to introduce him to her in-laws, relieved to have an excuse to direct attention away from herself.

She'd made it through the initial meeting without anyone pointing a finger and denouncing her as a fake, but there was plenty of time for disaster to strike.

"A Norman Rockwell kind of family" was how Max had described the Walkers. Until now, Nikki hadn't been willing to admit, even to herself, just how much that description had influenced her decision to marry Sam. Her own family had borne little resemblance to the sort of cozy images for which Rockwell was famous.

From the time she was small, the two stable figures in her life had been her grandfather and Lena, and, while she'd never doubted their love for her, she'd always had a wistful longing to be part of a big, close-knit family, the kind common on television and all too rare in real life.

And now, by virtue of a business deal cum marriage, she was part of such a family, at least for the next year. The Walkers bore little resemblance to the Brady Bunch, but there was no mistaking the affection between them.

Rachel, in particular, fascinated her. Her initial impression that her mother-in-law was a little on the vague side turned out to be far from accurate. Though she was barely five feet tall and looked as if a strong breeze might carry her away, it seemed as if Rachel had only to express a wish and one or more of her sons moved to fulfill it.

It was obvious that they adored her. Equally obvious that the feeling was mutual. Nikki tried to remember if Max had said anything about Sam's father, but could come up with nothing beyond the fact that he was dead. She wondered if Rachel had raised her sons alone.

Despite her certainty that disaster lurked around every corner, it was turning out to be the best Thanksgiving she could ever remember having. It took some time for her to dare to relax, even a little. She was vividly aware she was there under false pretenses and afraid of making a verbal slip that would expose the truth about her marriage to Sam. But as no one demanded an explanation for their hasty marriage or asked any questions she couldn't answer, she started to believe that Sam had been right about his family accepting their marriage at face value.

It had probably been ridiculous to worry so much. After all, what sane person would expect to find a genuine marriage of convenience in their own family?

Gage returned in about an hour. He brought a huge turkey, which happened to be frozen solid, two chickens and ten pounds of hamburger. Since it would be days before the turkey could thaw, there was a hasty reshuffling of the dinner menu.

The turkey went in the freezer, the two chickens went in the oven, and Sam and Cole threw coals in the barbecue to cook the hamburger. Within a couple of hours, they sat down to roast chicken and grilled hamburgers with all the traditional Thanksgiving trimmings. Nikki couldn't ever remember enjoying a meal more.

Chapter 8

The remainder of the day passed in a kind of pleasant lethargy. After dinner, everyone helped clear the table. With so many bodies in such a relatively small area, it might have been more efficient if the task had been left to one or two, but no one seemed concerned with efficiency.

Once the table was cleared and the first load of dishes was in the dishwasher, there was a general retreat to the living room. Nikki was amused by the way Jason rose when Rachel entered the room, offering her his chair with an old-fashioned gallantry that brought a delicate flush of color to the older woman's cheeks.

The television was turned to one of the many football games being played. With the score at thirty-five to three, there wasn't much suspense in the competition, but that suited the low-key mood just fine.

Nikki, whose interest in football was about on par with her interest in the sex life of tree frogs, wandered over to the baby grand piano that dominated one corner of the living room. She brushed her fingers soundlessly across the keys.

"Do you play?" Rachel's question startled her, since she hadn't been aware of the other woman's approach.

Nikki shook her head. "I had lessons when I was a child, but I was terrible at it. I could hear the music in my head, but I could never seem to get it from there to my fingers."

"I can't play a note and my singing is so bad that the boys used to cry when I'd sing lullabies to them." Rachel smiled at Nikki's chuckle, but shook her head. "It's true. I can't carry a tune in a bucket. But David, Sam's father, he had a voice like an angel and could play just about any instrument you'd care to name. The boys got what musical talent they have from him."

Nikki's mind boggled at hearing the four large men, currently sprawled on various pieces of furniture, called *boys*, but she supposed it was a mother's privilege to call them that.

"Does Sam play piano?" she asked.

"No. He played guitar when he was in college, but I don't think he kept up with it. I think he just used it to attract girls."

Nikki couldn't imagine that Sam Walker had ever needed any kind of accessory to attract the opposite sex. He came equipped with everything necessary for that, she thought, shooting a quick look at his long body, which was settled comfortably in a big, overstuffed chair. With an effort, she dragged her attention back to what Rachel was saying.

"Cole inherited his father's voice, even sang in the church choir when he was a boy. Gage is the one who plays piano. There was a time when we thought he might make a career of it, but...things changed." Something in her tone suggested that whatever it was that had changed, the memories weren't pleasant. Nikki sought to distract her.

"What about Keefe? Does he sing or play an instrument?"

"Only if you're in the mood for torture," Cole put in. He was sitting on the sofa. Mary had crawled onto his lap after dinner and was now fast asleep, her tiny body curled against his chest. It was a sweet picture.

"Torture?" Nikki asked, glancing at Rachel for an explanation. But it was Keefe who answered.

"What Cole is trying to say is that there isn't a musical bone in my body."

"Actually, dogs have been known to howl in pain when Keefe sings," Gage clarified. He grinned as he fended off the pillow Keefe threw in his direction.

"Please, don't anybody mention dogs," Cole said.

There was a general mutter of agreement as everyone remembered Hippo's impact on the holiday dinner. But Nikki noticed there didn't seem to be any real rancor behind the complaints. She had yet to meet the canine in question, since he'd been banished to the backyard for his transgressions. She wanted to get at least a glimpse of the fabled creature before they left.

There were half a dozen pictures in a motley assortment of frames sitting on top of the piano. Nikki picked up one to look at it more closely. It was a family portrait, taken when the brothers were in their teens. They were seated on a dark sofa and the four of them stared at the camera with varying degrees of tolerance. Sam couldn't have been more than seventeen or eighteen, but he'd had a look of maturity beyond his years.

It took a conscious effort to drag her gaze to the rest of the family. She glanced at the three other boys, but her attention settled on the little girl standing in front of them. Four or five years old, with hair that was a rich, deep auburn and thickly lashed, blue eyes, she wore a ruffled pink dress and had a pink ribbon threaded through her curls.

"Who is that?" Nikki asked, thinking it might be a niece or cousin.

There was an almost imperceptible pause before Rachel answered. "That's Shannon. My little girl."

There was old grief in her voice and in her eyes as she reached out to take the picture from Nikki. Her forefinger settled gently on the glass that covered the picture, almost as if she were touching the child's face.

Nikki became aware of the silence around them and realized that Rachel wasn't the only one who'd heard her question. She glanced at Sam, wondering if she should have known who Shannon was, if a real wife would have known. He shook his head slightly, giving her a look that she took as reassurance.

"I'm going to take a walk." It was Gage who broke the tense little silence. Nikki caught a glimpse of his face as he stood up. He looked older than he had moments before, his features hard, his eyes a wintry blue.

"It's raining," Rachel said.

"I won't melt." He gave his mother a quick, tight smile. If it was intended as reassurance, it fell short of the mark, because the worry stayed in Rachel's eyes as she watched him walk out the door.

He left behind him a strained silence. Cole's attention was on his sleeping daughter, his hand stroking over her golden hair. Keefe stared at the television screen as if riveted by the ridiculously unbalanced competition being played out there. Sam looked after his brother, and for a moment Nikki thought he might follow Gage, but if that was his intention, he changed his mind after a glance at his mother's face.

"He'll be all right, Mom."

"I know." Rachel turned to set the picture back down on the piano, her hand not quite steady.

Utterly bewildered by the undercurrents of the past few minutes, Nikki looked at Jason, forgetting for the moment that he might think it odd that she was so completely in the dark. He spoke up immediately.

"I don't know about anyone else, but I think I'm about ready for another slice of pumpkin pie."

"I'll get it for you," Rachel said, obviously grateful to have something to do.

"Coffee would be good right about now," Cole suggested.

"Coffee and pie coming up."

"Perhaps I can help," Jason offered. He rose and followed his hostess into the kitchen.

Nikki looked at Sam, her eyes full of questions. *Later,* he mouthed, shaking his head to indicate that this wasn't the time to discuss the odd little scene that had just passed.

Her shoulders lifted in an almost imperceptible shrug. It was really none of her business. Not the way it would have been if she were truly a member of the family. She started to turn away, but her eyes met Keefe's. There was something in his look that made her feel as if he had read her mind, somehow sensing the distance between herself and Sam.

What would a real wife do after the tense little scene just past? The answer seemed obvious.

Looking as casual as she could, Nikki walked over to Sam's chair and settled herself on the arm of it. Sam shot her a startled look, which she answered with a sweet smile, a fierce glare and a subtle twitch of her head in Keefe's direction.

He glanced past her at his brother. Nikki assumed Keefe was looking at them, which explained Sam's sudden smile as he realized the necessity for keeping up their charade. But it didn't explain the wicked amusement in his eyes when he looked back up at her.

"You don't look comfortable there, sweetheart," he said lovingly.

"I'm fine, honey."

"Well, I'm not. I'll get a crick in my neck looking at you." Before she could guess his intention, he slid his arm around her waist and dragged her off the arm of the chair and into his lap.

Nikki's first impulse was to scramble up and away from him. Her second was to plant her fist in his nose and *then* scramble away. She might—just might—have done it and left Sam to try to explain her actions to his brothers. But her entire inheritance was at stake. Reluctantly, she stayed where she was, shooting Sam a look that promised future retribution.

"Comfortable, sweetheart?" Sam asked.

"Perfectly," she said through clenched teeth. She shifted position and managed to plant her elbow firmly in his midriff. "How about you, honey?"

Sam's response was muffled. Acting in self-defense, he slid his arm around her waist and dragged her close against his chest, leaving her no room to maneuver. Nearly nose to nose with her husband, Nikki glared at him.

"Isn't this cozy?" Sam asked cheerfully.

"Terribly," she agreed without opening her teeth.

This close to him, she was vividly aware of the width of his chest, of the muscled strength of the arms holding her. His thighs were hard beneath hers. She could smell the faint woodsy scent of his cologne and see the narrow line of dark gray that rimmed the blue of his eyes. She felt surrounded by him, overwhelmed by his sheer masculinity. His mouth was only inches from hers. If she leaned forward just a little...

She jerked her thoughts back from that dangerous path, stiffening her spine as she looked away. Her gaze collided with Keefe's and she was surprised to read something that looked suspiciously like sympathy in his eyes. Again, she had the impression that he knew a great deal more than she might have expected.

Before she had a chance to pursue that thought, Rachel and Jason came back into the room. Keefe got up to clear a small end table so that Jason could set down the tray he was carrying.

"You two look cozy," Rachel said with a glance at the newlyweds.

Nikki forced a smile and murmured something noncommittal. She tried to angle her elbow into Sam's midriff again, but he was holding her too tightly. She felt the amusement in him and promised herself a suitable revenge. Something along the lines of a dip in boiling oil, perhaps.

The doorbell rang just then. Rachel went to answer it, returning with a tall, elderly woman. In the ensuing rush of greetings, Nikki twisted away from Sam's hold and stood, taking care to plant her foot firmly on his as she did so. His grunt of pain put a genuine smile on her face.

Though the newcomer was probably nearing eighty, her spine was ramrod straight and the cane she carried seemed to be more for effect than necessity. Her lined face showed traces of real beauty in the elegant arch of her cheekbones and the still bright blue of her eyes. She was wearing a pair of black wool trousers and a silk blouse of peacock blue. She wore her snow-white hair in a plain chignon and carried herself like a woman accustomed to having the world fall in line with her wishes. But there was a sparkle of humor in her eyes to soften the arrogance. She sat down with the grace of a much younger woman.

"Nikki, this is Molly Thorpe. She's a friend of the family. Molly, this is Sam's new wife, Nikki Walker." She hesitated. "I didn't even think to ask you if you were keeping your maiden name, dear."

"Are you kidding? The only reason I married Sam was so I wouldn't have to keep spelling Beauvisage for the rest of my life."

"Beauvisage?" Molly Thorpe looked at Nikki sharply. "You're too young to be Lyman's daughter. Must be the granddaughter."

"Did you know my grandfather?"

"We'd met a time or two. Heard he died a while back."

"Yes, he did," Nikki confirmed. "I miss him a great deal."

"Then he was a lucky man," Molly said. "Can't ask more out of life than someone to care enough to miss you when you're gone." She looked past Nikki. "Good bloodlines here, Samuel. You'll have fine children. No sense blushing," she added when Nikki's face flamed with color. "I'm too old to mince my words. Don't have enough time left to spend it finding polite phrases to spare people's sensibilities. Ain't pregnant yet, are you?"

"No." Nikki's denial was strangled.

She heard Sam laugh. "Mary already asked her that, Molly. I'm starting to think there's something you're not telling me, sweetheart."

Nikki shot him a look that would have slain a lesser man where he stood. Sam just grinned. She was grateful to Keefe for stepping forward to greet Molly, drawing attention away from her.

"You're incorrigible, Molly."

"I hope so. There's not much else to be at my age." She held out her hand to him, her eyes warm with affection. "Keefe. How are you?"

"Fine." He took her hand and bent to brush a kiss over her cheek. "I won't ask how you are. I can see the answer for myself."

"You could have seen it anytime these past three years if you'd taken the trouble to visit," she told him sharply. She didn't give him time to answer, but continued in a slightly softer tone. "Have you seen my great-niece lately?"

There was an instant of tense silence that told Nikki there was more to the question than what it seemed on the surface. She was aware of several quick glances being shot in Keefe's direction.

"I haven't seen Dana since the divorce," he answered calmly.

The old woman's ebony cane tapped the floor in a gesture of impatience.

"I expected better of you, Keefe Walker. Thought you were smarter than my great-niece," Molly said bluntly. "I was pleased as punch when you two got married. Thought you'd manage to hang on to her, keep her away from that silly goose of a mother and that mental midget of a father of hers."

"Sorry I didn't live up to your faith in me," Keefe said with a tight smile. He reached in his pocket for a cigarette, caught his mother's eye and thought better of it.

"I am, too. Dana's got a head on her shoulders, even if she don't choose to use it as often as I'd like. And she never will use it if her parents have their way. A more foolish pair I've never encountered." She peered up at him with a roguish smile. "And at my age, I doubt I'll live long enough to encounter a dumber pair."

"I suspect you'll outlive the lot of us, Molly." Keefe might not have wanted to talk about his ex-wife, but he was obviously quite fond of her great-aunt.

"I might at that." Bracing herself on her cane, she got to her feet, waving away Keefe's attempt to help her rise. "Day comes I can't get up on my own, they can take me out in the pasture and shoot me." She tilted her head back until her eyes met Keefe's. "When I was Dana's age, I wasn't stupid enough to let a man like you slip away. Married the only one I met. And if I were forty years younger, I'd give Dana a run for her money."

"I don't think Dana's in the running anymore," Keefe said dryly. "Besides, if you were forty years younger, I doubt I could handle you."

"'Course you couldn't," she snapped. "I'd do the handling. And damned lucky you'd be to get me."

"I don't doubt it. They don't make 'em like you anymore, Molly."

"Good thing, too," she said on a rich chuckle.

Molly didn't stay long. She'd just dropped in to wish the family a happy holiday, she said, refusing an invitation to have coffee and pie. Gage returned as she was leaving. He was soaked to the skin, but the haunted look had faded from his eyes.

It was after eight o'clock when Sam suggested that it was time they started the drive back to L.A. Rachel protested immediately.

"It's pouring rain. And it's such a long drive. You wouldn't be home till nearly midnight. Why don't you spend the night?"

"I don't think so, Mom. We really should be getting home."

"Why? I thought you said you had tomorrow off."

"I do, but—"

"Jason, do you have to go to work tomorrow?" Rachel asked, turning to the older man.

"The offices are closed for the weekend. But I couldn't impose myself on you like that."

"Nonsense. There's plenty of room. And I wouldn't be able to sleep for worrying about the three of you out on the roads in this kind of weather."

"I really would rather get home," Sam said. He glanced at Nikki. "I'm sure Nikki would, too."

"Actually, I'm pretty tired," she contradicted, ignoring the demand in his eyes. Obviously, he wanted her to say that she was anxious to get home, but after his annoying behavior earlier, she wasn't particularly in the mood to oblige him. In fact, she rather enjoyed thwarting him.

Besides, she *was* tired. She stifled a yawn. Her nap in the car hadn't been enough to make up for the week of poor sleep that had preceded it.

"If your mother doesn't mind putting us up, I'd like to stay, honey."

"Honey" looked less than happy, but he didn't pursue the argument. Nikki couldn't suppress the urge to give him a triumphant look. It was time he realized that he wasn't going to win every round. But Sam's response wasn't what she might have expected. Instead of looking annoyed, he looked resigned, and there was a kind of rueful laughter in his eyes which she didn't like at all.

She liked it even less a little while later when she realized why he'd been so adamant about driving back to L.A. and why he'd given her that amused look when she sided with his mother.

"The two of you can have the front room," Rachel was saying as she led the way to the back of the house. "It has its own bathroom."

The two of us? Nikki barely managed to swallow back the urge to repeat the phrase out loud. She wouldn't have been able to keep the horror from her voice. *The two of them? As in her and Sam? Together? In the same room? For an entire night?*

"It's only a double bed, but you two haven't been married long enough to mind being cozy," Rachel was saying indulgently as she pushed open the bedroom door. "The sun comes in this window first thing in the morning, so you'll need to draw the blinds if you want to sleep late."

"Oh no, I'm sure we won't want to do that," Nikki said, staring at the bed, which seemed to dominate the room. "I have to be back in L.A. before noon," she lied. "So we'll be leaving fairly early."

It was too bad she couldn't think up a plausible excuse to leave that minute. But no one was likely to buy the idea that she had an appointment in L.A. at midnight.

"If you wouldn't mind helping me make the bed," Rachel said, "then the two of you can call it a night whenever you'd like. I don't have guests very often, so I don't leave the beds made up. I think it's so much nicer to have fresh sheets. Don't you?"

Nikki murmured an agreement, but she wasn't thinking about sheets, fresh or otherwise. There was that phrase again, *the two of you,* as if she and Sam were a couple. Of course, Rachel had no way of knowing they *weren't* a couple, but it was still disconcerting to hear her refer to them as if they were a single unit, the way they would have been if this were a real marriage.

Rachel got a set of sheets out of the linen closet in the hall while Nikki stripped the bedspread off the mattress.

"I'm so glad the two of you decided to stay over," Rachel said as they eased the bottom sheet into place. "It's been a long time since I had a houseful of family like this.

It used to get very crowded when the boys were all married."

Nikki's head popped up. "*All* married?"

"Well, not Gage, of course. I don't know if he'll ever marry. And the way he spends all his time traveling, he's never in one place long enough to get to know anyone. But when the other three were married and they'd all come home for the holidays, this poor house bulged at the seams."

From her smile, it was obvious that she hadn't minded the crowding. She bent to smooth a wrinkle from the crisp white sheet. Nikki was grateful for the chance to cover up her shock. *Sam had been married before?* Why hadn't Max told her? Why hadn't *Sam* told her?

"It was nice having a houseful of people," Rachel said as she straightened. "But then Dana and Keefe split up, and Cole and Roxie. But Cole got custody of Mary, so that certainly could have been worse. The worst of it was when Sara died."

Sara? Sam's wife? He was a widower?

Rachel stared past Nikki, her expression pensive. "I wasn't sure Sam would ever marry again." She was silent for a moment and then seemed to shake herself free of her memories. She focused on Nikki, her smile warm. "I'm so glad he found you. It's good to see him happy again."

Nikki flushed and looked away, at a loss for words. The charade that had seemed so simple was getting more complicated all the time. She'd thought of it as affecting only her life and Sam's, but it was becoming obvious that she'd been ridiculously shortsighted.

Here was Sam's mother thanking her for making him happy again. If it hadn't been so painful, it would have been laughable. The only thing she'd done to make Sam happy was write a very large check. And the only other thing he was likely to want from her was her signature on the divorce papers when the year was up.

Chapter 9

The bedroom door had barely closed behind Sam before Nikki pounced.

"Why didn't you say something?" she demanded.

He didn't pretend not to know what she was talking about. "What should I have said? 'Sorry, Mom, we can't spend the night because we'd have to share a room.' Don't you think it would have looked a bit odd if we had separate bedrooms a month after the wedding?"

"Lots of married couples sleep in separate bedrooms."

"Yeah, but that doesn't mean they'd rather drive three hours in a rainstorm rather than face sharing a bed."

Nikki's spine stiffened and her eyes turned a pure, icy green. "We are *not* sharing a bed."

"If you speak a little louder, maybe the whole house will be able to hear you." The accusation was unfair since she'd been keeping her voice low, but he wasn't particularly concerned with fairness at the moment. It had been a long day.

He was tired and not particularly thrilled at the prospect of the night ahead.

"We are not sharing that bed," she repeated.

Sam had never before heard anyone make a whisper sound like a shout. It was a unique talent, but one he was a little too tired to appreciate at the moment. If it hadn't been such a long day, with an even longer night to follow, he might have dragged out the discussion for the sheer pleasure of watching her lay down the law. "You're right. We are not sharing that bed. I'll sleep on the floor."

Nikki was already drawing breath to argue with him when it registered that there was nothing to argue about. She gave him a look of mingled relief and annoyance.

"The floor isn't going to be very comfortable," she said.

"Do you have a better idea?" Sam unbuttoned his shirt cuffs.

"Maybe I should be the one who sleeps on the floor. After all, this is your home...."

"This is my mother's home," he corrected. "And I'm not going to arm-wrestle you for the right to spend a miserable night trying to get comfortable on the cold, hard floor, so unless you're desperate to sleep there, I'd suggest you don't argue. My chivalrous streak isn't very wide."

She stared at him consideringly for a moment. He could almost see the debate going on in her head. Did she protest politely and risk having to sleep on the floor or did she give in and let him have the last word? He should have known she'd find a way to do neither.

"As a strong nineties kind of woman, I should insist on equal-opportunity misery."

Sam's grin was slow. "As a nineties kind of man, I wouldn't dream of standing in your way." He swept one hand out in invitation. "The floor is yours if you insist."

"That's quite all right. It's enough that you respect my right to sleep there. You're welcome to it," she said graciously.

"Gee, thanks."

"Don't mention it."

"I won't," he said dryly. "I'm going to get ready for bed. If your sensibilities would be shocked by the sight of me in my underwear, then I suggest you turn the light out while I'm in the bathroom."

Their eyes met and he knew she was thinking the same thing he was, which was that she'd seen him in considerably less. Nikki looked away first, her cheeks a little flushed.

"Lucky for me that your mother had something I could wear," she said, gesturing to the nightgown she wore.

Sam wished she hadn't mentioned it. He'd really have preferred not to think about her in a nightgown, because that made him think about her in bed, and that didn't bear thinking about. At least his mother hadn't loaned her some silk-and-lace thing designed to drive a man wild. The garment was floor-length white cotton with a pattern of tiny pink roses scattered across it. Long-sleeved, high-necked, modest enough for a nun. And damned if she didn't look sexy as hell in it.

He cleared his throat. "Looks big enough for an entire family to sleep in," he said casually.

She laughed, a soft, husky sound that shivered down his spine. "The colors might be a little subdued, but I'm sure there's enough fabric for a circus tent."

"Gotta be close." He looked away and reached for the top button on his shirt. "I'm beat. I'm going to clean up and try and get some sleep."

"Okay." Nikki turned away and then hesitated, looking back over her shoulder at him. "Are you sure? About sleeping on the floor, I mean?"

Was she trying to drive him nuts? She was standing there with the light behind her and he could see the shadowy outline of her slender body beneath the prim nightie. The odd juxtaposition of modesty and sensuality was sexier than if she'd been standing in front of him completely nude. Sam was caught off guard by a wave of gut-level hunger.

"I'll be fine on the floor. Unless you want to share the bed," he said huskily.

His eyes met hers and saw them widen at the desire he didn't trouble to conceal. Something flickered in her eyes, an awareness that made it clear that he wasn't the only one conscious of the potential explosiveness of the situation. He had a moment to wonder just what he'd do if she said yes, and then she looked away and the moment was gone.

"The floor looks fairly soft," she said with a nervous half smile.

"Tell that to my back," he grumbled without heat.

He shut the bathroom door without waiting for her to respond. Leaning his hands on the edge of the sink, Sam stared at his reflection in the mirror, searching for signs of incipient insanity. Had he actually just suggested that he and Nikki might sleep together? Wasn't his life complicated enough without adding sleeping with his wife to it?

When he opened the bathroom door ten minutes later, he'd taken the time to give himself a firm talking to. His marriage to Nikki was in name only, which was exactly how he wanted it to stay. It was one thing to be civil. It was even okay to admit that there were moments when he thought he might actually like the woman he'd married. And he'd be a fool to try and deny her attractiveness. But that was as far as it could go. He didn't need the added problems that would come with acting on that attraction.

Nikki had taken his advice and the bedroom was dark. Before he shut off the bathroom light, Sam saw that she'd folded the heavy bedspread and laid it on the floor as a makeshift mattress. A blanket and one of the pillows completed his bed. He flicked out the light and then waited a moment for his eyes to adjust to the darkness before making his way across the bedroom.

He'd slept in more comfortable places, but he'd also slept in much worse, Sam thought as he laid his head on the pillow and pulled the blanket up around his shoulders. Listening to the rain beating against the side of the house, he had to admit that, floor or no, this was certainly nicer than being on a freeway somewhere between here and Los Angeles.

Now if he could manage to forget that a beautiful, sexy woman who just happened to be his wife was lying only a few feet away. If he could convince himself that he was all alone...

"Sam?"

The sound of her voice, pitched low and intimate, did nothing to relax his tense body. Maybe if he didn't say anything, she'd think he fell asleep the instant his head hit the pillow.

"Sam? Are you asleep?"

His eyes popped open and he stared at the ceiling. "I'm awake."

"I think today went pretty well, don't you? I mean, I don't think anyone suspects anything."

"I told you they wouldn't."

"It just seems so obvious to me that we're not really married that it's hard for me to believe it isn't obvious to everyone else. I guess it's just my guilty conscience."

"There's nothing to feel guilty about," he said firmly, ignoring the fact that his own conscience was less than comfortable with the deception they were playing.

"I can't help but feel guilty when your family has been so nice. They've accepted me as if I really was your wife."

"You *are* my wife." Funny how it was getting easier to think of her that way.

"Only on paper."

He heard the covers rustle as she turned over, and he closed his eyes, trying not to think about her in bed, with nothing between her and the sheets but that soft nightgown. Nothing between her and his hands... He opened his eyes and stared up the ceiling again. Maybe she'd go to sleep now. Maybe she'd—

"Sam?"

He closed his eyes in resignation. "Yeah?"

"I didn't mean to upset anyone when I asked about the little girl in the picture."

Sam felt his body tighten. "You couldn't have known it was a problem."

There was another silence from the bed, and he hoped she was going to drop the subject even when he knew it wasn't going to happen.

"Was Shannon your sister?"

It took him so long to respond that Nikki began to think he was going to ignore the question. Maybe she'd overstepped the undefined boundaries of their relationship by asking.

"Shannon is my half sister," Sam said finally.

"Is?" There was surprise in Nikki's voice. "I thought... The way your mother referred to her, I thought..." She let the words trail off.

"That she was dead? She's not." There was a fierceness behind the words, as if saying them could make them true.

"A year after my father died, Mom remarried." Sam spoke rapidly, wanting to get the the story over with. He didn't like talking about what had happened. "She was lonely, and I think she had some idea that the four of us needed a father. So she married Seth Hardesty. He was a cop, like my father had been, and she met him through a mutual friend.

"The marriage was a mistake. Seth didn't like sharing his wife with four children who weren't even his, and the feeling was mutual. He thought we were undisciplined little louts and we thought he was a complete bastard. We were probably both right," he admitted with bleak humor.

"We didn't make it easy for him, but his idea of discipline usually involved using his belt on one of us. I was thirteen and big for my age. He only tried to hit me once."

Nikki's heart ached for the boy he'd been. He might have been big for his age, but he'd still been a thirteen-year-old, still a child. It couldn't have been easy for him to stand up to a grown man.

"I warned him about hitting any of the others and I thought he'd listened. I told him I'd kill him if he hurt my brothers." There was something in his voice that told Nikki it hadn't been an idle threat. "I thought things were settling down, but Mom came home one day and caught him beating the hell out of Cole for some minor infraction of one of Seth's rules. I think she already knew the marriage had been a mistake, but that was the push she needed to end things. She divorced him, but she was already pregnant with Shannon."

He stared up at the darkened ceiling, remembering. Nikki was quiet, waiting for him to finish the story.

"I think we were all a little shell-shocked by then. First Dad dying, then Seth, then the divorce. Shannon was the first good thing that had happened to the family in a long time. We were all old enough that there was no question of resenting her, and we spoiled her rotten. It's a wonder she didn't become an obnoxious little brat. But she was a great little kid. As soon as she could walk, she'd follow one or the other of us around. We all adored her.''

He fell silent, as if lost in memories. Nikki wasn't sure she wanted to know what had happened anymore. Some memories were better left undisturbed. But now that he'd started, it seemed Sam intended to finish the story.

''Seth had visitation rights, of course. Not that he bothered to take advantage of them very often. But he popped in and out of Shannon's life, seeing her once or twice a year, just enough so that we couldn't forget him, which was probably why he did it.

''Shannon was about four when he tried to convince Mom to give the marriage another try. She wanted no part of him and told him so. He seemed to take it fairly well, but it must have rankled with him. A couple of weeks later, he came to pick Shannon up to spend the weekend with him. He never brought her back.''

He said it so simply that it took several seconds for his meaning to sink in.

''You mean he just disappeared with her?''

''Into thin air.''

''And you haven't seen her since?''

''No.''

''But that was years ago.''

''Nineteen.'' The way he said it told her that the wound was far from healed.

''Didn't he call? Let you know that she was all right? Give some explanation?''

''No.''

''Did you try to find her?''

''Sure. But thousands of children disappear every year and are never seen again. Shannon was one of them.''

Nikki knew that tragedies like the one he'd just described were more common than anyone wanted to believe. But it was one thing to know it on an impersonal level, something else to hear about it happening to someone she knew. She thought of the family portrayed in the photograph, of the smiling faces. And then she thought of the pain in Rachel's face, in Sam's voice. Nineteen years later, the hurt was still close to the surface. There wasn't enough time in the world to get over something like that.

"I'm sorry." The words seemed hopelessly inadequate, but there was nothing else she could offer.

"Yeah. Me too," Sam said softly.

They didn't speak again. Nikki lay awake for a long time, staring into the darkness. She was sorry she'd asked about the child in the picture, sorry she'd brought up something so painful to him. It would be a long time before she forgot the pain that had roughened his voice.

When she'd married Sam, she'd seen him as the means to an end. She hadn't given much thought to him as a person. But she was starting to realize that it wasn't possible to share a house and a marriage license with someone and avoid coming to know them as an individual.

She turned over and tucked the pillow under her cheek, frowning at the wall opposite the bed. She didn't want to know him as a person. It made things more complicated. Meeting his family complicated things. And the fact that she liked them only made it worse. It had been simpler when she'd disliked him, when he'd been nothing more than an annoying necessity in her life.

Nikki closed her eyes determinedly. Tomorrow they'd be back in L.A. and things could get back to normal. She and Sam would go back to being nodding acquaintances. She preferred it when there was plenty of distance between them.

* * *

The sound of someone knocking on the door woke Sam
out of a light sleep. He was momentarily disoriented when
he opened his eyes and found himself staring at the carpet
inches from his nose. But the fogginess lasted only a moment, and it hit him that, whoever was outside the door, he
didn't want them to see him sleeping on the floor while his
wife of barely a month had the bed all to herself.

He lunged to his feet, bringing his pillow and blanket
with him. He threw them at the bed and bent to snatch up
the bedspread that had served as a mattress. It hit the foot
of the bed in a jumbled heap and slid off onto the floor.

Nikki had been more deeply asleep when the knock
came, and she was just turning over and opening her eyes
when she felt a solid weight hit the bed. Her eyes flew open
and she found herself nose to nipple with a man's naked
chest. She opened her mouth, but the startled shriek
emerged as a muffled squeak as Sam's hand closed over her
lower face.

"It's me," he hissed in her ear. With his free hand, he
was shoving the pillow he'd used back against the head-
board and trying to pull the covers into place. The knock
came again, louder this time. He saw understanding in
Nikki's eyes and moved his hand.

"There's someone at the door," she whispered.

"No kidding." Sam jerked the blanket into position.
"Come in," he called. As the doorknob turned, he slid his
arm under Nikki and pulled her solidly against his side. She
immediately stiffened and tried to pull back.

"We're newlyweds, remember?"

"We're not *that* newlywed," she muttered between her
teeth just as the door opened.

Keefe stood in the doorway. His dark eyes skimmed over
the tangled covers and the couple nestled cozily in their

midst. He arched one brow in silent commentary. Nikki blushed, looking more angry than embarrassed.

Sam scowled at the amusement in his brother's eyes. "What do you want?"

The amusement deepened. Keefe propped one shoulder against the doorjamb, looking as if he planned on staying awhile. "I can see being married hasn't made you a morning person. You're going to have to work on that, Nikki. See if you can convince him that life begins before noon."

"Actually, I'm not overly fond of mornings myself," Nikki said. Shifting subtly, she tried to wedge a little space between herself and Sam, but he kept her firmly clamped against his side.

"Obviously the two of you are well suited." Keefe blandly ignored Sam's furious look and slouched a little more comfortably.

"I'm glad you approve," Sam said through gritted teeth. He'd had precious little sleep the night before and was not really in the mood for the game his brother was playing. Talking about Shannon had brought up a lot of old memories and it hadn't been easy to shake them. And he'd spent more time than he cared to admit thinking about the woman sleeping just a few feet away.

Now he was actually in that bed with her. And she was pressed against him with very little between them. The cotton nightgown, for all its modesty, was not a very effective barrier. He could feel every inch of her along his side, the softness of her breast pressed against him, the smooth curve of her waist under his hand. Sam shifted uncomfortably and felt the silky length of her bare leg against his where the nightgown had twisted up.

"Was there something you wanted?" Sam asked, not troubling to hide his annoyance. Damn it all, Keefe knew, better than anyone, what the true situation was.

"Actually, I—"

"Good morning." Gage looked over Keefe's shoulder and grinned at the couple in the bed. "You two look cozy."

"Thanks," Sam muttered. Nikki shifted, seeking some distance between them. The softness of the mattress defeated her, and she succeeded only in rubbing her leg against his. Sam swallowed the urge to groan.

"If you guys don't mind—"

"Uncle Sam!" Mary darted between Gage and Keefe and ran over to the bed. "You're awake."

"Yeah." Sam conjured a smile for his small niece. "Good morning, rug rat."

"I'm not a rug rat," she told him firmly. "Babies are rug rats. I'm not a baby." She perched on the foot of the bed and studied Sam and Nikki with the open curiosity of the very young. "You're in the same bed."

The simple observation turned Nikki's face pink and brought a snort of laughter from the two men in the doorway.

"Yes, we are," Sam said, shooting a killing look at his brothers.

"Is that 'cause you're married?"

"Yes." Maybe this was a sort of cosmic punishment for the deception they were practicing. "We'd really like to—"

"I told you not to wake them, Mary." Cole's tall figure filled in what little space was left in the doorway. "Morning, you two."

"What is this?" Sam snarled. "Is someone selling tickets?"

"What kind of tickets, Uncle Sam?"

"I think he means that the room is getting a little crowded," Cole suggested. He grinned at his oldest brother.

"Nikki might as well find out now what kind of a family she's married into."

"A bunch of voyeurs," Sam muttered in disgust.

"What's a voyer?"

"Never mind, urchin." Cole came into the room and lifted his daughter from the bed. "I think your aunt and uncle would like to be alone."

"So they can kiss?" she asked. "My friend Bambi says her big sister just got married and all they do is kiss and kiss and kiss. Do you kiss Aunt Nikki a lot?" Perched on her father's hip, she looked at them with bright-eyed curiosity.

"All the time," Sam managed in a strangled voice, torn between frustration and laughter.

"Can I watch?"

Gage and Keefe laughed out loud. Cole grinned. "Kissing isn't a spectator sport," he told his daughter. "That means it isn't for people to watch."

"How come? People kiss on TV."

"This isn't television," Sam told her. He didn't dare look at Nikki. From the rigidity of her body, he suspected she might be on the verge of bolting for safety.

"Don't you want to kiss Aunt Nikki?" Once she'd gotten an idea in her head, Mary wasn't inclined to let go of it.

"Yeah, Sam. Don't you want to kiss Aunt Nikki?" Keefe asked, his eyes gleaming with a wicked amusement.

Gage didn't know the truth about his brother's marriage, but he did recognize an opportunity for harassment. "I'd certainly want to kiss Aunt Nikki if I were married to her."

"What I want is to be an only child," Sam said, his glare encompassing all three of his brothers.

"But don't you *want* to kiss her?" Mary asked, showing a tenacity at odds with her delicate appearance.

Sam stared at her helplessly. There was more truth in his answer than he would have liked. "Of course I want to kiss her."

He sucked in a sharp breath as Nikki's fingers found the skin over his ribs and pinched viciously. The message was unmistakable and enough to make him give up the half-formed thought of using his niece's innocent curiosity to satisfy his own not-so-innocent urges.

"But I don't want to kiss her with everyone staring at us."

"We'd close our eyes," Gage offered helpfully.

"I wouldn't," Keefe said, grinning at his older brother.

It was just as well that Rachel entered the picture just then, because Sam's response would probably not have been fit for Mary's young ears.

"What have you got going—a convention?" she asked, poking her head in the door. Her gaze went from Nikki's flushed face to the temper simmering in Sam's eyes to the pure mischief in her other sons' expressions. "Out," she ordered briskly. "Stop harassing Sam and Nikki. Keefe, did you tell them breakfast would be ready soon?"

"Gage showed up before I got a chance to," he said.

"I don't remember putting my hand over your mouth to keep you from talking," Gage protested.

"Don't start squabbling," Rachel told them.

"He started it," Gage said, doing a creditable twelve-year-old whine.

Despite the situation, Nikki found herself laughing. The sight of Gage, at six foot two and looking like a Greek god, whining like a preadolescent brat was too ridiculous. He grinned at her, blatantly pleased with himself.

"Don't encourage him," Sam muttered, less in the mood to be amused by any of his siblings.

"Out," Rachel said again, making shooing motions. "Keefe, there's bacon on the stove. See that it doesn't burn. Gage, you can scramble the eggs."

"He always overcooks them," Cole complained.

"Then you can cook the eggs," she said promptly. "And your brother can take care of the pancakes. Mary, you make sure your father and your uncles do as they're told."

"I've always envied only children," Sam grumbled as the room emptied.

"Can't say I blame you," Rachel said, with an exasperated look at her departing offspring. "I asked Keefe to wake you, but I didn't expect it to turn into a convention. I hope they didn't embarrass you too much, Nikki."

"Not at all," Nikki lied.

Now that they were gone, she was less concerned with Sam's brother's teasing than she was with the fact that she was still plastered to Sam's body. A very warm, muscular, male body, one that set off tremors she had no business feeling.

"Why was Keefe supposed to wake us?" Sam asked. He rubbed one hand over his face to conceal a yawn.

"Because I knew you wanted to get started early."

"We did?"

"Nikki needs to get back to L.A., remember?"

"She does?" He gave his mother a blank look that sharpened quickly when Nikki's fingers found the tender skin over his ribs again. "Oh yeah. I forgot."

Rachel gave him a questioning look, but all she said was, "Breakfast will be on the table in twenty minutes, if your brothers don't start a food fight."

The door had barely shut behind her when Nikki wrenched herself loose from Sam's hold. He watched with unabashed interest as she scrambled off the bed. He caught only a glimpse of long legs before she jerked the night-gown down and into place.

"If you ever manhandle me like that again, I'm going to call the police," she snapped, shoving her hair back from her face.

"I am the police. Besides, I'm the one with bruises." Sam rubbed his side for emphasis. "You've got fingernails like a damned velociraptor."

"You're just lucky I couldn't get to your throat. You didn't have to hold me so tight."

"We're supposed to be newlyweds," he reminded her. He folded his hands under his head and watched as she stalked across the room to where her clothing lay in a neat pile.

"You had me squashed so close, we looked more like Siamese twins than newlyweds." But he noticed the heat had gone out of her voice.

"I wasn't the one who made up some story about having to leave early, which led to Keefe coming in to wake us."

"I thought we'd want an excuse to get out of here this morning. I don't think we should push our luck with this whole charade we're playing."

"Not a bad idea," he admitted. "But if you'd let me know, I could have made it a point to be up and about before anyone was likely to come knocking on the door."

Nikki turned to look at him, her fine brows drawn in a frown. Wearing the modest cotton gown, with her hair falling in tousled waves and not a scrap of makeup on her face, she didn't exactly look like a centerfold, but Sam had never seen a stapled-in-the-middle model who sent such a sharp stab of awareness through him. A quick surge of hunger made him want to pull her onto the bed again and not let her up until the sun went back down. Didn't he want to kiss her, Mary had asked. The problem was he wanted to kiss her too damned much.

"I think Keefe suspects something." Nikki's worried comment distracted Sam from his lustful—and completely inappropriate—thoughts.

"Keefe?" He stalled for time.

"There's something about the way he looks at us, as if he suspects something." Her teeth tugged at her lower lip. "Do you think he's guessed that we're not really married?"

"Guessed?" Sam hesitated, reluctant to tell her that Keefe hadn't had to guess. But she looked so worried and he was surprised to discover that he didn't like seeing her look that way. "Keefe doesn't suspect anything."

"How can you be so sure? The way he looks at us—"

"He knows the truth. I told him a couple of weeks ago."

"You *told* him? I thought we agreed that no one was going to know the truth about us."

"I suppose you didn't tell your friend Liz?" He arched one brow in question.

"I told Liz," she admitted.

"I told Keefe. We're even." He shrugged.

Nikki tried not to notice the way the movement drew attention to the furry width of his chest. For some reason, it was difficult to notice anything else. It wasn't as if she hadn't seen his chest before, she thought, exasperated by her wandering attention. It was an unfortunate reminder, bringing back memories of the day she'd walked into his room. She'd seen a great deal more than his chest that day.

She looked away, trying to marshal her scattered thoughts and drag them back to the conversation at hand. It probably didn't matter that Keefe knew the truth. And she could hardly blame Sam for telling his brother, when she'd told her best friend. Her eyes widened suddenly. "Keefe knows?"

"I thought we'd already established that." Sam stifled another yawn.

"Last night, when you dragged me onto your lap, you knew I was worried that he might suspect something, that that was why I sat down on the arm of your chair."

"I couldn't resist," he admitted without the least sign of repentence. "You were doing such a good job of playing the doting bride."

"You took advantage of me."

"You got your revenge," he reminded her. "You drove your elbow halfway to my spine, and I'm probably permanently crippled from the damage you did when you stepped on my foot."

"Good." She nodded in satisfaction. "Maybe that will teach you not to treat this situation like it's some kind of game."

She turned and stalked into the bathroom without giving Sam a chance to respond. He stayed where he was, his eyes on the closed door. The bed beside him was still warm and a trace of soft, floral scent clung to the sheets.

It occurred to him, not for the first time, that this marriage-of-convenience business wasn't nearly as simple as it had seemed at first.

Chapter 10

The rain of the day before had given way to deep blue skies and warm sunshine. Breakfast was a noisy affair, involving a great many good-natured insults tossed back and forth about who'd burned the bacon and who'd undercooked the pancakes, both of which were perfect as far as Nikki could tell.

After the meal, Nikki helped to clear the table. She and Rachel talked easily as they worked, and any silences were filled in by Mary, who seemed to never run out of questions about anything and everything.

"You're very good with her," Rachel commented, after Nikki had fielded a particularly convoluted inquiry.

"I like children," Nikki said, her face soft with affection as she watched the little girl carefully carry a plate from the table to the counter.

"Mary could use some cousins. Not that I'm hinting or anything," Rachel added, smiling.

"I... We haven't really discussed that." Nikki was pleased by the steadiness of her voice.

"Well, there's plenty of time," Rachel said comfortably.

Nikki murmured an agreement and made her escape as quickly as possible, retreating into the living room, which was momentarily empty. She couldn't take much more. Her conscience was already screaming bloody murder. How could she have been so incredibly blind? To think that this marriage wouldn't affect anyone but her and Sam.

She wandered around the room, touching a knickknack here and there but not really seeing anything. They'd be leaving here soon and she might never come back. It wouldn't be all that hard to avoid visiting Sam's family for the next eleven months. After all, she didn't care what they thought of her. Did she? She shied away from the answer to that question.

Finding herself next to the piano with its row of photographs, it occurred to her that there was probably a picture of Sam's wife. Seized by a sudden curiosity, she bent to look at them.

There it was. Picking it up, she carried it over to the window, where the light was better.

It was an informal shot, obviously taken at their wedding. Nikki guessed that Sam had been in his mid-twenties and the woman at his side looked a little younger. They were smiling at the camera, but there was something about them that suggested they were aware only of each other. They looked young and very much in love.

Her eyes skimmed over the quietly pretty brunette and focused on Sam's face. This was a different man than the one she'd married—younger, with fewer shadows in his eyes.

Nikki was so absorbed in the photograph that she didn't hear Sam's voice until he was right outside the living room. She couldn't be caught standing here with his wife's picture in her hand. In a panicked flurry, she stepped behind the open drapes. She regretted the move immediately. She was going to look like a complete fool if anyone caught her lurking behind the drapes like a second-rate burglar. But it was too late to change her mind.

"I don't want to argue with you about this. Just take the check," Sam was saying.

"I don't want it." It was Cole's voice, and he didn't sound happy. "I can come up with the money on my own."

"How? By selling your plane? Then how are you going to earn a living?"

"I'll manage," Cole said tightly.

"You don't have to manage. I've got the money. When the time is right for Mary's surgery, it will be paid for."

Mary's surgery? What kind of surgery? Nikki's heart clenched at the thought of something being wrong with the beautiful, dark-eyed little girl.

"Where did you suddenly come up with this kind of money?" Cole asked. "Unless they've started paying cops a helluva lot more than they used to, you don't have this kind of bucks."

"Nikki's rolling in the stuff. When I told her about Mary's surgery, she wanted to help." Nikki wondered if she was the only one who heard the strain in Sam's voice.

"No." Cole sounded adamant, and she heard him move abruptly away and then back again, as if he couldn't stay in one place. "It would be bad enough if it were your money, but I'm sure as hell not going to sponge off your wife. I'll pay for it myself," he insisted stubbornly.

"Don't be an ass." Sam didn't trouble to soften the sharpness in his voice. "Nikki is family now. She wants to do this."

Which was true, even if Sam didn't realize it.

"No." Nikki didn't need to be able to see him to know that Cole was shaking his head. "Absolutely not."

"Swallow your damned pride and think of what's best for your daughter."

"What's best for her is to have a father who doesn't take charity," Cole said sharply.

"This isn't charity, dammit! I'm family. And don't tell me you wouldn't do the same damned thing if the situation were reversed."

"It isn't reversed and I don't want your wife's money. I'll do it on my own."

"So your pride is more important than Mary's health?" Sam snapped furiously.

There was a brief silence, and Nikki half expected to hear it end with the sound of Cole's fist connecting with Sam's jaw. But the next sound wasn't that of a fist against flesh. Cole sighed, a quick, harsh sound that held both anger and resignation.

"I hate it when you're right. No, my pride isn't more important than Mary's health. I'll take the money." The words sounded as if they'd been pulled from him.

There was a pause, and Nikki imagined Sam handing him the check.

"This . . . means a lot to me, Sam, to both of us. Thank you."

"You'd do the same for me."

"Yeah, but I wouldn't be so obnoxious about it." Nikki was relieved to hear a trace of humor in Cole's voice.

"I'm oldest. I get to be most obnoxious."

"You're very good at it."

"Thanks."

"I'll catch Nikki before you guys leave and thank her," Cole said.

"No!" Sam must have realized that his response was too sharp, because he softened it immediately. "She'd be embarrassed. I'll pass on your thanks."

"I'd really like to say something to her myself. This means a lot to Mary and me. I'd like to thank her."

"No, really. She's . . . very self-conscious about having money and . . . I know it would just make her uncomfortable."

Nikki bit her lip to hold back a chuckle at the blatant discomfort in Sam's voice. Obviously, she wasn't the only one finding herself floundering under the false pretenses they'd created.

"If you're sure." Cole sounded doubtful.

"I'm sure. I'll tell her how much you appreciate it."

There was another silence, and Nikki mentally urged them to leave. Her nose was starting to itch and she wasn't sure how much longer she could resist the urge to scratch it.

"I've got to ask you something, Sam." Cole sounded uneasy. "You didn't marry Nikki to get the money for Mary's surgery, did you?"

Her itchy nose was immediately forgotten. Nikki held her breath, waiting for Sam's response. Would he tell Cole the truth?

"Have you looked at Nikki?" Sam's tone was rich with amusement. "Can you imagine anyone marrying her for her money?"

Cole's tone didn't lighten to match his brother's. "I can imagine you doing it if you thought it would help one of us," he said slowly. "You've been trying to protect us ever since we were kids."

"I was the eldest. There wasn't anyone else."

"Yeah, but we're not kids anymore. If you married Nikki so you could give me this money, I don't want any part of it. I can still figure out a way to pay for the surgery."

"I think you've seen too many movies." Nikki wondered that Cole didn't hear the false note in Sam's light tone. "I married Nikki because I wanted to. She's beautiful, she's intelligent, and the fact that she happens to be rich just worked out well for you and Mary."

"You're sure?" Nikki could imagine the searching look Cole gave his older brother.

"I'm sure. Now, will you put the damned check in your pocket? I don't think I've ever seen anyone so reluctant to take money. God help Ed McMahon if he ever tries to give you any."

Cole laughed reluctantly. "Maybe you should call and warn him."

"Maybe I should. I've got to find Nikki. We have to hit the road pretty soon."

Nikki waited until she was sure they were gone before leaving her hiding place. Thank heavens neither of them had seen her. It would have been a little difficult to explain why she was hiding behind the curtains with a picture of Sam and his first wife clutched in her hands.

She carried the photo back over to the piano, but before setting it down, she stared at it for a few more minutes, her thoughts spinning with all she'd learned. In the past couple of days, she'd seen the man she'd married in a whole new light. He'd been married and, from the way Rachel spoke, he'd loved his wife.

He was devoted to his family, enough so that he'd married a woman he didn't know to get the money for his niece's surgery. Why hadn't he told her that was what it was for? She'd assumed he was driven by greed, while holding her own motives up as pure and noble. The memory of her smug condemnation of Sam as a fortune hunter made her squirm inside.

"Sam's looking for you." Rachel's voice came from directly behind her. Nikki started and spun around, guiltily aware of the photo she held.

"I was just...looking at some of the pictures," she blurted out.

Rachel's dark brows rose in surprise. "You're family, Nikki. You're welcome to look at them all you like."

Aware that she'd reacted oddly, Nikki forced a smile. "Lena used to always accuse me of getting into things I shouldn't. I guess I still half expect her to catch me with my fingers where they don't belong."

Rachel smiled. "I haven't slapped anyone's fingers in a very long time."

"Oh, she never slapped my fingers. She just gave me this long-suffering look and then took me out to the kitchen and put me to work helping with dinner." Nikki's face softened with affection. "She spoiled me rotten, actually."

"Is Lena your mother?"

"Oh no. Lena is our housekeeper, only she's always been more like a mother to me. Marilee is my mother, and I doubt if she'd notice if I had my hand in a tank of piranhas." There was amusement rather than condemnation in her tone. "Not that she doesn't love me," she added, with more duty than conviction. "But Marilee lives in her own little world and she doesn't pay much attention to anything outside it."

If Rachel thought there was anything strange about the fact that Marilee's child apparently hadn't been a part of that world, she didn't comment. She held out her hand for the photo. "Which one were you looking at?"

Nikki reluctantly handed it over, wishing she hadn't given in to the moment's curiosity about Sam's wife. "I just wondered what she looked like. Sam...hasn't said much about her."

Which wasn't a lie. Sam hadn't said *anything* about her.

Rachel studied the photograph for a few seconds before lifting her gaze to Nikki's face, her eyes shrewd. "Did Sam mention Sara at all?"

Nikki opened her mouth to say that, of course, Sam had told her that he'd been married before. But she couldn't get the lie out. She shook her head.

"We...haven't really known each other all that long," she said quickly, trying to forestall the questions she saw in Rachel's eyes.

"Sam told me it was a whirlwind courtship," she murmured.

"I suppose it seems foolish to you—us marrying so quickly, I mean."

"I'd known Sam's father less than a month when we got married and we were very happy. Sometimes you just know something is right," Rachel said slowly.

"Yes."

And sometimes you know it's wrong and do it, anyway.

Rachel hesitated a moment longer, her eyes searching. Nikki felt as if she had the word *phony* emblazoned across her forehead in flashing neon lights. But she obviously didn't look as guilty as she felt.

"I think Sam's about ready to leave." Rachel reached past Nikki to set the photograph on the piano.

"I'll go find him." She was vividly aware of Rachel's eyes following her as she left the room.

* * *

"I think Jason finds your mother attractive," Nikki said, glancing at Sam as the truck pulled away from his mother's house.

"I figured that when he decided to stay in Los Olivos over the weekend. Should I be asking to see his credentials?" He took his eyes off the road long enough to glance at her with a quick smile.

"They're impeccable. Besides, I don't think they're heading for Vegas quite yet."

"I don't know. Mom was blushing like a girl."

Nikki had noticed the same thing, along with the fact that Jason had seemed younger than he had in years.

"Would you mind if they fell in love?"

"Why should I?" Sam gave her a surprised look. "Jason seems like a nice guy and Mom could certainly use some happiness in her life."

"But what about when we get a divorce? If they get together, won't that be awkward?"

"Let's worry about that when the time comes," Sam suggested. "They aren't married yet."

"True." Nikki stared down at her wedding ring, twisting her hand back and forth to watch the way the light changed on the gold band. She hadn't planned on saying anything, but the words were suddenly there. "I heard you talking to Cole this morning."

Sam stiffened, and she felt the look he shot in her direction. "Talking about what?"

"About the money. About Mary's surgery. What's wrong with her? Why does she need surgery?"

He took his time answering. This wasn't a topic he'd ever expected to discuss with Nikki. But she knew enough now that there was no reason not to tell her the rest of it.

"There's a hole in her heart."

"Will she be all right?" There was real concern in her voice, in her face.

"The prognosis is very good. They'll do the surgery sometime in the next couple of years probably. I don't know what all goes into deciding when to do it. But they generally wait until a child is a little older. It doesn't cause her too many problems. And once the repair is made, she should be fine."

"And that's what you wanted the money for? That's why you married me?"

"Yeah. Max knew about the situation with Mary, and he thought it would be a good solution." He flicked on his turn signal. Nikki waited until he'd made the turn before speaking again.

"What about insurance? Wouldn't that pay for the surgery?"

"Cole runs a delivery service. A one-man, one-plane operation, and he's still paying off the plane. No insurance, not a lot of ready cash. We'd have come up with the money eventually. Gage is the only one of us with any money in the bank, but it wasn't enough. Keefe was trying to sell his ranch. Our marriage made things a lot simpler."

"And you don't mind making that kind of sacrifice for your brother?"

"He'd do the same for me. We're family." The simple statement summed everything up for him. "Besides, it's a pretty decent salary for a year's work, not to mention it's only a part-time job. And the living conditions aren't bad."

He shot her a quick grin which she didn't see. She was staring out the windshield with an expression he couldn't read.

"Your family seems very close," she commented.

There was a wistful note in the comment that made Sam remember her surprise when he'd asked if her family would be getting together for the holidays. He hadn't given much thought to it at the time. He'd just been relieved that there was no conflict with spending Thanksgiving with his family. She'd commented that her family was not close. Apparently, she'd meant it. Which reminded him of something else.

"Did you mean what you said to Molly—about changing your name to Walker? I assumed you'd want to keep your own name."

"I don't know. It might be nice to have a name that I didn't have to spell every time I make a reservation or order something over the phone, even if it is only for the next year. If you'd rather I didn't..." She let the words trail off in question.

"I don't mind." In fact, he was finding that he minded less and less about this marriage. When it had begun, it had seemed like a year doing hard time. Once they'd called a truce, he'd begun to think of it as more of a minimum security sentence. But after the last couple of days, the prison analogy didn't seem apt anymore.

When he'd married her, he'd seen Nikki as a means to an end. But the longer he knew her, the more he saw her as a person, one he was coming to like.

He frowned at the highway in front of the truck. It was one thing to like her, but he didn't want to find her attractive. Unfortunately, he didn't seem to have much choice about it.

Chapter 11

Sam picked up the phone, tucking it between his chin and his shoulder so that his hands were free to keep shuffling through the papers on his desk. Where the hell had he put that report? "Walker."

"Sam?" The woman's voice was vaguely familiar.

"Speaking."

"This is Liz Davis, Nikki's friend."

"I remember." The redhead with the cute kid and the suspicious husband. He moved another stack of papers in search of the elusive report. "What can I do for you, Liz?"

"I'm sorry to bother you at work, but it's about Nikki, actually."

"Is something wrong?" The report was forgotten as his attention focused sharply on the conversation. "Is Nikki all right?"

"She's fine," Liz said hastily. "She's just stranded. Her car won't start."

"It's a wonder that thing ever starts." Sam relaxed back in his chair. He tuned out the bustle around him with practiced ease. Nearly fifteen years on the job had given him the ability to concentrate on the matter at hand, regardless of what was going on around him.

"That's what Bill says. But Barney is more reliable than he looks."

"Barney?" Sam's eyebrows rose. *Barney who?*

"Nikki's car. Michael named him."

"The car has a name?" *That rolling junk pile is named Barney?* "Isn't there a puppet or something named Barney?"

"A dinosaur. The most irritatingly happy creature you've ever seen. He's purple. Nikki's car is purple."

"So your son named the car Barney," Sam finished for her.

"Children aren't always as imaginative as they're cracked up to be," Liz said dryly. "Anyway, Barney has the croup, and Nikki's stuck for a ride. She called me and I told her Bill would pick her up, but it turns out Bill's working late tonight, and I really don't want her there after dark."

"Want her where?" It seemed as if he'd spent most of the conversation asking questions.

"At Rainbow Place," Liz said, sounding surprised that he had to ask.

"Of course." What the hell was Rainbow Place? A shopping mall? A restaurant? And why would Liz assume that he'd know what it was?

"I was hoping you might be able to pick her up. If you can't, I'm sure she can get a cab."

Sam glanced at his watch. He'd put in a good ten hours and there was nothing urgent pending—at least, no more than there usually was.

"I'll pick her up. Can you give me the address? I don't have it handy." Which was true enough, since he didn't have it at all.

"I have it right here."

Sam's brows shot up at the address she was giving him. He suddenly understood Liz's concern about Nikki being there after dark. He wasn't sure *he* wanted to be there after dark. So what was Nicole Beauvisage Walker, pampered rich girl, doing in a neighborhood like that?

"I know Nikki will appreciate this, Sam," Liz said, obviously relieved to have the problem solved.

"No problem."

He hung up the phone and stared at the address scribbled on the outside of a fast-food bag that had been lying on his desk. What was Rainbow Place? And what was his wife doing there? There was one way to find out. He got up and reached for the coat draped over the back of his chair.

Half an hour later, he pulled the Bronco up to the curb in front of the address Liz had given him. There had to be a mistake. *This* couldn't be the right address. But painted across the front of the building, in bright, crayon colors were the words *Rainbow Place,* complete with rainbow arcing across the wall.

Sam shut off the engine and got out, careful to lock the truck. The neighborhood wasn't as bad as he'd expected it to be, a small pocket of tattered respectability in the midst of urban blight. The houses nearby were shabby but neat— it was obvious that the occupants might not have much money, but they hadn't stopped caring about their homes.

He stopped in front of the tall chain-link fence that surrounded Rainbow Place and studied the assortment of playground equipment that filled the small yard. The fence itself had been painted in a variety of bright colors, which made it look a little less starkly functional. The scene was bright and welcoming. And completely bewildering.

A nursery school? What was Nikki doing at a nursery school?

The gate was locked, but there was a bell with a hand-lettered sign that read Ring Me. Sam took the suggestion and pressed his finger on the bell. A moment later, the door of the house opened and a slender young African-American woman came out. She stopped on the other side of the fence and eyed him suspiciously. Seeing her up close, Sam realized she was younger than he'd thought—probably not more than seventeen or eighteen.

"We don't allow solicitors," she told him firmly.

"I'm not a solicitor. I'm here to pick up Nikki. I'm her husband." It struck him that the words came more easily than he might have expected. More than he'd have liked?

"Nikki doesn't have a husband," the girl said flatly.

Obviously Nikki hadn't felt it necessary to tell everyone in her life about her marriage. Sam was surprised by the sharp little pinch of annoyance he felt.

"Yes she does, and I'm it." He tried a smile and got nothing but a cool look in response. "How about if you tell her I'm here and we'll see if she admits to knowing me?"

"What name shall I give her?"

He thought of pointing out that it was unlikely Nikki had more than one husband, but remembered that even that was under dispute. "Sam Walker."

"Wait here."

"I'm not planning on scaling the fence," he muttered as she turned and walked back up the path.

He shoved his hands into the pockets of his denim jacket and hunched his shoulders a little against the chill in the air. Thick gray clouds hovered overhead, blocking the late afternoon sun. Rain was predicted sometime before midnight.

But Sam wasn't concerned with the weather, present or future. He kept looking at the cheerful playground and the brightly painted stucco building. Just where did Nikki fit into this picture?

A few minutes later, the teenager returned. "Nikki says you can come in," she told him. Her expression was slightly more welcoming than it had been before his identity had been confirmed. "I'm Jade Freeman. I'm sorry about making you wait, but Nikki hadn't told us about getting married."

"We've only been married a little while." Sam stepped through the gate, waiting while she relocked it.

"Still seems odd she didn't say anything."

It seemed odd to him, too, but he couldn't say as much. He smiled and tried to look unconcerned. The look Jade gave him suggested she was wondering if Nikki had had a reason for concealing his existence. Under other circumstances, Sam might have been tempted to drag his knuckles on the ground and maybe drool a little to confirm her obvious suspicions, but at the moment he was more interested in finding out what Nikki was up to.

Jade pushed open the front door, which was painted an eye-searing shade of pink, and led him into a narrow front hall. The walls were a soft white, the better to show off the rows of crayon drawings and finger-painted masterpieces that covered them like one-of-a-kind wallpaper.

"Nikki said you could wait in the office," Jade told him.

Sam glanced through the door at the tiny room, which was nearly filled by a battered wooden desk. A personal computer and stacks of paper concealed its surface. There were more examples of children's artwork tacked to the walls and several boxes of disposable diapers stacked in one corner.

"Where's Nikki?" he asked.

Jade had already started to walk away, but she turned back at his question. "She's with the children, but she said you should wait here."

"I'd like to see her, please." Seeing the refusal in her expression, Sam tried a coaxing smile. "I gave up devouring small children years ago."

There was a flicker of humor in her dark eyes. "Found a new hobby, did you?"

"Hanging by my heels from rafters."

A smile tugged at the corner of her mouth. "We don't have any rafters handy."

"Then you don't have anything to worry about."

She studied him a moment longer, and then, with a half shrug, turned away. It wasn't exactly the warmest invitation Sam had ever had, but he wasn't complaining. He heard Nikki's voice even before Jade stopped in the doorway of another room. She looked over her shoulder and put her finger to her lips.

The warning was unnecessary. Sam didn't think he could have found his voice if his life depended on it. There were a dozen children in the room, ranging in age from toddlers to perhaps five-year-olds. They were sprawled on the floor or seated in child-size chairs, their attention firmly directed toward the woman sitting cross-legged on the floor at the front of the room.

Sam found his own attention similarly riveted. This was a Nikki he'd never seen, never even imagined. She was wearing a pair of faded jeans and a jade green cotton shirt, both decorated with assorted smears, courtesy of over-exuberant young artists. Her hair was pulled back in a

simple ponytail, but a few pale gold tendrils had escaped
confinement and lay against her forehead and neck.

This was not the woman he'd married. *That* woman wore
silk suits, tailored trousers and impeccable makeup. She
didn't wear jeans and sneakers and have a smear of red
paint along her jawline. And she didn't sit on floors, reading to a group of fascinated children.

While Sam was staring at her, the story came to an end.
Immediately, young voices were raised in a babble of comment and demands for her to read another story. She answered questions, told them that two stories were more than
enough and fished a tissue from her pocket to wipe a runny
nose, all the while looking cool and unflustered, as if she
did this every day. Which, for all he knew, she did.

It occurred to him that maybe he didn't know as much
about the woman he'd married as he thought he did.

"I had a hard time convincing your watchdog to let me
in the gate," Sam said.

"Jade is very protective of the children." Nikki moved a
stack of papers from one corner of the desk to the other.
Her office was far from spacious at the best of times, but
with Sam in it, the room suddenly seemed claustrophobi-
cally small. In fact, from the moment she'd looked up and
seen him standing in the doorway, she'd felt as if there
wasn't quite enough air in the building.

"She seemed surprised when I told her we were married."

His tone was neutral, but Nikki felt a surge of guilt. It
was completely irrational. She didn't owe him any expla-
nations, but she heard herself giving one, anyway. "I
thought it would be easier if I didn't mention it. It might
confuse the children when we...when the year is up, I
mean."

It sounded weak even to her own ears. Her marriage and divorce would be nothing more than an abstract idea to a four-year-old, causing not even a blip in their lives. But she didn't feel comfortable telling him the truth, which was that she'd wanted—needed—this one place to remain untouched by the charade her life had become. Ironic, really, since the charade had begun *because* of this place.

But Sam nodded as if it wasn't a completely ridiculous excuse. "Makes sense," he said. "If I'd known, I could have said I was your uncle from Australia or something."

"It's all right. It was a silly idea, anyway." She picked up the same stack of papers and straightened them by tapping them against the desk, concentrating on the task as if her life depended on having the edges perfectly aligned.

"You volunteer here?" Sam asked, probing carefully.

Nikki considered saying yes and leaving it at that. It was the truth—she *did* volunteer here. But she didn't want any more lies, even those of omission. Lately, it seemed as if her entire life was a tissue of lies.

"Actually, Rainbow Place is mine. Jade's mother manages the place, but I work here three or four days a week."

She wasn't sure whether or not to be insulted by the surprise in Sam's expression. Obviously, it had never occurred to him that she might do something useful.

"It looks like a great place," he said slowly, still trying to get his mind around the idea of her as a businesswoman.

"The kids like it." She set the slightly mauled stack of papers down. "I'm ready to go."

"It's not the greatest neighborhood," Sam commented as they walked to the gate. "Couldn't you have found a better location?"

"This is where there's need," she said simply. "Most of the children come from single-parent homes. Having a safe place to leave them makes it possible for their parents to work and stay out of the welfare trap. Some of our mothers are going to school full-time, getting a better education so they'll qualify for better jobs.''

''Is this why you wanted the money your grandfather left you?'' Sam asked slowly. That was a question that had lingered in the back of his mind—why Nikki would want the money so much that she was willing to marry him to get it.

She hesitated a moment and then nodded. ''Yes. Inheriting that money means I don't have to spend my time fundraising to keep Rainbow Place open. I may even be able to open a second day-care center somewhere else.''

Sam considered what she'd told him while she unlocked the gate, relocking it after they'd stepped through. It was a new facet to the woman he'd married, one he'd never expected.

''It's a lot of work,'' he commented, trying to shift his thinking to encompass Nikki as a philanthropist.

''It needs to be done. Do you know how hard it is to raise a child alone? If you don't have family or friends who can help, you're virtually forced onto the welfare rolls, and once you're there, it's almost impossible to get back on your feet again.''

She stopped abruptly, aware that she'd been all but lecturing him. ''Sorry. I didn't mean to sound off like that. It's just so frustrating to me when I think of all the people who fall through the cracks in the system.''

''I don't mind. Most cops have more than a few complaints about the system.''

''I suppose you do. But at least you know you're doing something to help.''

''Are we?'' Sam's mouth twisted in a mournful half smile. ''Sometimes I'm not so sure. What's wrong with your car?'' he asked, abruptly changing the subject before she could comment.

"It won't start."

"Now, that's a good, detailed description." His grin took any criticism from the words. "Give me the keys and I'll see if I can come up with a more specific diagnosis."

Nikki handed him the keys, then stood on the sidewalk while he slid onto the front seat and tried to start the car. The engine turned over, almost caught, sputtered and coughed, but refused to start.

"I think it might be the fuel pump," he said as he got out and shut the door.

"Can it be fixed?"

"Sure." He stared down at the battered purple vehicle. "It might be kinder to shoot it and put it out of its misery, though."

"Absolutely not," she said indignantly. "Barney is perfectly dependable most of the time."

"Except when it doesn't start," he pointed out dryly. He lifted his head and glanced around the neighborhood. "Of course, no self-respecting car thief would be caught dead trying to steal something this old. In that respect, it may be the smartest thing you could drive."

"That had occurred to me. I know I can park Barney just about anywhere and find him still there when I come out."

"It would be safer still if you didn't come here at all," he said as he handed her back the keys.

"It's not as bad as it looks."

As if on cue, a car full of tough-looking youths drove by, radio blasting out a drumbeat so loud the ground seemed to shake under Nikki's feet. As they passed, a beer can sailed out the window, bounced off Barney's hood and landed on the grass between Sam and Nikki. He waited until the car had disappeared down the street before giving Nikki a dry look.

"An example of some fine, upstanding citizens, I presume."

"There are a few troublemakers," she admitted. "But most of the people around here *are* fine, upstanding citizens."

He glanced at the tidy houses across the street. "That doesn't make it any safer for you to be here. I don't like the idea of you coming down here alone."

Nikki started to tell him that it was none of his business, when an extraordinary thought occurred to her. *He's worried about me.* She tried to remember the last time someone had been protective of her, but nothing came to mind. Lena, certainly, when she was a child. But no one since then. The realization softened her response.

"I've been doing it for three years and nothing has happened to me."

"It only takes once."

"Do they teach you that positive attitude at the academy?"

"Yeah. Reality 101. Come on. Let's go home. We can call your friend Bill and arrange for him to pick up this junk heap and tow it to a shop. If you need a ride tomorrow, I'll bring you."

"Thanks, but I wasn't planning on coming here tomorrow. I just had some shopping to do, and that can wait."

She climbed into the Bronco, aware of a warm feeling in her chest and the vague thought that if she'd *had* to get married, she could have done worse in choosing a husband.

Sam woke suddenly, hearing the sound of a crash echoing in his head, like something half-remembered from a dream. Only the sound hadn't been part of a dream. He stood, grabbing a pair of jeans from the foot of the bed and dragging them over his legs. He had no particular desire to deal with a burglar in the nude. Lifting his gun from the night table, he pulled it from the holster on the way to the door.

The house had a good security system—not the most sophisticated, but more than enough to encourage the average burglar to seek out an easier target. Since he hadn't heard the alarm, if there was someone in the house, they were professional enough to have bypassed it. It couldn't be Nikki—she'd gone to bed hours ago.

Sam headed for the stairs with long, silent strides. He held the .45 beside his head, pointed at the ceiling, where he could bring it into action quickly if necessary.

A quick scan of the darkened living room revealed everything apparently in order. He stepped into the foyer and immediately heard a sound from the direction of the kitchen. A few seconds later, he'd found the intruder, as well as the cause of the noise that had awakened him.

Nikki stood in the middle of the kitchen. The tile floor in front of her was covered with a pool of sugar and a powdery brown substance he couldn't immediately place. In one hand she held a stainless-steel canister, slightly dented. In the other she held a dark brown box which, after a moment, he identified as having once held cocoa—until very recently, judging by the mess at her feet.

He lowered the gun to his side. Apparently, he wasn't going to need it. "If you're planning on stealing that canister, I should warn you that I'm a police officer."

At the sound of Sam's voice, Nikki jumped and jerked her head toward him. Great. Just what she needed. Not only had she made a world-class mess but now there was someone to witness it. And not just someone, but Sam

Walker—the man who was and wasn't her husband, the cause of the sleeplessness that had brought her down to the kitchen in the middle of the night.

"Go ahead and shoot," she told him glumly. "It can't make any more of a mess than I've already done."

Sam grinned and came farther into the room. "I don't think it's worthy of capital punishment." He set the gun on the counter and studied the mess at her feet.

He hooked his thumbs in the belt loops of his jeans, and Nikki tried very hard not to notice when the denim slid dangerously low on his hips. The only light was the small one over the stove, but it was more than enough to show every inch of his bare chest. It was a dream about that chest—not to mention everything that went with it—that had caused her to flee her bedroom in the middle of the night in hopes that a cup of cocoa would bring less disturbing dreams.

"How about half an hour hard labor with a broom?" Sam said.

With an effort, Nikki forced her attention back to the disaster at her feet. "Half an hour?" She raised her brows. "Do you know how far five pounds of sugar scatters when dropped?"

"Well, I didn't see any in the dining room, so I think it's safe to assume that the spill is at least partially contained."

"That's a relief. I can quit worrying about filing an environmental impact report."

"That's a safe bet. Do you mind my asking what happened?"

"Should I demand to have my attorney present?" Nikki set the canister and the nearly empty box of cocoa on the counter.

Sam grinned again, and she felt her pulse take a jump. "I'm asking as an interested bystander, not as an officer of the law," he assured her solemnly.

"In that case, I'll admit that I'm occasionally overcome by an uncontrollable urge to come down to the kitchen in the middle of the night and drop canisters on the floor."

"Ah, a canister dropper." The laughter in his eyes belied the serious set of his mouth. "We studied them at the academy, but I've never had to deal with one before."

"Did your instructors offer any suggestions?"

Nikki couldn't remember having ever had such an utterly ridiculous conversation with anyone. If someone had told her that she'd be standing in a small sea of sugar, in the middle of the night, having such a conversation with the man she'd married, she'd have thought they were crazy.

"They advised us to use extreme caution," Sam said. He shook his head, looking worried. "Canister droppers are known to be unpredictable. You never know what they might do next."

"I don't suppose they said anything about helping them clean up the mess," she suggested hopefully.

"*That's* the worst possible approach. Sometimes they turn violent."

"But I'm unarmed," she protested, spreading her hands to emphasize her harmlessness.

Unfortunately, as far as Sam was concerned, Nikki didn't need a weapon to be dangerous. Someday, he'd figure out how it was that she managed to look so desirable wearing clothes that couldn't, even by the wildest interpretation of the word, be called *sexy*. The voluminous nightgown she'd worn Thanksgiving night certainly hadn't been designed with enticement in mind but he'd been enticed. Tonight she was wearing a pair of pink-and-white striped cotton pajamas that had an almost childlike sweetness about them. But there was nothing childlike about the body inside them. *That* was all woman.

And the response she inspired in him was all man.

Nikki saw Sam's eyes go over her in a slow, sweeping glance that started with her tousled hair and ended with her sugar-dusted, slippered feet. He took his time, letting his gaze linger on the way.

The look had the impact of a physical touch. When his look skimmed her breasts, it was as if he'd put his hands on her. She felt her breasts swell, her nipples hardening into tight peaks that pressed against the fabric of her pajama top, visible evidence of the effect he was having on her.

His gaze moved on slowly, tracing the curving indentation of her waist before sliding slowly across her hips and down the length of her legs. As if he hadn't already wreaked enough havoc with her breathing, he then proceeded to retrace his path.

By the time his eyes collided with hers, Nikki's knees were trembling so badly that she was in danger of sinking to the floor, sugar and all. The blatant male hunger in his look sent a wave of heat through her like nothing she'd ever felt before.

"I—I should get a broom." She spoke more out of a need to break the tense silence than out of housewifely concern for the mess at her feet.

"If you walk through the sugar, you're going to track it even farther." Sam's words were reasonable, but his tone and the look in his eyes suggested that tidiness was not the main thing on his mind.

Without giving her a chance to respond, he stepped closer, his bare feet crunching on the edge of the spill. Leaning forward, he closed his hands around her waist. Nikki gasped as he lifted her as easily as if she'd weighed nothing at all. To steady herself, she put her hands on his arms, feeling the corded strength of his muscles as he stepped back from the grainy brown-and-white pool on the floor.

Nikki's breath caught when he drew her close before lowering her, so that her body brushed against his every inch of the way. Her eyes remained locked with his, mesmerized by the searing blue flame of his gaze. She felt that warmth as if it were a touch, spreading heat through her body, warming her in ways she'd never felt before, never imagined.

He was going to kiss her. She knew it as surely as if he'd stated the intention out loud. The thought sent a shiver of anticipation, mixed with something very close to fear, rushing down her spine. She couldn't analyze the fear—it wasn't physical. She knew, with every fiber of her being, that Sam would never hurt her. But there was a deep, emotional trepidation, a feeling that his kiss would change her life in ways she wasn't sure she was ready for.

"I don't think—"

"Don't think," he ordered, his voice a soft rasp. His hands, still at her waist, slid around her back, one pressing against her spine, the other sliding upward to tangle in the thick, pale gold of her hair. He tilted her head back. "Don't think at all."

The last word was a breath against her mouth. It was an unnecessary order. Every semblance of rational thought fled the moment his lips touched hers.

She'd been expecting him to take possession of her mouth, as much triumphant conqueror as lover. Instead, his lips were gentle, asking rather than demanding, coaxing her to let go of her uncertainties, to give him the response he wanted, to give herself to him in a way she'd never allowed herself to do.

Nikki was aware of a feeling oddly akin to despair. This was what she'd been afraid of—that once the door was opened, it might be impossible to close it again, to keep a safe distance. She felt as if carefully built walls were crumbling to dust. But it was impossible to resist. If she were honest with herself, she didn't *want* to resist. She wanted this, had wanted it from the first moment they'd met.

With a breath that was nearly a sob, she opened her mouth to him. Sam accepted her invitation immediately. His tongue tasted the fullness of her lower lip, brushed across the smooth surface of her teeth and found the honey-eyed sweetness of her mouth, taking possession.

Nikki's fingers dug into the heavy muscles of his upper arms, clinging to him as the world tilted and spun around them. It was everything she'd known it would be. It was the fulfillment of every guilty fantasy she'd had over the past few weeks. This was the dream that had driven her from her bed, that had sent her downstairs. She'd been seeking the gentle comfort of warm cocoa and found instead the hot passion of Sam's kiss.

She was everything he'd imagined she'd be, warm and soft, fitting in his arms as perfectly as if made to be there. Sam deepened the kiss, drawing Nikki closer until not even a shadow could have slipped between them. He could feel the fullness of her breasts crushed against his chest, the cotton of her pajama top proving a thin barrier at best.

He'd been waiting forever for this, waiting to taste her, to feel her against him. She'd created a hunger in him like nothing he'd ever known. One taste and he was rock hard and aching.

He slid his hand under the hem of her pajama top, flattening against the satiny skin of her back. Her skin warmed beneath his touch. His mouth slid restlessly from hers. Nikki gasped when his teeth closed on her earlobe. His tongue tasted the taut arch of her throat, settling on the pulse that beat raggedly at its base. He felt an echo of that pulse in his own heartbeat. God, he wanted her.

He wanted her here and now. He didn't care if she was sprawled beneath him on the table or sitting on the counter. Hell, he'd have her on the floor in the midst of the damned sugar, for that matter. As long as he could bury the aching heat of his arousal in the tender warmth of her. The thought of it made him shudder with need.

Nikki felt as if she'd been snatched up in a whirlwind. She could feel the hunger in him, feel herself being pulled into it, overwhelmed by it. Her skin felt sizzling hot beneath his hand. That heat radiated outward until her entire body was flushed with it. Her fingers curled into the thick dark blond hair at the base of his skull as her tongue came up to curl around his, teasing and tantalizing, fanning the heat higher still.

Sam shuddered against her. His hands shifted abruptly, and Nikki gasped in shock as she felt them slide beneath the fabric of her pajamas and flatten against her bottom. She started to protest, but all that came out was a soft moan against Sam's mouth as he lifted her half off her feet, pressing her lower body against his, letting her feel the swollen length of his arousal.

Nikki's bones seemed to melt. There was a throbbing pressure in the pit of her stomach, an aching emptiness that only he could fill.

"I want you." The words were a low growl against her throat, as much felt as heard.

"Yes." Nikki arched her head back, trusting Sam to keep them both upright. His tongue swirled across the pulse that beat wildly at the base of her throat.

"Come upstairs with me."

Yes. It was the natural conclusion to what they'd begun, and she wanted it as much as he did. She wanted to lie in his bed, to feel him over her, within her. There was nothing to stop them, no reason to hesitate. They were married and, in a few short minutes, they would be husband and wife in fact as well as name.

The thought penetrated Nikki's fevered absorption in the taste and feel of the man holding her.

Husband and wife? Married? For real? That wasn't the way it was supposed to work. This was a marriage of convenience, not passion. If they made love, all the rules would change. She'd be Sam's wife in every sense of the word. There'd be no more pretending that they were strangers linked by nothing more than their names on a marriage license. No more pretending that, at the end of the year, she was going to walk away untouched by regret. No more pretending that she wasn't falling in love with the man she'd married to get her inheritance. The thought was terrifying.

"No." The word was barely audible, and she had to repeat it, as much for herself as for Sam. "No."

"No?" He echoed the word against her mouth, and Nikki was helpless to prevent a response. "No?" He rocked his hips gently against hers, sending a shiver of need racing down her spine. "No?"

It took every ounce of willpower she possessed to turn her head away. Her hands slid from his hair to his shoulders, pressing against him. "No."

Sam held her a moment longer. She wanted him. He could feel it in her, in the way she trembled in his arms, in the ragged edge to her breathing. He could change her mind. It wouldn't take much to have her begging for him there and then, to hell with going upstairs.

He shuddered as he eased his hands away from her, steadying her until her feet were solidly on the ground. He drew an unsteady breath and stepped back. She was still too close for his peace of mind, but at least he didn't inhale the scent of her with every breath he drew.

They stared at each other across the rubble of their tidy marriage of convenience.

"It's going to happen," Sam said quietly. "Not tonight. Not until you're ready. But it is going to happen."

Nikki opened her mouth to deny what he was saying and then closed it without speaking. She knew he was right. She couldn't pretend otherwise. Now that the hunger, the need, was out in the open, it was inevitable that they'd come together.

She looked away from him, staring down at the fine white grains of sugar and the powdery brown cocoa that dusted the dark tile floor.

"I should get this cleaned up," she said. It seemed like the accident had happened a thousand years ago.

"Why don't you leave it till morning?"

"Lena will have a fit if she walks in on this in the morning. Besides, I'm . . . not really sleepy."

Sleep was the last thing on Sam's mind, but he wasn't such a glutton for punishment that he was going to offer to stay and help her. His self-control was stretched to the limit. As it was, it was going to take an hour or two in a cold shower before he'd cooled down enough to think about going back to bed.

"I'll leave you to it, then," he said.

Nikki nodded without looking up. Sam hesitated a moment longer before turning away. He picked up his gun on the way out of the kitchen. All in all, he might have been better off finding the burglar he'd been expecting. It certainly would have done less damage to his peace of mind.

Chapter 12

"So, are you two sleeping together yet?" Liz asked, eyeing Nikki with cheerful curiosity.

Nikki choked on a mouthful of ice tea. When she managed to regain her breath, she glared at her friend out of red-rimmed eyes. "*What* did you say?"

"You heard me." Liz twisted her fork in the fettuccine Alfredo on her plate, looking as if she didn't know she'd just asked an utterly outrageous question.

"I heard you, but I thought I must be hallucinating."

"No, you didn't. We've been friends too long for me to surprise you." Liz popped the fork in her mouth.

"That's what I thought. But I can't believe you just asked me if... what you just asked me." Nikki couldn't bring herself to repeat the question. The images it brought to mind were simply too powerful. "You know this isn't a real marriage."

"I know he's a man and you're a woman."

"You sound like a bad pop song," Nikki muttered.

"And I know chemistry when I see it," Liz finished, ignoring the interruption. "There was definitely chemistry between the two of you at the wedding."

"All bad," Nikki snapped. "I despised Sam then."

"Aha!" Liz pounced on the weak point. "*Despised.* Past tense. Obviously, your feelings have changed."

"For heaven's sake, Liz, you've got to get out more. You're starting to sound like a talk-show hostess." Nikki dropped her voice in imitation of a television announcer. "'Today our show is about women who marry men they dislike in order to get inheritances that should have been theirs in the first place.' And I always thought they made all that stuff up."

"Truth is stranger than fiction," Liz said imperturbably.

"*You're* stranger than fiction." Nikki jabbed her fork into a broccoli floret.

She'd thought about canceling her monthly lunch with Liz but had decided she was better off occupying her time with something more productive than thinking about Sam. Now she wished she'd listened to her instincts. This conversation wasn't doing anything to help put him out of her mind.

It had been three days since The Kiss. Nikki had counted herself fortunate that her path and Sam's had crossed only briefly in that time. Sam was apparently putting in long hours at work, because he didn't seem to be home much. Either that or he was no more anxious to see her than she was to see him.

She had mixed feelings about that thought. He was the one who'd said that they were going to end up sleeping together, and she hadn't been able to deny it. Shouldn't he be putting some effort into convincing her? Not that she *wanted* him to convince her. At least, she didn't think she did.

And it really didn't matter, anyway, because she was very busy with the day-care center. With Christmas just around the corner, many of the parents were working extra hours, which meant Rainbow Place stayed open later, which meant everyone was putting in more time.

It was an unfortunate fact that, despite the additional work, it seemed there was still plenty of time to brood about Sam. And now, when she thought she'd be able to escape her own thoughts for a little while, her best friend was dragging him into the conversation.

"You can insult me all you like," Liz said calmly. "But I know you well enough to know when you're hiding something from me. You can tell me it's none of my business—"

"It's none of your business."

"But something's bothering you, and I think it's Sam. I thought it might be that the two of you were starting to get involved."

"We're married. I think that's plenty involved."

"You know what I mean."

Nikki knew exactly what she meant. She'd had a graphic demonstration a few days ago of what Liz meant.

"I don't want to get any more involved with Sam than I already am," she told Liz firmly. But even as she said it, she knew it wasn't entirely true. Her head didn't want to get involved with him, but the rest of her didn't seem to feel the same.

"What you want and what you get aren't always the same thing." Liz waved a forkful of fettuccine for emphasis. "Look at *me*."

"What about you? You wanted to marry a nice guy and have one or two kids and a home of your own, and that's exactly what you got."

There was a brief silence.

"Okay, so that wasn't a good example," Liz admitted. "But that doesn't change the essential truth of what I said. Life doesn't always go the way you plan."

"Tell me about it." Nikki looked down at the gold band on her finger. At the moment, almost nothing in her life was going as planned. Liz must have read something of that in her expression, because she dropped the faintly teasing tone she'd been using.

"Look, Nikki, all kidding aside, I worry about you."

"Why?" Nikki gave her a surprised look.

"You're so directed, so focused on what you want and how to get it. You always have been."

Nikki raised her eyebrows. "This is bad?"

"No, it's good," Liz said quickly. "You know how much I admire the work you do with Rainbow Place. I didn't even argue when you told me you were going to marry some guy you'd just met to get your inheritance so you'd have the money to expand the program."

"Maybe you should have argued," Nikki said. At least then she wouldn't have to worry about the possibility of falling in love with a man who'd only married her for her money. No matter how noble his intentions for that money, it still wasn't a comfortable feeling. Even now, he hadn't so much as hinted that he loved her, just that he wanted her.

"Maybe I should have," Liz agreed. "But I knew how much getting this money meant to you. And then I met Sam and I thought there might be other benefits besides just getting the money."

"You figured that because he was good-looking, we were going to fall in love and live happily ever after?"

"I figured that the two of you struck too many sparks off each other for this to remain a cold business deal. I was really hoping it might lead to something, if you'd let yourself be distracted."

Distracted? That doesn't even begin to describe the effect Sam has had. "The only thing I want it to lead to is me getting my inheritance a year from now," Nikki said firmly.

"What about Sam?"

"What about him?" Nikki toyed nervously with her silverware.

"Is he just going to walk out of your life? Disappear forever?"

The question caused a sharp pain in Nikki's chest. She swallowed hard. "That was the plan."

"But plans can change. That's what I mean by you being so focused. Sometimes I think maybe you don't look at the possibilities." Liz leaned forward, her hazel eyes intent. "Wouldn't it be wonderful if Sam turned out to be the love of your life?"

"I've only known him six weeks." Nikki's protest sounded weak, even to her own ears.

"I knew a week after we met that Bill was the only one for me."

"Not everyone has your ability to make snap judgments."

"You don't have to make a snap judgment. You've got a whole year to make up your mind." Liz poked her fork in a slivered carrot and then waved it at Nikki. "Think of how much time you could save if you and Sam stayed together. You wouldn't have to spend time dating another guy or planning another wedding."

"So you think I should try to fall in love with Sam because it's efficient?" Nikki's mouth twitched at the corners.

"It's as good a reason as any. Besides, you'll either fall in love with him or you won't. You won't have to *try* to do it."

That's just what I'm afraid of, Nikki thought. She ran her thumb over her wedding band. She was very much afraid that she wouldn't have to try to fall in love with Sam at all.

It just might be happening already.

With an effort, she looked away from the ring and fixed Liz with a look that held both determination and warning. "Enough about me. Tell me what my wonderful godson has been up to lately."

To Nikki's relief, after only a momentary hesitation, Liz followed her lead and the topic of her marriage was dropped. But Liz's comments stayed with her.

She was still thinking about them a couple of hours later when she turned into the driveway and saw Sam's truck sitting in front of the house. She shut off the engine on the rental car—Barney was at Bill's garage awaiting a new fuel pump—but didn't immediately get out.

So Sam was home. She hadn't seen him since yesterday morning when they'd bumped into each other in the entryway, both on their way to work. They'd exchanged polite greetings, but she'd been vividly aware of the way his eyes had lingered on her lips, making her mouth feel as flushed and swollen as if she'd just been thoroughly kissed.

Of course, maybe she'd imagined the look. Maybe he didn't even remember the kiss and his promise that they were only postponing the inevitable. Or had it been a threat?

Muttering under her breath, Nikki pushed open the car door and got out. Accustomed to Barney's quirks, which included cranky latches, she slammed the door too hard and the little rental car shuddered under the impact.

"Wimp." She scowled at the car. It might have air-conditioning and a heater, but it was boring. But she knew it wasn't the rental car's lack of personality that was bothering her.

With a sigh, she walked up to the house. Maybe she'd be lucky and she wouldn't even see Sam. The door had barely shut behind her when she heard him call her name.

"Nikki? Is that you?"

She briefly considered the possibility of not answering. She wasn't ready to see him. Not when her head was full of Liz's comments about letting herself fall in love with him.

"It's me," she said.

"Could you come here a minute? We're in the living room."

We? Who's we? Her curiosity stirred. Nikki shrugged out of her coat, hanging it over the newel post on her way into the living room.

Sam was standing by the fireplace, and Nikki felt her breath catch a little when she saw him. He was wearing a pair of dark blue running shorts that came perilously close to qualifying for indecent exposure. He also wore a tank top that left his arms and a good portion of his chest bare. He looked like a poster boy for the benefits of working out.

Distracted by the flagrant display of muscle, she needed a moment to get her mind on what he was saying.

"This guy broke into the house and I caught him trying to get out with that vase." He nodded to a Sevres vase that usually sat on a side table. It was now lying on its side on the sofa. "I'd have hauled him off before now, but he claims he's your brother."

"My brother?"

A slightly stout young man of medium height rose from the wing chair where he'd been sitting and turned to face her. "Nikki, would you tell this ape who I am?" he demanded petulantly.

"Alan?" She stared at him in disbelief. She hadn't seen him since her grandfather's funeral. He'd put on at least forty pounds. Despite the extra weight, he looked smaller than she remembered. Or maybe it was just the fact that Sam loomed over him that made him look small. "I thought you were in Monte Carlo or Rio or some such place."

"So he was telling the truth?" Sam didn't trouble to conceal his disappointment.

"Of course I was telling the truth." Alan adjusted the lapels of his pale gray suit and drew his shoulders back, his soft mouth settling into a self-important little sneer. "Now you'll know what it means when I tell you that you're fired."

"It means the same thing it meant a few minutes ago when you threatened to fire me," Sam said, looking more amused than angry. "Nothing."

"You obnoxious, overbearing, overgrown—"

"Sam is my husband, Alan," Nikki said quickly. She came forward to stand next to Sam. "We were married six weeks ago."

The announcement cut through his tirade like a hot knife going through butter. "You're married?" His voice came out on a wheeze.

"We're married," she confirmed.

"I don't believe you." His eyes narrowed, and he shot an accusing look from her to Sam and back again. "You did this just to get around Grandfather's will. Just so you could keep your hands on my money."

"Your money?" Nikki felt a shaft of anger go through her, stiffening her spine. "*Your* money? Grandfather left you half of his estate, which you received on his death. The money I inherit when I marry is *my* money."

"That's a matter of opinion," he sneered. "But it really doesn't matter one way or another, because Grandfather's will specifically stated that it had to be a genuine marriage, not some stranger you picked up off the street and paid to marry you."

Nikki hoped he'd take her guilty flush as a sign of anger. He'd come uncomfortably close to the truth.

"Not that it's any of your business, but our marriage *is* genuine." Sam put his arm around Nikki and drew her against his side. The look he gave her held such blatant hunger that Nikki felt herself flushing again, but for a different reason. "*Very* genuine."

"I don't believe it." But Alan's protest was weak.

Just like the man, Sam thought, surveying him with unconcealed contempt. It was hard to believe that this whiny little specimen was Nikki's brother.

There was, he supposed, a certain physical resemblance. Both were fair, and Alan's eyes were a slightly paler shade of green than his sister's. But the resemblance ended there. It didn't look as if Alan had any of his sister's strength and determination.

"Maybe you'd like to tell us why you broke into our home and tried to steal that vase," Sam said to his brother-in-law.

"I don't have to tell you anything," Alan snapped.

"Okay." Sam dropped his arm from Nikki's waist and took a step forward. He pretended not to notice when Alan flinched away from him. "Keep an eye on him, honey, while I call 911."

"You wouldn't," Alan said. He took one look at Sam's expression and all the bluster drained out of him.

"I needed some money," he muttered. "I was going to sell the vase."

"You were going to sell Grandfather's favorite vase?"

"He's not around to care anymore," Alan said. "I didn't know you'd cooked up this marriage thing, and I figured it was going to be mine in a few months, anyway."

Sam considered arguing with his choice of phrasing, but he didn't think Nikki had any desire to drag out this scene.

"Well, now you know it isn't going to be yours, so unless Nikki wants you to hang around to reminisce about old times, why don't you leave?"

"I can't."

"Why not? You know your way to the door, don't you? Or do you normally enter houses through the window?"

Alan shot Sam a resentful look. "I came by cab," he said sullenly.

Sam's brows rose. "You had a cab bring you here to commit burglary? That's one I haven't heard before."

"Burglary!" Alan looked alarmed. "What are you talking about?"

"When someone jimmies a latch, climbs in a window and tries to make off with valuable items, that's what it's usually called."

"I had to come in the window because I lost my key," Alan told him furiously. "But this is my home and I have a right to take anything I want. This should all be mine, anyway. If she hadn't married you, it *would* be mine." The look he shot Nikki was venomous. "She owes me."

It took Sam a moment to control his temper. With every fiber of his being, he wanted to plant his fist in Alan's face. He might even be doing the jerk a favor. A broken nose might add some character to Alan's pretty-boy looks. On the other hand, Alan obviously had no character, so it would be false advertising, and from the sick look in Nik-

ki's eyes, he suspected that the best thing he could do for
her was to end this scene as quickly as possible.

"Nikki doesn't owe you a damn thing," he said, keeping his tone level with an effort. "I want you out of here
and I don't ever want to see your pasty, overfed face in this
house again."

"You can't throw me out. I have just as much right to be
here as she does." Alan jerked his head in Nikki's direction.

"Does he have any legal rights to the house?" Sam
asked, without taking his eyes from Alan's.

There was a moment's pause, and then, out of the corner of his eye, he saw Nikki shake her head slowly.
"Grandfather left the house to me. Alan has no legal claim
on it."

"Then that makes this a definite case of breaking and
entering." Sam's smile held all the friendliness of a wolf
contemplating a particularly juicy rabbit. "Isn't it handy
that I'm a cop."

"You're a cop?" Alan paled to the color of skim milk.
He glared at Nikki. "You married a cop?" He made it
sound as if she'd committed a heinous social solecism.

"It happens in the best of families," Sam said cheerfully.

"How could you marry a cop?" Alan seemed to be taking it as a personal affront.

"I wouldn't worry too much. I don't expect we'll be seeing much of each other." Sam dropped the good-humored
facade. "Out. And don't come back."

"Are you going to let him do this, Nikki?" Alan turned
an appealing look in his sister's direction. "We're family.
Are you going to let this gorilla you married force me out
of your life?"

Nikki looked at her older brother and felt nothing but a cold emptiness inside. They'd never been close, but she'd always felt a certain tie to him. It was obvious that she was the only one who'd felt that bond. Alan's sole concern was for himself, just as it always had been and just as it always would be. "Goodbye, Alan."

Shock flashed across his face. "You're choosing him over your own family?"

"We've never been a family," Nikki told him. She thought of the Walkers, of how close they were, of how they'd opened their arms to her. She'd never known what a family was until she became part of theirs.

He must have seen the finality in her eyes because he didn't attempt to argue any further.

"Can I at least have the vase?"

"I don't believe you!" Sam's hand closed over the smaller man's shoulder, and from Alan's sudden pallor, Nikki assumed his grip was no gentler than it looked. She considered—briefly—protesting on Alan's behalf.

"Out!" Sam ensured Alan's obedience by marching him from the room. A moment later, Nikki heard the door slam shut, cutting off Alan's protest that he needed to call a cab.

"We could have let him call a cab," she said as Sam reentered the room.

"The walk will do him good," Sam said without the least sign of remorse. "Are you okay?"

"If you mean, am I devastated by the loss of my only brother's warm affection, no. I told you before that we weren't really close."

"I guess that's an understatement."

"I suppose it is." It was only recently that she'd realized just how much of an understatement it was. "I hope he wasn't too obnoxious before I got here."

"He wasn't exactly charming, but I doubt I'd have won any awards in that respect myself." Sam shrugged. "When I caught him trying to make off with the vase, I guess I wasn't as civil as I might have been."

Despite the nasty scene just past, Nikki found a smile tugging at her mouth. She walked over to the sofa and picked up the vase to return it to its place. "Don't they teach you to be civil to burglars at the academy?"

"I think I was sick that day."

Sam watched her walk around the room, straightening things that didn't need straightening. Whether she wanted to admit it or not, the scene with her brother had obviously upset her. He wished he knew what to say to make her feel better, but he couldn't think of anything.

She finally turned to look at him. "I think I'm going to go for a run. I need to blow the cobwebs out of my brain."

"It's almost dark."

Nikki followed his glance out the window and hesitated, but she was desperate to get out and feel the fresh air in her face.

"It'll be okay. This is a pretty safe area."

"No area is safe, especially not for a woman alone. I'll go with you."

"No, really, Sam. I'll be all right." Since he was part of what she was running from, it wouldn't do much good to have him with her. But she couldn't tell him that, so she sought another excuse. "I've been running for almost five years and I set a brisk pace."

She realized her mistake immediately, but it was too late. There was a slight but visible stiffening of Sam's spine. Male pride radiated from every inch of him.

"Do you think I couldn't keep up with you?"

"Do you run?"

"I've done my share," he hedged, not wanting to admit that it had been almost ten years since he'd run on a regular basis. "Besides, I'm in damn good condition. I bench-press two-twenty before breakfast. In fact, Alan's arrival interrupted my workout, so a run sounds like a good idea."

Nikki hesitated a moment and then nodded. "Let me get changed."

Sam watched her climb the stairs, hoping he hadn't just bitten off more than he could chew.

Chapter 13

"I feel much better," Nikki said brightly. "A good run always clears my mind and leaves me with so much energy. Isn't this great?"

Sam glared at her. He didn't have the breath to spare to answer her and, even if he had, his mother had taught him not to use those kinds of words in front of women. He was about to die right here on the street, and she was still bounding along like a damned gazelle.

He'd never been so grateful to see anything in his life as he was to see the familiar driveway up ahead. He knew he just might make it that far without humiliating himself by collapsing in a heap.

"I feel good enough to make another round," Nikki chirped.

Sam's heart dropped. His knees threatened to follow suit. He'd never make it. One more hill—up or down—and he was going to die. There was no question in his mind.

"I guess it's a little late for that, isn't it?" she asked.

"Yes." He put as much force behind the word as possible with his lungs on fire. When had he gotten so out of shape? Or was this a symptom of encroaching age?

To his enormous relief, Nikki turned in the driveway. The thought of reaching the end of this torture renewed Sam's energy to the point where he was able to keep from staggering his way up the drive.

"I always do a little bit of cool-down out by the pool," Nikki said, bounding past the house.

Sam gave the front door a longing look, thinking of the hot showers, cold beers and soft beds that lay beyond it, but he forced himself to follow Nikki.

"You look a little tired," she said as she began a series of stretches that made him ache just to look at.

"It's...the damned...hills," Sam got out between gasps for air. He braced his hands on his knees, his back rising and falling in a rapid rhythm as he struggled to catch his breath.

"Am I hearing correctly?" Nikki asked incredulously. "Is the iron man saying that a little run was more than he could handle?"

"That wasn't a 'little run.' We must have covered at least six miles."

"Three and a half," she corrected. She jogged in place a little. "I've measured it."

The look Sam shot her suggested that he didn't appreciate her precision. "And it wasn't more than I could handle. I'm just a little winded, that's all. Would you stop bouncing up and down!"

With a barely concealed grin, Nikki stopped. She stretched out one leg and leaned her weight toward it, stretching the muscles. There was a brief silence filled only by the sound of Sam's ragged breathing.

"Shall I get you an oxygen mask?" she asked politely.

For a moment, Sam remained in the same position. Nikki waited, her teeth tugging at her lower lip as she fought the urge to grin like a clown. After his comments about what great condition he was in, she couldn't help but enjoy the picture he made.

"You have just made the mistake of your life," Sam said as he straightened. The look he gave her held the promise of retribution.

"Now, Sam, there's no reason to get hostile." She took a cautious step backward.

"No reason? You just tried to kill me by running me up and down every hill in Los Angeles and now you're making fun of me?"

"I ran up and down those hills, too," she protested.

"Yeah, but don't think I haven't figured out your secret." He moved toward her. Nikki backed away.

"Secret?"

"You're wearing rocket-powered running shoes."

"Rocket-powered shoes?" She bit her lip to hold back a giggle.

"That's the only possible explanation. And after taking unfair advantage of me, you had the nerve to laugh."

"But, Sam, I wasn't laughing *at* you. I was laughing *with* you."

"Do you see me laughing?" he demanded sternly.

"If you hadn't made such a point of what great shape you were in and how you could bench mark a thousand pounds, I wouldn't have cracked so much as a smile."

"That's bench-*press* two-twenty," he corrected her. She thought she saw a smile tug at his mouth, but he suppressed it.

"Can't we talk about this?" She held out one hand in a pleading gesture.

Sam seemed to hesitate, as if considering the possibility.

"No, we can't." He moved with a speed that left Nikki blinking, his hand closing over hers and dragging her forward. She squeaked in surprise as she felt her feet leave the ground and she found herself cradled against his chest, his blue eyes only inches away.

"I know a really quick way to cool down," he said, smiling wickedly. Nikki glanced over her shoulder and saw where he was heading. The tiled pool was only a few feet away.

"Don't you dare!" She threw her arms around his neck, determined to take him with her. It was a wasted effort.

Instead of dropping her in the pool, Sam simply stepped off the edge and into the water. Nikki held her breath as the water closed over her head. Sam released her when they hit the water and Nikki surfaced first, drawing in a deep breath. She jerked her head to the side to flip the hair out of her eyes and saw Sam surface next to her. Acting on pure instinct, she put her hand on top of his head and promptly dunked him.

She brought her legs together in a scissor kick, heading for the side of the pool, but her fingertips had barely brushed the tiled edge when she felt his hand close over her ankle. Her shriek was abruptly silenced when he dragged her under.

For the next few minutes, they played like a pair of children, chasing each other through the water, laughing and shouting. They called an unofficial truce just long enough to toe off their running shoes, letting them sink to the bottom of the pool for later retrieval. And then the game was on again. Sam's greater strength and longer reach were balanced out by the fact that Nikki was a better swimmer. Her speed and agility made the contest more even than it would have been on land.

"You'll never catch me, copper," she cried defiantly as she swept her hand across the water, sending a miniature tidal wave in Sam's direction.

When he ducked underwater to avoid it, she took the opportunity to make a wild escape dash toward the shallow end. Her feet had just touched bottom when a long arm caught her around the waist, jerking her backward against a hard, male body.

"You'll never take me alive!"

She struggled to escape, but Sam used his superior height to unfair advantage. With his feet planted solidly on the bottom, he controlled her effortlessly. He turned her to face him and wrapped his arms around her, stilling her wild struggles.

"You're cheating," she protested breathlessly. She thrust out her lower lip and glared up at him. "The water's too deep."

"Funny, it seems about right to me." He grinned down at her, his teeth gleaming in the shadowy illumination of the pool lights. "I should have warned you that I always get my man."

Nikki shoved experimentally against his chest. It was like pushing a solidly built wall. Next, she tried to touch the bottom of the pool. With her foot pointed, her toes just brushed the tile, which wasn't nearly enough to give her the leverage she needed.

Her movements, small as they were, were enough to make Sam aware of the soft curves he was holding. His hold shifted, gentling subtly. One hand flattened against the small of her back as he widened his stance. The pressure of the water brought Nikki's hips against his.

Her head came up, her wide green eyes meeting his blue eyes. In the space between one heartbeat and the next, the playful mood was gone. In its place was a sharp awareness, a vivid realization of how close they were, of how fragile a barrier their clothing was.

And hunger—hard and powerful and overwhelming.

"I don't want to play any more games," Sam said huskily.

Nikki knew he wasn't talking about their childish romp in the pool. She swallowed hard, trying to gather her thoughts together. Hadn't she spent the past few days considering just this possibility? She should have had a response ready, known just what she wanted to say.

But the choice wasn't one she could make based on careful thought. It was made for her by the aching need deep inside her, by the desire to feel his touch again, to finally assuage the hunger that had haunted her for so long. She was tired of playing games, too. She wanted him, had wanted him from the very beginning. There was no more lying to herself, no more lying to him.

She didn't need to say anything. Sam saw the answer in her eyes, felt it in the way her body softened and molded itself to his. With a muffled groan, his mouth covered hers.

There was a rapacious hunger in the kiss. They couldn't get enough of each other. The need they'd been denying, once acknowledged, exploded into a white heat at the first touch.

Nikki didn't realize Sam had moved them into shallower water until she felt the bottom of the pool come up under her feet. His hands were impatient with her clothing, stripping her T-shirt and bra over her head, without bothering to unhook the latter.

Nikki whimpered with pleasure when his hands closed over her bare breasts, his thumbs flicking across nipples already puckered by the coolness of the water. A moment later, her shorts and panties floated languidly toward the deep end.

"Aren't you overdressed?" she whispered.

He was most definitely overdressed, Sam thought, staring at her naked body beneath the water. He could strip off his shorts and take her right here and now. He'd never made love in a pool before, but he was sure he could handle the logistics.

On the other hand, he'd spent the past few days fantasizing about having her in his bed and he wasn't quite ready to give up that fantasy. Besides, the pool might be heated, but it wasn't exactly balmy.

"Not like this," he groaned.

"I don't mind." Nikki reached for the waistband on his running shorts. She was impatient with the last barrier between them, impatient to feel him against her.

"I mind." Sam's hand closed over her fingers, stilling them. He waited until her eyes lifted to his face. "I want our first time together to be in a bed, where I can hold you and touch you and not have to worry about one of us drowning. I want to make love to you all night without risking hypothermia."

"I don't think you can get hypothermia in a heated pool," she whispered, dazed by the intensity of his look.

"You can if all your body heat is being used elsewhere." He scooped her up against his chest and started up the steps. "And for what I have in mind, we're both going to need plenty of body heat."

The darkly sensual promise in his voice warmed Nikki so that she hardly noticed the chill of the night air against her bare, wet body. She planted nibbling little kisses along the line of his shoulder. His skin was cool and damp beneath her mouth. She licked the droplets of water from his collarbone, smiling with satisfaction when she felt him shudder.

Later, Sam wondered how he'd made it as far as his room. The feel of her, wet and naked and trembling in his arms, made it difficult to remember basic skills like putting one foot in front of the other. It seemed like forever before he pushed open the door of his room and carried her inside.

"Hurry," she whispered.

Sam didn't need her urging. He was nearly shaking with the need to be inside her. He couldn't remember ever wanting a woman this much, so that it was a gnawing hunger, an all-consuming need that drove out all rational thought.

He had to have her.

Now.

He tumbled Nikki onto the bed. Hot as the flame burned, he didn't immediately move to join her, but stood over the bed, looking down at her, savoring the knowledge that she was there, that she was about to be his in the most elemental way possible.

Nikki flushed beneath the heat in Sam's eyes. Feeling suddenly shy, she reached out to turn off the light. He stopped her with a word.

"Don't."

She hesitated, flicking him an uncertain look.

"I want to look at you," he said. "I want to see your breasts swell under my mouth and the way your skin flushes when I touch you. I want to watch your face when you take me inside your body."

Nikki's hand dropped to the bed, all the strength gone from her fingers. The erotic images he'd painted in her mind were as powerful as a touch. Her skin felt hot and sensitive and a throbbing ache settled deep in the most feminine heart of her.

"Aren't you overdressed?" she whispered again, her voice trembling.

He hooked his thumbs in the waistband of his shorts and slid them down over his hips. His erection sprang free of confinement, thick and hard, visible proof, if she'd needed it, of just how much he wanted her.

"Oh my," Nikki breathed, feeling the words catch in her throat.

"I'll assume that's not a complaint," Sam said, with a grin that suggested he already knew the answer. Nikki couldn't imagine he'd ever had any complaints. There was pure male arrogance in his smile, in the way he stood there, hands on his hips, without a stitch of clothing—or modesty.

At another time, Nikki might have felt compelled to take a jab at that arrogance, to deflate it just a little. But at the moment, she had much more important things on her mind.

"Now," she said fiercely, opening her arms and legs to him.

Sam groaned. "Give me a second."

Nikki waited with barely controlled impatience while he opened the nightstand drawer and took out a condom. Later, she'd appreciate his responsible behavior. At the moment, the small delay seemed almost unbearable. But it was only a matter of moments before he came to her.

There was no need for further foreplay. It was as if all the weeks since their marriage had been a kind of extended foreplay, leaving them both aching and ready now that the moment was finally here.

Sam tested himself against her. Nikki groaned and arched her hips in a wordless demand. A demand he answered immediately, sheathing himself in the moist heat of her body with one thrust. He shuddered with pleasure as he felt her close around him.

Nikki felt herself filled, completed in a way she'd never known, never imagined possible. The pleasure was more than physical. It was as if a piece of her soul had been missing and was now found. Her fingers clung to Sam's back as he began to move over her and the world rocked around her.

The fire was too hot to burn long. They strained together in a headlong rush toward fulfillment. And when they found it, it was shattering in its power, tossing them both toward the stars, leaving them breathless, able only to cling to each other in the aftermath.

This was what he'd ached to know; this was what he'd had to have. She was made for him and him alone.

This was what she'd ached to know, had to have. He was hers and hers alone.

Chapter 14

"I've got a great idea. Let's spend the rest of the day in bed," Sam suggested.

The morning sunlight filtered through the curtains, creating intriguing patterns of shadow and light across Nikki's bare body. With his fingertip, Sam traced an imaginary line from Nikki's belly button up between her breasts to the hollow at the base of her throat. He let his finger rest there, feeling the delicate flutter of her pulse.

"Sounds great, but I can't," she said on a sigh.

"Why not? It's Saturday. They can do without you at the day-care center. I have the day off, and unless the criminal element rises en masse and lays siege to city hall, I don't have to think about work. Play hooky. I'll make it worth your while."

He provided a vivid demonstration of just how worth her while it might be by leaning over to replace his finger with his mouth. He retraced the path he'd blazed moments before, with a few side trips along the way. Nikki shivered as he swirled his tongue over the side of her breast, teasing but not quite touching its peak.

"You're . . . very persuasive." For some reason, it was suddenly difficult to form a coherent sentence.

"I took a course in negotiation at the academy." The tip of his tongue teased her nipple.

"You're . . . you're very good at it." She arched her back in a silent plea.

"Not everyone has the necessary skills." His breath brushed across her damp nipple, like a feather going over her skin. "You have to know when to be gentle." He stroked the taut bud with the tip of his tongue. "And when to be more firm."

Nikki moaned as his mouth opened over her breast, drawing the nipple inside and suckling strongly. Her fingers slid into the dark gold thickness of his hair, pressing him closer.

Sam's original intention had been more teasing than passionate. After all, they'd made love not more than an hour ago. And last night—

Just thinking about last night made his head spin. They'd slept in each other's arms, woke to make love again and slept again, only to wake in the dark hours after midnight, ravenously hungry. They'd raided the refrigerator, feasting on cold chicken, marinated artichoke hearts and a package of Twinkies Nikki found in the pantry.

Watching her lick traces of sticky filling from her fingers, Sam had felt desire rise as fast and hard as if it had been months rather than hours since he'd touched her. She'd seen the look in his eyes, and her own had grown heavy and slumberous, her mouth parting a little as if she were having trouble breathing.

Nikki hadn't offered any objection to the hardness of the table against her back.

They'd staggered upstairs, giggling like a pair of guilty children, and fallen into bed and gone instantly to sleep, wrapped in each other's arms. When they'd awakened less than an hour ago, they'd made love again.

Yet he had only to touch her, to feel her arch beneath him, feel her skin heat beneath his fingers, and he wanted her again. It was as if he could never get enough of her, as if he were trying to slake a lifetime of hunger. With a groan, he dragged his mouth from her breast.

"Do you give in or am I going to have to get tough?" he asked unsteadily.

"I think you're going to have to get tough." She tugged his face up to hers.

A considerable time later, Sam collapsed on the bed next to Nikki. A fine sheen of sweat coated both their bodies. Sam slid his arm under her and pulled her close so that her head was cradled on his shoulder.

"Maybe next time you won't force me to take such drastic measures."

"I think I may be one of those habitual criminals," she confessed. "The kind that can't be rehabilitated."

Sam groaned. "I can see this is going to be a tough assignment."

"I'm counting on you not to give up." Nikki threaded her fingers through the crisp hair on his chest.

"I'd better start taking more vitamins," he muttered. "Extrastrength."

They fell into a comfortable silence. Sam eased his fingers through the tangled gold of Nikki's hair. He tried to remember when he'd last felt so utterly content. It had been years. Since before Sara died.

The thought of his first wife brought a sharp pinch of guilt. Not at the idea of betraying Sara. She'd neither expected nor wanted him to spend his life tied to her memory. No, the guilt wasn't for Sara, it was for Nikki, who didn't even know that he'd been married before.

His previous marriage had held no relevance when they'd made their original deal. Now everything was changed, but that change had come about so quickly there hadn't been a moment when it seemed appropriate to bring up the fact that he'd been married before.

This certainly wasn't the time or the place. But soon. Very soon. He didn't know where the two of them were headed, but he didn't want any big surprises coming out at an inopportune moment.

Nikki shifted slightly, settling into a more comfortable position against Sam's large body. She'd gone to sleep wrapped in his arms and awakened the same way. But it seemed the more he held her, the more she wanted him to hold her. It was as if she'd been starved for this, for having his arms around her, his body pressed against hers.

She slid her fingers through the hair on his chest, watching the lazy movement through drowsy eyes. Her body was satiated, replete with satisfaction. There was a pleasantly tender ache that spoke of thorough loving and a certain awareness just beneath her skin. She felt exhausted, fulfilled, full of energy and thoroughly indolent, all at once.

Underlying it all was a stunned awareness of the drastic change that had just taken place in her life. She hadn't just gained a lover. She'd gained a husband in fact as well as in name. In one night, all her plans for a marriage of convenience and a tidy divorce had crumbled to dust.

Wherever they went from here, they couldn't go back to the way they'd been. There'd be no returning to separate bedrooms and polite nods as they passed in the hallway. Last night had changed everything, and only time would reveal all the ramifications of that change.

Nikki searched her mind for some sense of regret and found none. Other than the fact that Lena was going to be unbearably smug when she found out how well her matchmaking had turned out, there was nothing to regret. How could she possibly regret something that had felt so right? She felt an uneasy twinge. There was more to that feeling of rightness than the purely physical satisfaction she'd experienced. She felt a sense of completion that went much deeper than that. Half-afraid of what she might find, she decided not to examine her feelings too closely. At least, not right now.

"So it's settled," Sam said, interrupting her thoughts. "We're spending the rest of the day right here, pursuing your rehabilitation."

"I really can't." Nikki sighed with regret and rolled away from him to sit up on the edge of the bed. She glanced back over her shoulder. "I promised Liz I'd take Michael for the day to give her and Bill a little time alone. I'm taking him to the zoo."

Sam thought briefly. "It's not exactly what I had in mind, but I haven't been to the zoo in a while."

"You'd go with us?" Nikki hadn't even considered the possibility that he might want to join them.

"If you have no objections."

"*I* don't have any objections, but I don't know how you'll feel after a day with Michael. Kids his age aren't exactly restful."

"I like kids," Sam said easily. "Mary tells me I'm her very favoritest uncle." He frowned slightly. "Of course, I've heard her tell Gage and Keefe the same thing, but I know she means it when she's talking to me."

Nikki grinned. "I'm sure she does. If you're sure you want to come with us, you're welcome."

Actually, it might be interesting to see him with Michael. Her godson had seemed to take to Sam at the wedding and Sam had been good with him, but it would be interesting to see how Sam's patience lasted over the course of an entire day. In the back of her mind, unacknowledged, was a deep curiosity to see what kind of a father Sam might make.

If it was possible to judge by a day at the zoo, Sam would make a wonderful father. His patience with Michael seemed endless. He answered questions, wiped sticky hands and laughed at terrible, five-year-old jokes. But he also didn't hesitate to pull Michael up short if he threatened to get too wild. Michael might not know Sam very well but he knew the voice of authority when he heard it, and Nikki was disgusted to find him much more inclined to listen to Sam than he was to her.

"It's a manly thing," Sam told her with a grin. "You wouldn't understand."

Nikki shook her head. "I think it's just that you're bigger than I am. He probably thinks you'll squash him like a bug if he doesn't obey. You've terrorized him."

Since Michael was currently perched on Sam's shoulders, his small fingers firmly entwined in his mount's hair, the terror theory seemed a little shaky, but Nikki stuck with it, finding it more palatable than some secret man-to-man understanding.

When they reached the tiger enclosure, Michael demanded to be set down.

"I wanna see 'em up close."

Sam obediently deposited him on the ground but kept a close eye on him, suspecting that the boy's idea of "up close" might not stop at the railing. He was aware of a feeling of quiet contentment.

He'd been disappointed when Nikki had told him that she already had plans that precluded spending the day in bed. But he had to admit that he was enjoying himself. Michael was a handful, but he was a great little kid.

"You meant it when you said you liked kids, didn't you?" Nikki asked suddenly.

"What's not to like?" He reached out and caught Michael by the back of the collar before the boy could attempt to work his way through the barrier surrounding the tiger enclosure.

"How about the endless stream of questions, the demands to possess every item they see, the fact that they never stop talking?" Nikki reeled off promptly.

Sam chuckled. "I didn't say they were perfect. But I kind of like their questions. It makes you look at things in a different way. Who else but a kid would ask why polar bears have fur instead of feathers?"

Nikki laughed. "True. But you've got to admit that children aren't exactly restful creatures."

Sam kept his hand firmly on Michael's collar, but took his eyes off the boy long enough to shoot Nikki a curious look. She seemed awfully interested in his opinion of children. Was she pondering his suitability as father material? The thought was intriguing. What would it be like to have a child with Nikki?

He had a sudden image of her, her stomach rounded with his child, and felt a wave of hunger so powerful that it nearly staggered him. Good God, when had he started to think of Nikki in those terms? A few weeks ago, he would have said he didn't even like her. Now he was picturing her as the mother of his child and finding the picture startlingly right.

"I always planned on having a couple of kids," he said slowly. He glanced to make sure Michael was still fully occupied with watching the big cats. He returned his attention to Nikki. "I never told you that I was married before."

The zoo wasn't exactly the setting he'd envisioned for telling Nikki about Sara, but maybe handling it casually was better than anything he could have contrived.

She looked surprised but not particularly shocked. "I know. Your mom mentioned it. She was surprised that I didn't already know."

Sam winced. "That must have been awkward. If it had occurred to me that Mom might mention it, I would have told you myself."

Nikki shrugged. "I don't think she suspected anything out of the ordinary, if that's what you're thinking."

"It isn't. I was just thinking that it was a hell of a position to put you in—we're supposed to be madly in love and you didn't even know about Sara. What did she say?"

"Not much. Only that your wife—that Sara—died." Nikki was pleased by the even tone of her voice. They might have been discussing the weather. Certainly, no one would have guessed that there was a knot the size of a small car in her stomach.

"She had cancer," Sam said, speaking almost as if to himself. "By the time we knew she was sick, it was too late to stop it."

"I'm sorry," Nikki said sincerely. "That must have been terrible."

"I've had better years." He was looking at Michael but Nikki had the feeling he was seeing something—or someone—else.

"You must have loved her very much." As soon as the words were out, Nikki wished she could call them back. She wasn't sure she wanted to hear what he might say in response.

He took his time about answering, and shook himself free of memories. When he looked at her, his eyes seemed clear of shadows.

"I loved her deeply," he said simply. "When she died, I couldn't imagine ever loving anyone that much again. I figured it was a once-in-a-lifetime kind of thing."

Nikki struggled to conceal the effect his words had on her. Better to know now, she told herself. Better to know before she let her heart get any more involved than it already was. But Sam wasn't done speaking.

"I'm not so sure anymore," he said slowly, his eyes searching her face. "I wonder if it can happen twice, after all."

Nikki's heart stumbled, her breath catching in her throat. Was he saying what she thought he was? That *she* was the reason he was changing his mind? That he might be falling in love with her? The possibility was enough to make her feel light-headed.

She didn't know whether to be relieved or sorry when Michael interrupted.

"I want to see the elephant," he announced, having seen his fill of the tigers. "Can I ride, Uncle Sam?"

Sam's eyes held Nikki's a moment longer and then he dragged his gaze to Michael's pleading face. "What do you think I am—a horse?" he complained as he swung the child up, settling him easily on his shoulders. Michael giggled happily.

"Giddyap," he cried, apparently taking to the idea of Sam as a two-legged horse.

"I had to mention it," Sam said, throwing Nikki a rueful look.

She smiled, but it didn't reach her eyes. Walking beside Sam and Michael, she listened with half an ear to Michael's endless stream of commentary and questions and Sam's patient answers.

Nikki tried to sort out what had just happened. Had Sam implied that he was falling in love with her or was that wishful thinking? And how could it be wishful thinking when she didn't even know if she *wanted* him to be in love with her?

If she hadn't been in the middle of a busy walkway, Nikki might have been tempted to tear her hair in frustration. This wasn't the way it was supposed to work. She'd had everything planned out, and falling in love with Sam—and she wasn't saying she had—wasn't part of that plan.

Perhaps Sam sensed something of what she was feeling. He stopped in the middle of the crowded pathway, oblivious to the eddy they created. He reached out to catch her hand in his, and Nikki had no choice but to stop also.

"We're causing a traffic jam."

"Los Angelenos are used to traffic jams. Makes them feel at home."

"I'm not so sure," Nikki commented, catching the exasperated look thrown them by a mother who had to push a stroller around them. "Is there a reason we're halting traffic?"

"Yes. A very important reason."

Nikki waited and, when he didn't continue, she looked at him, raising her brows in question. She caught just a glimpse of his smile, and then his lips covered hers in a kiss that made only marginal concessions to the fact that they were standing on a public pathway in broad daylight. When he finally lifted his head, Nikki had to set her hand against his chest for balance.

"What was that for?" she asked, blinking up at him.

"Just a little something to tide us both over until tonight."

If he'd been looking for a way to distract her, he'd certainly done a good job, she thought dazedly. The distant future didn't seem nearly so worthy of concern when the near future held so much interest.

"Are you guys gonna do mushy stuff? Can't ya wait till after I see the elephants?" Michael asked in a tone of such disgust that both his companions burst out laughing.

"We'll try to hold off until after the elephants," Sam promised, but there was another, sensual promise in his eyes for Nikki.

Maybe Liz was right, she thought as they continued to walk. Maybe she did spend too much time planning her life. It seemed that there were some definite advantages to allowing the unexpected to happen. Perhaps it was time to try living life one day at a time and see what happened.

Though there was no discussion, it seemed as if both Sam and Nikki had the same idea. Over the next couple of weeks, there was no discussion of the future, no questioning what might lie ahead, no speculation about where the sudden change in their relationship might be going, if anywhere. Like lovers on a desert island, with no expectation of rescue, they lived life wholly in the present.

They made love. They talked about everything, from politics to movies, sometimes agreeing, sometimes agreeing to disagree. They made love. They swam in the pool. They made love.

Sam talked Nikki into trying her hand at weight lifting. Her brother, Alan, had bought the gym equipment when he was in high school, installing it in an unused bedroom on the ground floor. Probably the only useful thing he'd ever done, in Sam's opinion.

Nikki was a little uncertain about picking metal bars up only to set them down again, but Sam was persuasive, promising that she'd love it once she got the hang of it. He'd guide her every step of the way. He was true to his word, giving her an extremely hands-on demonstration of technique, which resulted in the discovery that an exercise mat was soft enough to make possible aerobic activities beyond the ones for which it had been intended.

Nikki sprawled across Sam's chest, listening to the rapid rhythm of his heartbeat beneath her ear. Her body tingled with the aftershocks of their lovemaking. They were still joined together, and she liked the feel of him inside her.

She'd never in her life felt so utterly replete as she had in the days since she and Sam had become lovers. He'd shown her a side of herself that she'd never known existed, a deeply sensual side that she found just a little shocking.

"I never realized that lifting weights was so much fun." The words came out just a little breathless.

"Building strong muscles is an important part of a solid program of health improvement," Sam said in a pedantic tone that made her giggle.

She suddenly laughed harder. "I just thought of something."

"What?" Sam smoothed his hand down her back, less interested in what she'd thought of than in the interesting vibrations caused by her laughter.

Nikki lifted her head and looked down at him, her green eyes bright with laughter. "I finally understand the meaning of the term *pumping iron.*"

Sam stared at her for a moment before her meaning sank in, and then he started to laugh.

Having someone to laugh with was one of the things he'd missed most after Sara died, Sam thought hours later. And it was one of the best aspects of his relationship with Nikki—a relationship that had yet to be defined. Nikki was sprawled on her stomach beside him, taking up a ridiculous amount of room for a woman her size.

They'd eaten dinner together, then watched an old movie on TV, arguing all the while about who the killer would turn out to be. When the ending had proven him right, he hadn't been able to resist the urge to point out his superior powers of deduction. Nikki had proven herself a poor loser by hitting him with a pillow. The ensuing battle had ended with him carrying her upstairs draped over his shoulder, issuing threats in between giggles and demands to be put down.

The sex was certainly spectacular, he thought. And he'd be a liar if he said it didn't add a considerable amount to his current contentment, but he'd lived without sex before and could do so again, if necessary. But he really needed someone to laugh with, someone to talk to.... He hadn't realized how lonely he'd been until now.

But that was all in the past. At least, he thought it was in the past. Sam frowned at the darkened ceiling, considering the unsettled state of his marriage. A marriage in the legal sense of the word, but not yet one in the less easily defined terms of commitment.

He eased onto his side and looked at Nikki. Her face was turned toward him, and he let his eyes trace the smooth lines of her profile. She really was a beautiful woman, but it wasn't her beauty that he'd fallen in love with. And he was through pretending to himself that he didn't love her.

He loved her. He wasn't sure just when it had happened—maybe even that first time he'd met her in Max's office. Maybe that was why he'd disliked her—because he'd looked at her and seen his own personal Waterloo.

Now that he'd admitted to himself how he felt, he wondered how *she* felt. Sam frowned and reached out to brush a lock of hair back from Nikki's cheek. It curled around his finger like a pale silk ribbon, like the most delicate of chains.

Chains of a sort were part of marriage, bonds that tied two people together, creating a whole that was stronger than its separate parts. They'd started out this marriage with the intention of avoiding all but the most superficial of those ties. But everything had changed.

At least, it had for him. He knew what he wanted. He wanted Nikki as his wife. For now. For always.

The question was: Did she feel the same?

With Christmas almost upon them, it was easy for Sam and Nikki to postpone any discussion of their future together, a discussion they both knew was inevitable. But neither wanted to disturb the idyll they'd been granted. And the upcoming holidays gave them as good an excuse as any to avoid rocking their personal boat.

Christmas with the Walkers was like no Christmas Nikki had ever known. Feeling as if she wanted to return the hospitality she'd received at Thanksgiving, Nikki had invited the family to Pasadena for the holiday, broaching the subject very hesitantly over the phone with Rachel, afraid the other woman might think she was intruding. But Rachel had cheerfully consented to the change of venue, as long as Nikki allowed her to help with the food.

Since Lena was to spend the holidays with her son's family in Detroit, Nikki was more than happy to have the assistance. Though she was a better than average cook, thanks to Lena's tutelage, she'd never cooked a meal for so many people before.

Her own family's holiday celebrations had been modest. Her grandfather had not been fond of lavish celebrations of any sort. Nikki had sensed that even the tree seemed a bit much to him. A pleasant meal, a restrained exchange of gifts, a glass of fine sherry, and he'd considered the holiday sufficiently celebrated.

There was nothing restrained about the Walkers' Christmas celebration, however. They arrived together the afternoon of Christmas Eve and immediately seemed to fill the big house. There were hordes of presents, most of them haphazardly wrapped.

The tree had been put in its stand but had yet to be decorated, a lack that was soon remedied. Lena had been the one to decorate the tree, which was invariably small and sat neatly in a corner of the entryway. Lena decorated a tree the way she did everything else—with care. One strand of tinsel at a time, carefully chosen ornaments and the lights arranged just so.

This year, Sam had chosen the tree, a huge affair that swallowed half the living room. And it didn't seem to occur to anyone in the Walker family that tinsel had been designed for any purpose other than *hurling* at the tree, where it settled in drifts and occasional clumps that no one seemed to mind. Bulbs were hung with a similar abandon, and no one seemed to care if three red lights happened to wind up in close proximity to one another.

When it was finished, Nikki thought it was the most beautiful Christmas tree she'd ever seen.

Lying in bed that night, cuddled against Sam's side, she realized she couldn't remember a time when she'd been happier than she was right at this very minute. She couldn't imagine ever wanting anything more than what she had right here and now.

Nikki felt a twinge of worry at that thought, but she was already half-asleep, cradled close in Sam's arms.

Christmas morning began early. Mary saw to that. She woke her father at six o'clock. Cole made sure everyone else got up.

"I'm not suffering alone," he announced firmly.

There was some obligatory grumbling, but no one wanted to be anywhere other than where they were, which was emptying stockings and opening presents. The mound of presents turned out to contain everything from hand-knitted sweaters to a rather greasy drill that Cole had borrowed from Sam and decided to return as a Christmas gift.

Jason Drummond arrived in time for Christmas dinner, and Nikki was amused to see the usually unflappable Rachel flush like a schoolgirl when she heard his voice in the hall.

Dinner was reminiscent of Thanksgiving—everyone seemed to talk at once and yet no one seemed to lose the thread of the conversation. The food was wonderful, and Nikki flushed with pleasure at the compliments she received.

After the meal, there was a general slowdown. Cole tried to coax Mary into lying down for a nap. She consented only after everyone obediently promised not to do anything fun while she was gone. She was so obviously humoring her father that it was all Nikki could do to keep from laughing out loud.

But she felt a lump in her throat as she watched Cole carry the little girl upstairs. It just didn't seem possible that there could be anything wrong with Mary. She was suddenly quite fiercely proud that Sam had cared deeply enough about his niece that he'd been willing to make a marriage of convenience to ensure that Mary got the help she needed.

Even if it did leave Nikki with a niggling sense of uncertainty about the future of a marriage that had begun on such a basis.

By the time Mary got up from her nap and demanded to go in the pool, her uncles had recovered enough from their overindulgences at the table to accommodate her. With the temperature in the mid-seventies and not a cloud in sight, it seemed the perfect way to celebrate the holiday in true Southern California style.

Nikki, Rachel and Jason chose to remain on dry land, but they did move outside to the comfort of heavily padded redwood loungers, choosing a vantage point where they could watch the antics in the pool without running the risk of being splashed.

"I want to thank you."

Nikki took her eyes off the group in the pool and looked at her mother-in-law. Jason had gone into the house, and she and Rachel were more or less alone.

"Thank me?" Nikki asked. "For what?"

"For making my son smile again." Rachel's eyes were on the pool, where her sons and granddaughter were all happily attempting to drown each other. "It's been a long time since I've seen Sam so happy."

"I can't take any credit for that." Nikki shifted uncomfortably on the lounger, her contented mood shaken. She didn't want Rachel thanking her, not when her very presence in the woman's life was based on a lie.

"I think you can." Rachel's dark eyes settled on Nikki. "I was worried when Sam told me he was getting married so quickly and that he hadn't known you very long," she admitted quietly. "Sam's never been the impulsive type. I think it comes of him feeling that he had to try and take his father's place."

Rachel smiled a little, remembering. "He grew up so early. I worried about it, but I'll admit there were times when I leaned on him a bit, too. All my boys are strong, but Sam was the eldest and I depended on him, maybe more than I should have."

"I'm sure he didn't mind." Nikki reached out to touch the older woman's hand, which was restlessly smoothing the cover of the lounge pad. "I think Sam was very lucky to grow up in a family like yours. I think anybody would be," she added a bit wistfully.

"I think so, too," Rachel admitted. "It's not that I think Sam's life was blighted, but I do think he learned to control any impulsiveness in his nature at a young age. When he married you, it was so unlike him that it worried me."

If only Rachel knew that she'd had every reason to be worried, Nikki thought. And she still did. "It was rather sudden," she said simply.

"But obviously, it wasn't *too* sudden. It's been years since I've seen Sam laugh the way he has this weekend. Not since..."

"Not since Sara?" Nikki finished the sentence for her.

"Not since Sara," Rachel confirmed quietly. Her dark eyes were searching. "I thought he might have made a mistake, but you've helped him find the joy in life again and I thank you for that."

"What are you two looking so serious about?" Jason's voice preceded him as he walked toward them from the direction of the house. He was carrying a tray that held a pitcher of ice tea and a stack of colorful plastic glasses. "You're both much too lovely to be frowning," he chided as he set the tray down.

Gracious of him to include them both, Nikki thought, especially when he couldn't take his eyes off Rachel. From the delicate flush that rose in the woman's cheeks, Nikki assumed that Rachel had noted—and was not averse to—Jason's distinct partiality.

As far as Nikki was concerned, the interruption couldn't have been more timely. A few more minutes and she'd probably have been on her knees confessing the truth to Rachel.

She stared at the pool, picking Sam out easily, feeling something twist inside her when she heard his shout of laughter. For the past couple of weeks, she'd been pretending that everything was as it should be, that her marriage was just like anyone else's. It had taken Rachel's words to remind her of how false that was.

The dreams she was building were like houses built in an earthquake zone. And she just might find those dreams crashing around her ears.

Chapter 15

Sam felt the mattress shift and opened his eyes a crack, watching as Nikki got out of bed. A week ago, he might have grabbed her around the waist and dragged her back into it. But a week ago, he'd have known exactly how she'd react. There'd be a brief, laughing struggle, and it would be at least a half an hour before either of them made it out of bed.

But this morning he watched her tug on a soft cotton robe and tiptoe from the room without even letting her know he was awake. The soft snick of the door closing behind her sounded almost painfully loud. Sam opened his eyes and stared at the ceiling

Something had changed. He didn't know what it was, but he could almost see the walls she was building between them. Whatever it was seemed to have begun at Christmas, but, no matter how he racked his brain, he couldn't come up with a reason for it. Nikki had appeared to be enjoying herself. His family liked her. She liked them. As far as he could tell, it had been a terrific holiday.

But something had obviously happened, because in the week since then, he'd felt Nikki starting to slip away from him. It was a subtle change. She was still sharing his bed, still responsive to his touch, but there was a new element in their lovemaking. He couldn't put his finger on exactly what was different, but he knew it was there. She was holding herself back from him, keeping a little distance.

Sam swung his legs off the bed and stood. He'd spent too many hours lying awake the night before, trying to figure out what was wrong, and his eyes were gritty from lack of sleep. Naked, he crossed the bedroom and pushed open the bathroom door. He braced his hands on the counter and stared at his reflection, grimly satisfied to see that he looked just like he felt—tired and rumpled.

He suddenly thought of a conversation he'd had with Keefe late Christmas day.

"Looks like your marriage of convenience has turned out to be a lot more convenient than you'd expected," Keefe had said, nodding to where Nikki sat cross-legged on the floor, intent on the Lego tower she and Mary were building.

Gage was offering suggestions on the tower's construction. Normally he charged for this kind of consultation, he'd pointed out. Cole was sprawled in an easy chair, unabashedly asleep. Rachel and Jason were playing a game of gin rummy, and, from the barely audible complaint, she seemed to be beating him quite soundly.

Sam had directed his look to where Nikki and Mary sat, and his face creased in a smile that said more than words possibly could have. "She likes kids. Did I tell you she runs a day-care center?"

"Twice." Keefe's tone had been dry, but there was a smile in his eyes.

"It's worth repeating," Sam had said unrepentantly. He returned his attention to the bottle of wine he was opening, twisting the corkscrew into place.

"You're in love with her." The words were more comment than question, but Sam answered him, anyway.

"Very much." Applying steady pressure, he eased the cork from the bottle with a muffled pop. He set the bottle aside to allow the wine to breathe before looking at Keefe. "I wish I could say I was clever as hell and planned it this way."

"I haven't noticed that planning does much good when it comes to love," Keefe said. From the shadows in his eyes, Sam knew he was thinking of his own marriage and subsequent divorce.

"I thought you and Dana were going to make it," Sam said quietly.

"Yeah. So did I." Keefe's smile held a bitter edge. He reached for his cigarettes, remembered where he was and let the pack drop back into his pocket. "Lousy habit," he muttered. "One of these days I'm going to have to quit again. Tell her you love her," he said abruptly. He gave Sam an intense look. "Don't wait."

Sam had muttered something about it being too soon, but Keefe had simply repeated his advice. Maybe Keefe had been right, Sam thought now. Maybe he should tell Nikki how he felt. He'd planned to wait. Married or not, they hadn't known each other very long. It wasn't that he doubted his own feelings, but he didn't want to rush Nikki.

"Face it, Walker," he said to his reflection. "You're scared to death she doesn't love you. *That's* the real reason you don't want to tell her how you feel."

The man in the mirror offered scant reassurance. After a moment, Sam turned away, no closer to an answer than he had been. He pushed open the shower door and turned the water on full blast. His jaw was set as he stepped under the hot spray.

The only thing he was sure of was that he wasn't going to let Nikki slip away. He didn't know what had caused the change in her. Hell, maybe there *was* no change. Maybe it was all in his head. But he wasn't going to lose her, not without a fight. He hadn't been able to fight Sara's illness. He'd had to stand by and watch her slip away from him. But that was different. Nikki wasn't dying of cancer. And whatever the problem was, they could solve it.

Unless he was the only one who wanted it solved.

Everything had just happened too quickly, Nikki thought as she dressed. They'd gone from cordial foes to tentative friends to lovers in a few short weeks. It was too much, too soon. She wasn't ready for this.

She tugged a soft gold cashmere sweater over her head, tucking it into the waist of a pair of slim black trousers. This wasn't supposed to have happened. It hadn't been part of the plan.

Nikki stopped, a hairbrush suspended over her head, hearing an echo of Liz's comments about her being too wedded to her plans, about missing out on something wonderful because it wasn't part of her plan. But that wasn't what she was doing.

Was it?

She scowled at her reflection and yanked the brush through her hair in a quick, jerky stroke that pulled at her scalp. There was nothing wrong with having plans, nothing wrong with trying to direct your life. People who didn't have plans generally ended up going in circles.

Look at her mother. Marilee wouldn't know a plan if it slapped her in the face, and she'd spent her entire life drifting from one marriage to another, looking for something she probably wouldn't recognize even if she found it.

And Alan. Another perfect example of someone who just let life happen to him. He certainly hadn't planned to run through his inheritance the way he had. But because he hadn't planned on doing anything else, that's what had happened. Now he was reduced to trying to steal vases from his own sister. And if he'd done a little planning before attempting to rob her, he might have gotten away with it. But he'd just stumbled into burglary the way he stumbled into everything else in his life, and the result was he'd ended up with nothing. Even committing a decent crime required a plan.

Nikki brushed her hair back from her face and secured it at the base of her neck with a soft black ribbon. There was nothing wrong with having a plan and nothing wrong with trying to stick to that plan. It wasn't that she was going to walk away entirely from whatever it was she and Sam had together—she just wanted to step back a little. She didn't want to rush into anything.

She'd planned to get married, not to fall in love. Contrary to what Liz thought, it wasn't that she was so focused on her goal that she couldn't let anything intrude on her plans.

"I just want to be sure that what I think is happening is really happening and not just some flash-in-the-pan attraction," Nikki told her reflection. "After all, how do I know I'm *really* in love with Sam? It could be propinquity or animal magnetism or... or practically anything."

The woman in the mirror looked doubtful. Something in her eyes suggested that she thought Nikki was hiding her

head like a scared rabbit, making excuses for her own cow-
ardice.

"What do *you* know?" Nikki snapped. "It's my life and
I know exactly what I'm doing." She turned away from the
mirror, not wanting to see the doubts in her reflection's
eyes.

She picked up her watch and slipped it on. She needed to
talk to Sam, needed to try and explain how she felt, how she
wanted just a little distance. Though how they were going
to manage that when the terms of the will said they had to
live in the same house, she didn't know.

Pushing her feet into a pair of black loafers, she remembered that it was New Year's Eve and Sam had to work.
Which meant she could put off talking to him for a little
while longer. He'd understand. She knew he would. If he
loved her—which he hadn't said he did—he'd understand.

Nikki left her room and went downstairs. She'd planned
to spend the day at the day-care center. If she was lucky,
maybe she could grab a quick breakfast and be out of the
house before Sam came down.

The phone rang just as she reached the bottom of the
stairs, and she detoured into the living room to answer it.

"Nikki? It's Alan."

Nikki's brows rose. After the way Sam had nearly thrown
him bodily out of the house, she hadn't expected to hear
from her brother this soon, if ever.

"This is a surprise."

"I know. I ... ah ... wanted to see how you were."

Nikki's brows rose. "You called to ask how I am?"

"Don't sound so surprised. I *am* your brother."

"I am surprised, Alan. After grandfather's funeral, it
was a couple of years before I heard from you, and then it
was only because Sam caught you stealing from me. This
sudden concern for me is a bit unexpected."

"I *wasn't* stealing it," he snapped. "And that gorilla you married had no business treating me the way he did. He's lucky I didn't press charges."

"Seems to me your case would have been a little thin." Nikki didn't trouble to hide the amusement in her voice. "He did catch you breaking into the house. What would you have charged him with?"

"I don't know. Police brutality, maybe." Alan's tone was sullen, and Nikki could envision the pouty, dissatisfied expression on his face. "I'm sure a good lawyer could have come up with something, but I didn't want to cause any trouble for you."

"Gee, thanks," she said dryly. "I appreciate the brotherly concern."

"Well, I am your brother." Her sarcasm seemed to have gone right over his head. "I know we haven't always been close—"

"Try *never.*"

"—but that doesn't mean I don't care about you," he persevered, ignoring her interruption. "With Grandfather gone, I am the man of the family—"

"God help us."

"—and it's my duty to look after—"

"Cut to the chase, Alan," Nikki interrupted ruthlessly. "What do you want?"

There was a short silence on the other end of the line, and she knew that Alan was running through his options, debating whether to stick with the concerned-brother act or to try a new tack.

"I need money," he muttered sullenly, apparently deciding that honesty was the best policy.

"You expect me to give you money?" Even knowing him as well as she did, Nikki found it hard to believe his gall.

"After you tried to steal from me, you turn around and hit me up for a loan?"

"The money would have been mine if you hadn't gotten married." He made it sound as if she'd committed a crime.

"But I *did* get married, and that makes it *my* money."

"I was counting on that money."

"Didn't you ever hear the phrase 'don't count your chickens before they're hatched'? What did you do? Spend money you didn't have?"

If he thought she was stupid enough to give him money, he had another think coming. Undoubtedly, he was going to try and bully her into giving him what he wanted, the way he'd bullied her when they were children, the way he'd bullied his way through life. But she wasn't a child and she wasn't afraid of him anymore. She waited, her jaw tight and angry.

"I'm in trouble, Nikki." There was no bravado in Alan's voice, no bluster. Just fear, real and startling.

"What kind of trouble?" Nikki felt her stomach clench.

"I owe money to some people. I told them I was going to inherit a bunch of money next year, and they were willing to wait. But now that you're married, they know that's not going to happen and they don't want to wait anymore."

"Gambling?" she asked, her voice softening despite herself.

"Yeah. I know it was stupid, but I can't go back and change anything now. I know we haven't been close—"

Nikki's snort of laughter cut him off. *Close?* They'd barely been civil.

"How much?"

He named a figure and she winced.

"Must have been a hell of a poker game."

"Roulette," he muttered. "I lost most of it playing roulette."

"Oh, well, that's different, then. Roulette is much more respectable than poker."

Alan didn't respond, and she stared blindly out the window, her fingers knotted around the receiver. She couldn't shake the suspicion that he was suckering her, that this sincere act was just that—an act he could put on or take off at will. Maybe he didn't owe any money; maybe he just wanted more money to gamble with.

But what if he was telling the truth? What if he really did owe a lot of money to people who didn't like to wait. She didn't like him, but she didn't want him to end up at the bottom of a river wearing cement shoes, either.

"Give me one good reason why I should give you that kind of money."

"I'm your brother. We're family."

Nikki closed her eyes. She heard an echo of Sam saying much the same thing about his willingness to do whatever it took to get the money for his niece's surgery. *We're family,* he'd said, as if that answered all questions. And maybe it did.

"Okay," she said wearily. "I'll give you the money, Alan. Give me an address and I'll see that you get it in the next few days. But this is the only time," she added, ignoring his whoop of pleasure. "Don't come to me again. I'm not going to spend the rest of my life financing your gambling habit."

He ignored that comment and gave her the address. "I need it right away," he said, and she was almost amused to hear the old arrogance back in his voice. He hung up the phone without saying goodbye.

Nikki set the receiver slowly back in place, wondering if she'd just saved her brother's life or been played for a fool. It was something of a moot point, since she'd agreed to give him the money, but it would be nice to know, one way or another.

She turned away from the phone and found herself looking straight into Sam's eyes.

"Did I just hear what I think I heard? Was that your brother? And you just agreed to give him money?" He sounded both disbelieving and angry.

Nikki immediately felt like a child caught with her hand in a cookie jar and was just as immediately furious with herself for feeling that way. She didn't have to ask Sam's permission to give Alan money. She didn't have to ask anyone's permission to do anything. "That's exactly what you heard."

At another time, Sam might have heard the cool tone of her voice and taken heed, recognizing that this was not the time to pursue the subject. But he'd spent the past week feeling as if she were slipping away from him, and his sense of judgment was not what it might have been. "I can't believe you're actually going to give money to that jerk." Sam paced away from Nikki and then spun on his heel to look at her as if not sure who he was talking to.

"He's in trouble." It sounded weak. Worse, it sounded as if she were making an excuse. Nikki felt a quick flare of anger. It was her money and she could do anything she wanted with it.

"Guys like him are always in trouble," Sam snapped impatiently. "It's like pouring water into a bottomless pit. You give him money now and he'll just come back for more. If not next week, then next month or three months from now or six months from now. Are you going to give him more money every time?"

"Maybe." It wasn't the strong, mature response she would have liked. It was more the response of a sullen three-year-old.

He was right, of course. Alan wasn't going to suddenly become a model of fiscal responsibility. He was, always had been and always would be the kind of person who avoided responsibility of any kind as if it might be injurious to his health.

"Maybe?" Sam repeated. "So you're thinking of supporting him for the rest of his life?"

"I don't know. I haven't thought that far ahead."

"Well, you should. Because after setting a precedent like this, you're going to have him banging on your door every time he runs out of pocket change."

"I'll deal with that when the time comes."

"Why deal with it at all? Why not just nip it in the bud now?"

"I've already told him I'd give him the money." And even if she regretted it—and she certainly wasn't saying she did—she wasn't going to go back on her word, especially not with Sam insisting that she do just that.

"Call him back and tell him you've changed your mind." He knew immediately that he'd made a mistake. The words had come out like an order, and he saw Nikki's spine stiffen in response.

"I'm not doing anything that you wouldn't do," she said in a painfully controlled tone. "You'd do the same for any one of your brothers."

"None of my brothers would break into my house and try to steal from me," Sam snapped. "He's using you, Nikki. He doesn't give a damn that you're related—all he cares about is that you're loaded."

Though it was nothing that she hadn't thought herself, hearing Sam sum up her relationship with Alan so bluntly stung. She struck back. "I seem to bring out that tendency in people," she said softly. "You can't exactly throw stones at my brother. At least Alan doesn't have to marry me to get money from me. And at least he's not pretending to feel something he doesn't, just to stay close to my checking account.''

The minute the words were out, she'd have given anything to call them back. Sam's face whitened, his eyes a stark blue against the sudden pallor. His jaw tightened until it looked as if it had been carved from solid granite.

"I apologize," he said levelly. "It's none of my business whether or not you give your brother money."

Nikki stared at him, trying desperately to come up with the words to say she was sorry, that she hadn't meant anything she'd said.

Sam glanced at his watch. "I've got to get going."

"Sam, I—"

He looked at her, looked through her, and Nikki found the words drying up in her throat. He nodded as if she were a casual acquaintance. A moment later, she heard the door close quietly behind him.

What had she done?

Feeling as if she were running in quicksand, Nikki ran to the door, dragging it open just as she heard the truck's engine roar to life.

"Sam. Wait!"

Either he didn't hear her or he chose to ignore her. She didn't know which it was, but the truck pulled away even as she stepped out onto the porch. She stood there, watching it disappear down the driveway and turn out into the street. After a moment, she turned back into the house, shutting the door behind her and leaning against it.

How could she have accused Sam of pretending to care for her just for her money? She'd had her doubts about the speed with which things were moving between them, but she'd never thought he was a fortune hunter—not since she'd found out about Mary's illness, anyway.

How could she have hurt him like that?

*   *   *

Ten hours later, Nikki was still asking herself the same question. She'd finally decided that it had been less Sam's autocratic tone that had triggered her response than all the fears and uncertainties that had been plaguing her recently. She'd resented him telling her what to do, but that had been simply the spark that lit the fuse. She'd lashed out at Sam because she was afraid. She'd felt her life slipping out of her control and she'd responded like a frightened child.

She owed him an apology. She just hoped he'd be willing to listen to it.

Lena was still on vacation, so Nikki spent the afternoon and evening setting the table and cooking a special meal. The way to a man's heart was supposed to be through his stomach. She didn't think it was that simple, but perhaps a little candlelight and wine would help make her apology more vivid.

Once the meal was in progress, she went upstairs and changed into a little black dress—a very little black dress. She wasn't above using a touch of seduction if it would help soften Sam's mood. She didn't know what she'd do if he refused to accept her apology.

Nikki dabbed a touch of perfume behind her ears, carefully avoiding her reflection in the mirror. She was afraid of what she might see in her own eyes, afraid she might see something that would make it impossible to pretend there was any doubt about her feelings for the man she'd married.

She glanced at her watch as she left her room. If Sam had mentioned what time he expected to be home, she didn't remember. Since it was New Year's Eve, she assumed he'd be working late. But she'd wait up. The New Year didn't really start until after bedtime, and she wasn't going to bed until she'd talked to Sam. She didn't want to start the New Year off with those hurtful words between them.

She'd just reached the bottom of the stairs when some-one rang the doorbell. Sam. She felt her heart slam against her breastbone as she hurried across the foyer. Maybe he'd forgotten his key. Or maybe, after the fight they'd had, he'd hesitated to use it.

Nikki wrenched open the door, ready to throw herself into his arms, all her plans forgotten for once.

But it wasn't Sam standing on the porch, though it *was* a police officer. Two of them, in fact. She stared at them blankly for a moment, trying to shift her thinking to en-compass the fact that they weren't Sam.

"Mrs. Walker?"

"Yes." Their solemn expressions set off warning bells. Her fingers tightened around the edge of the door, and she had to fight the urge to slam it in their faces. She didn't want to hear what they had to say.

"I'm afraid we have some bad news."

Chapter 16

It was the waiting that was the worst, Nikki thought. It gave her too much time to think, too much time to wonder what was happening. Sam was somewhere beyond one of those doors, and it was all she could do to keep from jumping up and running down the hall, pushing open doors until she found him.

He was in surgery, the nurse had said. No, she didn't know the extent of his injuries. Officer Walker had been shot in the chest, but no one could tell Nikki anything beyond that. She huddled deeper into the plastic chair, only vaguely aware of the two police officers who shared her vigil. They'd introduced themselves, but she couldn't remember their names. Friends of Sam's, fellow officers. They didn't talk much to each other and they didn't seem to expect her to talk, which was just as well. Polite conversation was beyond her right now.

She'd lost track of how many hours she'd been sitting there, waiting, praying, when the door opened. Nikki jerked upright in her chair, hoping desperately to see the doctor and just as desperately frightened of what she might see in his face. But it wasn't the doctor. It was Rachel.

Nikki was out of her chair and in the other woman's arms in a heartbeat. They clung to each other for a long moment, not crying but drawing strength from the contact.

"Keefe and I asked at the desk, and they said he's still in surgery," Rachel said as she drew back.

"Keefe. I didn't see you." Nikki held out her hand but found herself drawn into his arms. He gave her a solid hug before setting her away.

"Sam's going to pull through," he told her firmly.

"Of course he is," Rachel added, her voice sounding a little shaky around the edges.

Nikki nodded, hoping her fear didn't show. "I know."

"Cole is in Oregon and Gage is somewhere in Africa," Rachel said. "I spoke to Cole and he's on his way home, but I didn't want to worry Gage. He's so far away. By the time he got my message, I'm sure Sam will be back on his feet."

When Rachel said it, Nikki could almost believe it. Rachel looked past her and saw the two officers. "You must be friends of Sam's," she said, moving toward them. "I'm Rachel Walker."

Nikki envied her her ability to keep up a facade of normalcy, to hide the fear she must be feeling.

"Don't look so scared," Keefe said quietly. "Sam's too mean to die."

"He's been in surgery for hours," she whispered, her eyes haunted. "And we quarreled right before he left. I had dinner planned and I was going to apologize."

"Must have been some apology," Keefe said, eyeing her dress. "Sam will definitely appreciate it. I'd try a different pair of shoes, though."

"What?" She looked at him blankly and then followed his glance to her feet. With the skimpy little black dress and cobweb-fine black hose, she wore a pair of battered brown loafers.

"They really spoil the look," Keefe said solemnly.

Despite herself, Nikki gave a snort of laughter. "Maybe I'll start a new fashion trend."

"I wouldn't count on it." He put his arm around her shoulder and hugged her again. "I should warn you that Sam's really obnoxious when it comes to accepting apologies. He can never resist the urge to rub it in that he was right and you were wrong."

"He can rub it in all he wants, as long as he comes through this." Nikki glanced to where Rachel was talking with the two officers. She looked up at Keefe, her eyes haunted. "I . . . I accused him of pretending to care about me because of my money."

Keefe winced. "You don't pull any punches, do you?"

"I was upset. Nothing's gone the way I planned it," she wailed in a whisper. "This was supposed to be a business arrangement. I didn't plan on falling in love with him."

Keefe's mouth twisted in a sympathetic smile. He brushed a lock of hair back from her face with gentle fingers. "Sam said just about the same thing to me at Christmas."

"He did?" Nikki's eyes widened with a mixture of fear and hope.

"I'll tell you the same thing I told *him,* which is that I don't think planning does much good when it comes to loving someone. I don't think you can schedule it."

"I just didn't think it would happen like this. I wasn't ready."

"Who is?"

Before Nikki could respond to that, the door opened again. This time it was the doctor, a tall, thin man, who looked much too young to have Sam's life in his hands. Nikki felt Keefe stiffen and knew that, for all his positive words, he was just as worried as she was.

"Mrs. Walker?"

Nikki took a half step forward, feeling as if her knees were going to collapse at any moment. "How...how is he?"

"He's going to be fine," he told her immediately. "It took us a while to get the bullet out and repair the damage, but the prognosis is excellent."

"Thank God." Nikki felt light-headed with relief. She barely heard the others' exclamations. All she could think of was that Sam was going to be all right.

"When can I see him?"

"It's going to be a few hours before he regains consciousness," the doctor said. "I'd suggest that you all go home and get some rest." He read the immediate refusal in her expression and held up his hand. "I'd suggest it, but I know it wouldn't do any good. You're welcome to wait here. Someone will let you know as soon as you can see him."

It seemed like days, rather than hours, before a nurse finally came to say that Sam could have a visitor. But just one, and only for a short while, she added hastily when Keefe and Rachel and Nikki all stood. After a moment's hesitation, Rachel sat back down.

"Give him our love," she told her daughter-in-law, forcing a smile.

"I will." Nikki gave her and Keefe both a grateful look and followed the nurse from the room.

Maybe she wasn't being fair. Maybe she shouldn't be the one to see Sam. After all, Rachel and Keefe were his family. She was the woman with whom he'd made a marriage of convenience. But it was so much more than that now. She loved him now. And Keefe had said that Sam loved her. She clung to that thought as the nurse pushed open the door to Sam's room and waved her inside.

"You can only stay for a few minutes," she said before she stepped back into the hallway.

Nikki barely heard the warning. All her attention was focused on the man lying in the bed across the room. As she walked toward him, she had to keep reminding herself that the doctor had said he was going to be fine. Connected to an assortment of tubes and equipment, he looked anything but fine.

She stopped next to the bed and looked down at him. His eyes were closed, and for a moment she thought he might be asleep. Needing reassurance, she put her fingertips against his arm, which lay on top of the sheets. Immediately his eyes flicked open.

"Sam? It's me. Nikki."

"Nikki."

She'd spent so many hours thinking she'd never hear him say her name again that she felt tears flood her eyes. She hadn't planned on saying anything; she'd just wanted to reassure herself that he was really all right. They could wait until later to straighten everything out. But the words came tumbling out. "Oh Sam, I'm so sorry. I didn't mean it. I know you wouldn't pretend you cared for me because of the money."

He blinked, trying to clear the lingering drugged haze from his brain. It took him a moment to remember the quarrel they'd had. It seemed a thousand years ago.

"What day is it?"

"What?" Nikki stared at him as if he'd lost his mind.

"What day is it?" he repeated, more clearly.

"January first. Why?"

"You don't expect me to remember something that happened last year, do you?"

"Last year? But it was just yesterday."

"Last year," he repeated firmly.

His chest felt as if an elephant were sitting on it and his entire body ached. He knew he'd been shot and he supposed he should be demanding to know what happened. But at the moment, that didn't seem as important as the fact that Nikki was standing next to his bed, looking rumpled and beautiful and—surely it wasn't the drugs that made him see love in her eyes.

"It's a new year. Let's start over again. Hi. My name is Sam Walker."

Nikki stared at him for a long moment. He saw her throat work as she swallowed, saw a flush come up in her pale cheeks and saw uncertainty in her eyes.

"I don't want to start over," she said. "I liked where we were, before we quarreled."

"It's not a bad place to start," Sam agreed. "But it could use some fine-tuning."

He wanted to pull her into his arms, but was limited by the assortment of tubes that tied him to the bed. He turned his hand up and waited until she threaded her fingers through his.

"What kind of fine-tuning?" she asked quietly.

"The kind that starts with me telling you that I love you." Maybe it was the drugs, but it suddenly seemed incredibly easy to say. He decided to say it again. "I love you, Nikki."

She was silent so long that he began to think he'd misread her, that it hadn't been love in her eyes. The sudden pain in his chest had nothing to do with the bullet he'd taken and everything to do with his heart cracking.

"This wasn't the way I had it planned," Nikki said slowly. "But I guess maybe it's time to change my plans a little." She lifted her eyes to his face, and Sam was dazzled by the love he saw there. "I love you, too."

She squeezed his hand, her heart swelling with love.

She'd never dreamed that her marriage of convenience would turn out to be so perfect.

Epilogue

If anyone had told Sam that something good could come out of taking a .38 slug in the chest, he would have thought they were crazy. But if he hadn't been shot, God knew how long it might have taken he and Nikki to admit their feelings for one another. He wasn't exactly *glad* he'd been shot, he thought a week later, but he couldn't say he was entirely sorry either. Getting shot seemed a relatively small price to pay to find out that Nikki loved him.

As if thinking about her had conjured her up, the door to his hospital room opened and she came in. Looking at her, Sam wondered how it was possible that he'd gotten so lucky. He married for mercenary reasons and ended up with something money could never buy.

"How are you feeling?" Nikki asked as she approached the bed.

"Like a rat in a trap." He caught her hand in his and tugged her down for a kiss. "If they don't let me out of here this afternoon, I'm going to make a break for it."

"If the doctor thinks you should stay another day..."

"I'm still coming home," Sam interrupted. "I can't take another day in this place. Every time I turn around, someone's coming at me with a needle or a thermometer. It's a wonder I have any blood left, considering the amount they've drawn off."

"Poor baby." Nikki gave into the urge to brush his hair back from his face, loving the feel of it beneath her fingers. She'd come too close to losing him to take even the simplest of contacts for granted. "I'm sure they're taking good care of you."

"And I'm sure the nurses are some kind of coven of vampires," Sam muttered.

"I don't think vampires come in covens."

"They do at this hospital. They've obviously got some kind of competition going to see who can draw the most blood out of me—the night shift or the day shift.

When Nikki laughed, he gave her an indignant look. "Go ahead and laugh but, I tell you, one more night in this place and I'm not going to have enough blood left to shake a stick at."

"What are you complaining about now?" Rachel Walker asked as she entered the room.

Nikki turned to smile at her mother-in-law. "He thinks the nurses are bloodsucking vampires."

"They probably are," Jason Drummond said as he followed Rachel into the room. "The one time I was in the hospital, they seemed to have a sadistic fascination with my veins. I was lucky to escape with my life."

"And you thought I was imagining it," Sam said. The triumph in his voice was at odds with the laughter in his eyes.

"Don't encourage him, Jason," Rachel said as she bent to kiss her son's forehead. "I suspect he's making the nurses' lives hell. He always was a terrible patient."

"Thanks for the sympathy, Mom," Sam said with heavy sarcasm.

"You're welcome, dear," she said serenely. She moved to the foot of the bed to stand next to Jason. "Nikki, you have my sympathy when it comes to seeing that he obeys doctor's orders when he gets home. I suggest you buy a whip and a chair if you expect to keep him in bed for more than a few minutes."

"I bought some good strong rope," Nikki said. "If he gets out of hand, I'll just tie him to the bed."

"Now that's the first interesting suggestion I've heard in days," Sam said, giving her an exaggerated leer.

"Behave yourself," Nikki told him, flushing a little. "If I tie you to the bed, it will be for strictly medicinal purposes."

"That's what they all say." Sam's grin was wicked.

"I still think the whip and the chair are your best bet," Rachel commented, watching the byplay between her son and daughter-in-law. "You're going to have your hands full with him."

"I don't mind." Nikki brushed her fingers against Sam's cheek and he caught her hand in his, bringing it to his mouth and pressing a soft kiss into the palm. The look they exchanged was so full of love that it seemed almost an intrusion for anyone else to witness it.

There was a moment's silence and then Jason cleared his throat. "Seems like the two of you made a better bargain than you expected."

"Bargain?" Nikki looked at him curiously.

"When you decided to get married. Your marriage of convenience," he clarified when they continued to look at him blankly.

"You know?" Nikki asked incredulously.

"I know. We both do," Jason added, glancing at Rachel.

"When did you figure it out?" Sam asked.

"I suspected before I met you," Jason told him. "When Nicole called to tell me she was getting married, I did some checking and couldn't find any connection between the two of you. It was pretty well confirmed for me when I saw the two of you together. Next time you're pretending to be madly in love with someone, Nicole, you'd do well to avoid grinding your heel into his foot," he suggested kindly.

She was too shocked to appreciate the humor. "But...if you knew . . . You gave us your blessing."

"You mean I knew you weren't fulfilling the terms of your grandfather's will? I suppose that's true, in the strictest of legal terms. When Lyman told me he wanted that provision in the will, I told him I'd have nothing to do with it. I told him he was going to force you to make a marriage of convenience, that you were too stubborn to let him beat you out of your inheritance. He said it was strictly up to me to decide whether or not you were making a mistake."

"And after I stepped on Sam's foot, you thought I *wasn't* making a mistake?" she questioned, bewildered.

"That wasn't exactly the moment when I made my decision," he admitted. "But there was something between the two of you that made me think you might have a chance. I'd never seen you so interested in a man, Nicole."

"Interested? I detested Sam then!"

"It was more reaction than you'd ever shown before. I'd learned enough about Sam to know you'd be safe with him, even if the two of you continued to detest each other. I decided to take a chance. And I was right," he added, nodding to their linked hands.

There was a silence while Sam and Nikki adjusted to the idea that their secret hadn't been a secret at all.

"Mom?" Sam didn't have to complete the question.

"Oh, I figured it out pretty early on. The way you got married without so much as introducing Nikki to the family. And the fact that you hadn't told her anything about the family, not even that you'd been married before. And of course, when Cole told me you'd given him the money for Mary's surgery, that cinched it. You've always had such a strong sense of responsibility toward the family, Sam. I guess I wasn't really surprised that you'd take such a drastic step."

"Why didn't you say anything?"

"Well, it was really none of my business. Besides, I liked Nikki and I hadn't seen you look so alive since before Sara died. I thought there was a pretty good chance that you'd find out that you'd made a better deal than you knew."

Sam looked up at Nikki, seeing his own shock reflected in her eyes. "So much for our acting abilities," he muttered.

"I guess we aren't going to have to prepare that Oscar speech after all. We thought we were fooling everyone." She giggled. "And they knew all along."

Sam grinned, looking from his wife to the older couple at the foot of the bed. "I suppose the two of you feel very smug, figuring out that we were meant for each other before we knew it ourselves."

"Actually, I did comment to your mother that you seemed a bit slow-witted," Jason admitted with a smile.

"I told him you'd come to your senses eventually," Rachel assured them.

"Gee, thanks." Sam's hand tightened over Nikki's.

He thought of his mother's comment that he'd made a better bargain than he knew. Looking up at his wife, he knew that he'd never heard truer words. He'd made the best bargain of his life.

* * * * *

COMING NEXT MONTH

NIGHT SMOKE Nora Roberts

Heartbreakers

Rugged arson inspector Ryan Piasecki wasn't prepared for the blaze of desire that coolly beautiful Natalie Fletcher had swiftly ignited in him. Could he stop Natalie's dreams from going up in smoke...and could he melt her icy reserve?

WHOSE BABY? Suzanne Carey

Sweet little Kassie had been abandoned before, and adoptive dad Jack Kelleher was determined that she wouldn't lose her family again. So when the death of his wife caused the authorities to take away the child he'd come to love, Jack knew he'd try anything to keep her, *including* marrying Liz Heflin—his wife's sister.

MAN OF STEEL Kathleen Creighton

The bottom dropped out of Rhett Brown's comfortable world when he found himself facing parenthood alone. Eventually he asked Dixie Parish to be a temporary nanny to his motherless children. Suddenly his children were smiling again—and *his* heart was stirring with long-forgotten sensations...

SOMEWHERE IN TIME Merline Lovelace

Spellbound

Air force pilot Aurora Durant's emergency landing had somehow transported her back to the flourishing Roman Empire—and straight into the arms of soldier Lucius Antonius. Though countless centuries stood between them, they soon discovered a love that defied time. But how long could it survive when destiny had different plans?

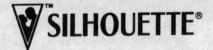

™ SILHOUETTE®

Who needs mistletoe when Santa's Little Helpers are around...

SANTA'S LITTLE HELPERS

We know you'll love this year's seasonal collection featuring three brand-new festive romances from some of Silhouette's best loved authors - including Janet Dailey

And look out for the adorable baby on the front cover!

THE HEALING TOUCH   by Janet Dailey
TWELFTH NIGHT   by Jennifer Greene
COMFORT AND JOY   by Patrica Gardner Evans

Available: December 1996   Price £4.99

COMING NEXT MONTH FROM

▼™SILHOUETTE®

Intrigue
Danger, deception and desire

KEEPER OF THE BRIDE Tess Gerritsen
UNDERCOVER VOWS Judi Lind
THE OTHER LAURA Sheryl Lynn
THE RENEGADE Margaret St George

Special Edition
Satisfying romances packed with emotion

MEGGIE'S BABY Cheryl Reavis
NO LESS THAN A LIFETIME Christine Rimmer
THE BACHELOR AND THE BABY WISH
Kate Freiman
FOUND: ONE RUNAWAY BRIDE Stella Bagwell
NATURAL BORN DADDY Sherryl Woods
NEW YEAR'S DADDY Lisa Jackson

Desire
*Provocative, sensual love stories for the
woman of today*

THE COWBOY AND THE KID Anne McAllister
FATHER ON THE BRINK Elizabeth Bevarly
GAVIN'S CHILD Caroline Cross
TWO WEDDINGS AND A BRIDE Anne Eames
THE BRIDE WORE BLUE Cindy Gerard
DONAVAN Diana Palmer

SINGLE LETTER SWITCH

A year's supply of Silhouette Desire® novels— absolutely FREE!

Would you like to win a year's supply of seductive and breathtaking romances? Well, you can and they're free! Simply complete the grid below and send it to us by 30th June 1997.

The first five correct entries picked after the closing date will win a year's supply of Silhouette Desire® novels (six books every month—worth over £160). What could be easier?

S	T	O	C	K
S	T	A	C	K
S	L	A	C	K
B	L	A	C	K
B	L	A	N	K
P	L	A	N	K
P	L	A	N	E
P	L	A	T	E

Clues:

A To pile up
B To ease off or a reduction
C A dark colour
D Empty or missing
E A piece of wood
F Common abbreviation for an aircraft

Please turn over for details of how to enter ☞

How to enter...

There are two five letter words provided in the grid overleaf. The first one being STOCK the other PLATE. All you have to do is write down the words that are missing by changing just one letter at a time to form a new word and eventually change the word STOCK into PLATE. You only have eight chances but we have supplied you with clues as to what each one is. Good Luck!

When you have completed the grid don't forget to fill in your name and address in the space provided below and pop this page into an envelope (you don't even need a stamp) and post it today. Hurry—competition ends 30th June 1997.

Sihouette® Single Letter Switch
FREEPOST
Croydon
Surrey
CR9 3WZ

Are you a Reader Service Subscriber?   Yes ❑   No ❑
(I am over 18 years of age)

Ms/Mrs/Miss/Mr _____

Address _____

_____

_____ Postcode _____

One application per household.

You may be mailed with other offers from other reputable companies as a result of this application. If you would prefer not to receive such offers, please tick box.   ❑

C6L